Small Acts
of Vengeance

Seren Black

Clink
Street

Published by Clink Street Publishing 2023

Copyright © 2023

First edition.

ISBN:
978-1-915229-59-5 - paperback
978-1-915229-60-1 - ebook

Contents

A Digression on Lovers and Other Strangers   113

Preliminaries

CHAPTER 1.

Generation Me

BETTY

Scroll up, scroll up for all the fun of the snare – the look-at-me era with trillions of images of you, you and you again. Puckering up and pointing at your pouty lips. Welcome to the big, crushing, share-and-despair epoch. It disgorges and churns out a toxic mix of emoji-mad, bogus-news-spreading screenagers, hashtag crazy sharers, influencers and followers that rate and berate.

The frenzied attention seeking and unhealthy drive to attract gazers and gawkers and to eke out as much 'look, look, it's me' time has gone a billion steps too far. That is where we begin. We are looking at you.

So, pucker up selfie stick suckers, we are going on a journey where the ending can only be bittersweet and totally twisted.

CHAPTER 2.

A Demented Madrigal

BETTY

Show-and-tell narcissists and hypocrites rile me, but here I am, on the verge of spilling *my* story. Undoubtedly that makes me a pretentious egotistical phony, although unlike some others, I will move swiftly on. You will think all the better of me for it.

Deep breath, on your marks, here goes everything…

Upfront, I have to confess that I have an identical twin. Sylvie my unfinished half is annoying, exquisitely ethereal and despicable. I used to taunt her by telling her that the words 'evil' and 'vile' play hide-and-seek in her name.

Unfortunately, I have to endure two Sylvies; the one who lives in the mews house opposite mine *and* the one that chirrups away in my head. She is often a parasitic, uninvited hostile guest in my crammed cranium. Both variants are equally abhorrent.

As for me: I am permanently miffed, manipulative and compulsive. Indecision and procrastination cohabit within me like a vulture on a rotting carcass. There are too many distractions: work for one, and nights out another.

Enough about that – now after two years of meticulous planning, I am poised and ready to act. There will be no more excuses. My plan is to execute several grisly deaths, eight to be precise. An auspicious number. Sylvie will play a bit part. Not that she knows that, what with all the disinformation I feed her. Our lethal stories are about to unfold.

*

It was a freezing January night. I was heading home from my first day back at work after the Christmas break. My prospective prey preyed on my mind. I was hyper-focused until a rat-sized lapdog beady-eyed me. The sight did nothing to quell my furnace-hot rage. Fortunately, thinking about the many odious types I would like to see wiped off the face of the earth helped me get through the day.

I had made a list of prey; it was quite long, two pages in fact. Four names are written neatly in capital letters on the first page. Temptation, compulsion and opportunity had left me with no choice. Before long the air would be profuse with crematorium ash and the cold, damp earth fuller still of decomposing bodies.

With me sauntering like a slow wave-sleeping swift – half-alert, half-not – Sylvie intrudes into my seething head, as she does.

She had emerged, ranting, from her cocoon-like, hibernating state. I suppressed her, thought of anything but her. It took a while. She tried to stop me; she screamed and waved frantically.

All I caught was, '*And you say I'm the vile one?*'

Then she was gone.

CHAPTER 3.

Time might tell

BETTY

Every clock in my house is wrong, out by minutes here, hours there. I, however, am always punctual despite the unreliable timepieces.

Sebastian Spiers – my more-off-than-on boyfriend of two years, four months and three days – was late again. He rarely called, could not manage one call or DM a day even.

Sylvie said I should ditch him.

I informed her that when you are hooked on someone it is too much of a wrench.

'Timekeeping is not Sebastian's forte,' she declared, not for the first time, making me bristle.

'Stating the obvious,' I replied, bristling some more.

'Flakiness is his main flaw. He needs behavioural training. I have something in mind,' she added, alarmingly.

I ordered her to keep away from him. He was so evasive; she would be lucky to locate him anyway.

What exasperated me about Seb was that no matter what I was doing or where I was, he was in my thoughts. He always halted me in my tracks. Once I got over my obsession with every molecule of his body and mind – and even with the air that he breathed and left behind – I would do something about it. Bad conduct left a bad taste; it needed addressing, but not by Sylvie.

I stared back at her. 'Keep your big fat nose out of my business,' I said tartly.

SYLVIE

Despite what my evil twin says, my nose is *not* big or fat. It is exactly the right size and deftly upturned in my elfin face, a face she happens to share with me. I am serene in my surroundings. She, my so-called superior half, on the other hand, is having a bad face day; I tell her as much.

'Your hair,' I add, 'looks like you just stepped out of a salon.'

'That is because I *have*,' she snaps back. 'I am heading to the Black Bar.'

And out she goes.

BETTY

A few Sambuca shots later, I staggered home. When I removed my inexpertly applied mascara, my eyes looked pink, dry and sore. I fleetingly fretted about my corneas. Unable to look myself in my repugnant eyes, I averted my gaze. I reflected on all the hours of research on my prey. Some of it had been interesting, the bulk of it was tedious – all of it would hold me in good stead. I felt a surge of confidence oozing from every pore; I was ready to take out the first of many prey.

Annoyingly, Sylvie gatecrashed my thoughts.

Rarely sparing with her words, she barely took a breath:

'*Your anger will topple you. Put your dumb show-off plans on hold until you have learnt how to exert self-control. You are unstable and deranged; your rage will undo you. What goes around, comes around, karma.*'

Then to infuriate me further after the tautology, she continued.

'*Your demented imagination has created a warped, hate-fuelled reality. The bad thing about reality is that it does not just bite; it scratches and cuts you and hits you where it hurts. Have you considered the consequences? I cannot see you thriving or surviving in prison. For a start you'd have to leave all your handbags and your freakish froufrou gowns behind.*'

I would not survive in prison, as if. She enraged me as much as the prey I had in my sights.

*

Fair do's must be given: sporadically Sylvie was on point. I was not only angry; I was miserable too. But killing would fix all that.

My life was hideous; work was dreary and things were always breaking. Nearly everything I owned had a flaw: a stone missing from my green amber necklace, a droplet fallen from my chandelier. All that imperfection was unbearable. It was time for things to change. I would not get this wrong; this undertaking was my chance to be devastatingly flawless.

Once again – whether for my imminent or past sins, I wasn't sure – I suffered another of Sylvie's fulminations:

'*No one ever winds up flawless,*' she began, her voice silky for a change, luring me in. '*Those who try are perfectionists; control freaks like you are born flawless, but develop faults. Even if not immediately apparent, failings linger; they rankle, and one day they are exposed. Your missing stone and abandoned droplet are both precedents of wrong.*'

I stared at my reflection in the mirror, giving myself a cold, sharp shock. I did look rather scary.

Sylvie, unwaveringly inhabiting the ridges and folds of my brain, rasped within, most unpleasant it was.

'*You will be caught, and deep down you know it.*'

So negative and pessimistic.

It was hard to believe we were formed from the same egg, or *jumeaux monozygotes* as mama used to say. Mama's words, devoid of affection, made me recoil every time she uttered them.

By the way, I never did tell you my real name, did I? All you need to know is that it is 666, six letters in each of my names. It was like my ice-cold mama predestined my murderous ways. I was born Blaise Carrel-Allard. It is rather magnificent (*merci*, mama), but you can call me Betty. The office knows me as Betty Ellard, I quite like that too.

CHAPTER 4.

'Alive and Kicking' (for now)

BETTY

As I awoke on a crisp breezy Saturday morning in mid-January, an all too familiar wave of insecurity and fear wrapped around me. I felt unsafe. Sylvie was out for blood, mine. She had been since her first day in the psychiatric unit way back.

I have had to watch her like a ready to swoop hawk since she stormed back into my life.

I never regretted orchestrating her incarceration over a decade ago. She had a habit of erasing unpleasant things and rewriting her life. She was on an endless inane happy path anyway. I savoured the serenity of every second of every minute, hour, week and month of our separation. It altered our affiliation for good; and it shook our parents up to their very cores.

Mama's voice trilled loud and clear in my ear: 'She doesn't see the world as we do.'

Although I too did not see the world in the same way as most others, I kept that to myself.

At the age of thirteen, Sylvie was like a seven-year-old, all sweet and wondrous but with an inexplicable flaw, a cruel streak. We used to live in France where 'kill it, skin, gut it, and eat it' was rife. But she took it a few indecorous steps further: catch it, toy with it, kill it, and leave it for someone else to clean up.

It was not surprising then, that I didn't trust the once-beguiling sibling who turned up on my doorstep, six years after our last encounter. Beneath her open façade, I felt Sylvie's deceit. Her motives were clear; her gleaming eyes gave her away. She was here to toy with me, kill me and leave me for someone else to clean up.

I had to keep an eye on her and watch my back at the same time. I imagined myself twisting and turning for the rest of my potentially brief life.

*

To increase my chances of staying alive, I shared my plans with her in a piecemeal way. What with me being an opportunist, it dawned on me that Sylvie's unwelcome arrival might be a disguised blessing. I was overstretched, what with work and my social life. She would be my facilitator, enabling me to be less fraught and more productive. Her role would be minor; for she was, after all, a minor me. I hated admitting that I needed help, but it was a filthy, putrid mess out there – rife with trolls, lager louts, touts, trippers, dippers, fly tippers and ignorant talentless wannabes. They all needed binning and that would be time consuming.

You see, I hated disorder. I wanted that sense of smug self-satisfaction, the feeling you get when you clean your house from top to lowermost, skirting boards and all. I knew that feeling deeply. I used to have a compulsion to clean, and had to get treatment. An excellent therapist cured me. I quickly hired an obsessive to come in twice a week or I would literally have had no time to kill.

*

Integral to getting away with murder, would be adopting many disguises. I tried several in the spare room at my mews house – and so had Sylvie (I sometimes let her near me, in person.) Amongst many, there was that of an old woman.

No one noticed women over fifty. Unless, they looked like Helen Mirren, Charlotte Rampling, Sophia Lauren or maybe our mama: head turners still. Most blended into the background (it sometimes applies to men too), overlooked, not particularly important with little prospect of any leg spreading. That was the perception; the perfect guise.

All we needed was a few sleepless nights, some clever contouring, one of those awful grey wigs, and a quick rummage in the charity shop. I felt my heart surge as Sylvie gave her two pennies' worth.

'We are on the same sentence on the same page, for once,' she said, as she stood in my hallway, no way was she getting any further. 'Those detestable stats that appeal so much to someone on the spectrum – women over fifty are the least fucked demographic in our unequal, judgemental society. It is a clever ploy to look a few decades older. You have something there.'

At that moment, even though we were diametrically opposed to each other, I felt that together we could outwit everyone.

'Do not go on a killing spree, it will end in tears,' she said.

My heart plunged, we are not even in the same library, let alone the same page. Why, I wondered, did she always ruin everything?

'Sylvie, the list of malefactors is long,' I explained, 'and I have spent years planning. Oh, and there will be no tears, not mine anyway.'

I shooed her out, and she scurried back to her house opposite mine. I closed my eyes, willing sleep to come so the other Sylvie could no longer invade. My new mantra was on repeat.

Slowly, slowly, catchy prey.

CHAPTER 5.

Pesky Pigeons

BETTY

It was a perfect day for a winter walk, so we decided to stroll in Greenwich Park. The two of us heavily disguised, looking like no other. We rarely stepped out together, too risky. Sylvie was excitable. The pigeons annoyed her, particularly the mangled ones; they were closing in as I fed them.

Pigeons are undervalued. In my view, they should get a reward for tidying up our filthy streets. They are bonded labourers with not much to cheer about – apart from the occasional frenzy around a bag of chips, a dropped, partially masticated sandwich, or any detritus spewed by drunks who could not handle their drink: big offence.

Sylvie reminded me of the mess they made; the pigeons that is, not the louts. Then she strode off. I surmised she was thinking about me – vengeful thoughts, no doubt. Getting even for my past transgressions against her being the key theme. Yet, I had made her into the adept, unhinged, underhanded being I saw before me. She should be grateful.

I ran up the hill and caught up with her. She was still harping on about the pigeons.

SYLVIE

I say, 'Whilst sporadically called flying rats in sprawling cities, in North America, a pigeon denotes an easily fooled sucker, an unwitting target for a con trick.' When I ask her if she thinks I am a mug, Betty looks away. I don't stop there, of course; there is going to be more. It surprises me that she lets me get a word in edgeways.

'Pigeons belong to the same family as doves,' I tell her. 'I consider myself blessed, pure. I am on a path to utopia, spun of platinum and gold thread, a bit like my hair.' I shake my head from side to side to annoy her, my wig whirling.

Unfortunately, there are a few misdemeanours in my past, hardly any of them my fault. Betty is overfond of poking her thin accusatory index finger at me, and time after time, mama believed her.

'You are a dirty pest,' I suddenly say. Betty laughs, sounding like a distressed raven.

I continue, for she needs to hear it. 'We may well be melded, but like pigeons and doves, we are a world apart. This does not bode well. May the universe bring forth the doves.'

I have more to say; much of it I keep to myself (I want to live and breathe after all), but I feel compelled to spill more of my thoughts.

'If I were in North America, where therapy is de rigueur, I would be supine talking about you in hushed tones, no doubt. Our balance of power is skewed. I'm the one with the brains, you are the vicious one that has been one step ahead, till now. Be wary,' I tell her. 'This is transient. I will have the last laugh. You are very careless, especially when sloshed.'

Next time she has a few, I would like to push her down the stairs and see if she gets up again. I didn't tell her that.

BETTY

I admit, I was ruffled, for I had been lying low, quite persistently, and not been out drinking, as my snide twin had inferred. As for being cleverer that me, well the cheek of it, we are on a par. Regrettably, her latest deflating words had set me on edge. Some of the things she said ate away at me, from craw to core.

To compound matters, my work makeup was clownish again – not scary clown, but sad, clowning-days-should-be-over clown. This would not do. I was having a bad face day for the second time in as many days. Maybe I needed to employ a makeup artist.

I removed my mask and started all over again.

THE MURDEROUS PATH

CHAPTER 6.

Prey One: Alby Fry

BETTY

For prey one I carefully selected Alby Fry, the talentless 'reality star' who appeared on a dire TV talent show. The next two preys were on the back burner – and prey four too.

Preys two and three, Kevin and Tracy Wilkins, were on that *Great Fat Britain* show; the one with the smug-thin fuck presenter and that whippet-like ferret of a personal trainer. We had never met them, but that meant we were less likely to be caught.

Besides, who would ever suspect an upstanding paralegal like me?

My work was both necessary and evil; meaning the execution of my plans would take ages, years maybe. I had been at the same law firm for three years. The only plus point, it was reassuring; you knew where you were with lawyers. Every interaction was on an unequal footing; that suited me, what with all my facets and assets.

SYLVIE

I, on the other hand, do not and cannot work. I am covert, have been since my time in the unit near the middle of the hexagon that is France. When I get out at age eighteen, Betty hands me a false passport and ten thousand dollars (from our parents' safe). I dye my naturally flaxen hair black and flee to Naha, Japan. Why? To escape the talons of my pernicious twin – oh, and to work out how best to pay her back for her heinous crime of having me locked up. I will rear that ugly head soon.

BETTY

Two years ago, when Sylvie knocked on my door, aged twenty-four, I expected her to stab me right through the heart, or maybe the eye. Instead, she dropped her bag on my foot and re-entered my life without a how do you do.

I helped her unpack her full-to-brimming backpack. It was bursting with designer clothing, two wigs made of real hair, and a latex mask. But she would not let me touch a rather crushed but exquisite looking silk kimono nestling at the bottom of the bag.

We ate together, in silence that first day and the next and nearly every day after.

Within weeks, I ensconced her in the mews cottage across the way. Mama and papa willingly paid a sizeable deposit and the subsequent monthly payments from one of their offshore accounts. There was no need for me to support her. She was adept at theft, mainly online – she clicked and collected – or waited for deliveries. Prada and Chanel packages and light rum and handmade chocolates were carried furtively into her place, always under the cover of night. Every time she went out, it was in disguise, her eyes and hair a different colour or shade, obeying my strict instructions.

*

A mere two months later, my plans to clean up society became more cohesive. Not only could Sylvie assist me, but, being a carbon copy, she could also provide me with an alibi (or I could frame her again). Not that I envisaged either of us being in the frame; sloppiness was not an option.

My heart raced as I shared my high-level plans to kill a total of eight prey. She would play a part. First she would go to Marrakesh for a night and a day. She glowered. Disconcertingly I saw myself in each of her glassy eyes.

Surprisingly, she did not react to my generous offer of a free holiday, instead she said, 'One, three, six, nine.' Sadly, Sylvie was a fan of disquieting odd numbers. 'What is to stop you killing everyone in sight? Once you start, you won't be able to stop,' she insisted. 'The thing about patterns of behaviour is that they become addictive. They become engrained in our psyche. Like riding a bike; once there is a blueprint for an activity, it is difficult, almost impossible, to cease.'

'I am not addictive,' I replied. 'I know when to stop.'

Once prey eight is dead, I thought. Easy enough.

That night I played online bingo. I could have quit when I was ahead; it was just that I needed to win big, as they say in the ads.

As Sylvie departed for her mews house, she told me that she had had enough of watching me in front of the screen with a vacant look on my expressionless face.

I wanted to slap her maddening head, twice and both cheeks, for good measure.

CHAPTER 7.

The Marrakesh (Poison) Express

SYLVIE

I agree to help Betty with her preposterous plans, but I am only here for the twisted ride. I could kill her now and escape her sharp-nailed clutches and nasty remarks, but that would let her off lightly. Whatever erratic path she takes, I will derail her and undermine her every step of the way. In the meantime, I act complicit.

Her maleficence initially leads me to Morocco. Her offer of a free break in the land of spices sways me. I am an accomplice, soon to be an accessory.

Colourless, odourless, tasteless, untraceable poison is what Betty wants. I acknowledge that I am the one taking a risk; she is a fraidy-cat.

The poison is for Alby, the first name of Betty's list. I foolishly tell her that I had a one-night stand with him – or more accurately a one-hour stand, over a year ago. She raises her eyebrows as I ask her to remove him and pick someone else. No chance; Betty is on a mission, or eight to be precise.

She orders me to also source enough poison for prey two and three whilst I am at it: Kevin and Tracy Wilkins.

'They are feeders; both waddle like toddlers,' Betty says. 'When they rouse from their slumber, that is.'

They are morbidly obese. Betty read about them in a tittle-tattle magazine. (Why she reads that rubbish I will never know.) She says it's to relax her overworked brain, liar.

BETTY

Kevin and Tracy's ten-year-old offspring was the human equivalent of a foie-gras duck, her liver turning to pâté with each fatty or sweet treat. What a warped way to show love.

They would be easy to dispatch of; just a case of waving a tasty morsel in front of them. They were on their way out anyway, a heart attack or stroke waiting to happen.

SYLVIE

She is wrong to target them. Obesity is an illness. I tell her that. Rasping, she accuses me of being a maggot crawling in the sulcus of her brain. Gross.

Anyway, off I go to Morocco. On the way, I obsess about the perfect dish; it makes me salivate all the way there.

I conclude that an effective way to disguise life-destroying poison is to dress it up in a steaming, brightly coloured tagine. Pungent turmeric and paprika covering a delicious chicken with olives. The Feeders will not be able to resist. (Or maybe they will; Betty is a terrible cook.)

In Marrakesh, I head straight to Jemaa el-Fnaa the throbbing heart of the city. Viagra, frankincense and myrrh are thrust my way at nearly every turn. As I am not making offerings, I only succumb to the Viagra purchase. You just never know; it might come in handy.

Twenty-nine hours later, I am home. A lightning visit. We convene to discuss Alby, the minor celeb, or sleb, as everyone seems to say these days (one syllable or letter less saves space and reduces effort.) I suggest to Betty that she spike Alby's mojito at the XO, that club he goes to, with Viagra, rather than killing him.

I recommend a dress rehearsal. A dummy run on an unsuspecting male. I put my hand up.

'I will do it, Betty, the dry run, or should I say wet run,' I snigger.

I'm the rude twin, in case you haven't guessed.

BETTY

'No dry runs, Sylvie, and certainly no wet runs. Death, like life, is not a rehearsal,' I told her as she placed two small brown paper packages on my kitchen table. I took a peek. The contents of these packages will be used on Alby, *my* first kill. 'We will not be following your lily-livered plan,' I insisted.

I clapped excitedly; I could not help it. I squared it away by thinking I looked more like a super-fast, competent cymbalist than an imbecile making like a seal. Sylvie gave me a filthy look.

I reflected on what she told me the previous week. She knew Alby intimately, before he became an abhorrent attention seeker. I shuddered as she shared the sordid details. She met him at a club in Essex a year before she barged her way back into my life.

Alby Fry was an average ex-footballer. A reckless tackle cut short his playing career and saw him embark on a new career in the media (or meejah as some call it). He appeared on many excruciating reality shows, how egregious. My hatred propagated every time I saw his ochre face – pumpkin orange in some lights, yellow in others – like the edges of an old newspaper. As for his blinding bling teeth and the rippled torso he took every opportunity to display – well, they were equally nauseating.

The hordes of wannabes that want to fuck the wannabe made me rage too. His current squeeze was a giraffe-legged unnatural blonde, and there were several others at the ready.

He was always in those gossip mags; I only read them so I can keep up with the dim-dims. Sometimes he was even on the front page. It made me squirm. Being famous for being a halfwit is not on. He invariably spouted banal crud and stupid catchphrases that he undoubtedly rehearsed in front of one of his many mirrors.

Naturally, he was a serial cheat. The likes of Alby would never attain fulfilment, what with all that striving for validation. It must be exhausting to try to be flawless, with a constant craving for the two-in-the-bush. He would never be happy with his lot.

My act would be one of compassion. He obviously had to make an early exit from his miserable, vacuous vanity fuelled life. Once dead, the wretched wretch would be famous beyond the wildest of his fanciful dreams. Pity he would not be around to see it.

CHAPTER 8.

We Are Watching You

SYLVIE

It is July, my favourite month – six weeks after my trip to Marrakesh.

According to Betty, we are still in the planning phase.

I spend the week like this: glum, glum (and bored), glum, glum, glum; not glum, glum.

Saturday is a day of frenetic activity, followed by clubbing, where I watch Alby from not afar – quite near actually. I get home tired and delirious at 5 am.

Sunday is a hangover write-off, but I have no plans anyway. I end up watching the long- tongued mad dog from next door, sheltering (rather precariously) from the sweltering heat under a parked car. Intent dog-watching is no mean feat. It takes dedication and focus, but the rewards can be plentiful. It is pure meditation. Online forums I frequent advocate that our way of life should reflect that of animals; in turn, this brings us closer to our true calling and spirit. Each one of us has an animal inside; the key is to discover our inner animal. Betty belongs to a savage genus.

She watches dogs too, probably feels an affinity with them, but she takes it a little further; she always does, whether its learning yoga moves or training herself to catch prey. Rather than simply watching a dog at play, sleeping and stretching, she pays attention to how it seeks out quarry. She observes the opening of its mouth, the gnashing of teeth, the foaming spit. The combination is enough to strike fear in any victim, usually a squirrel or bird.

I watch as she tries to replicate the look in a Doberman's eyes when it is about to pounce. Her eyes glaze over and become transfixed on the prize. All her energy pours into the chase and the kill. Before committing the act, she knows the prey is all hers. I tell her it seems like she can almost taste the juice of the meat as she imagines the hunting dogs ripping and gnawing. Catching prey, for her, is an orgy of unadulterated pleasure. I can see it in her scary eyes.

BETTY

Once again, unable to keep herself to herself, Sylvie relayed her views of my study of dogs.

'Enough about meat juices, sis,' I uttered. I felt nauseous.

Anyway, dilly-dallying would not do. I needed to act fast if I was going to stick to Alby's flatlining deadline.

SYLVIE

Operating on the assumption that one should canvass all modus operandi of unsolved crimes, I peruse several cold-case records that Betty has piled on her desk. Yes, I know she does the same – I saw her reading at least ten murder files – but she rushes things and leaps and falls head first to the wrong conclusion. She will fail, what with her workload and erratic nature.

Nevertheless, a wave of uneasiness permeates me. Treading a fine line does that to you; the frayed nerves and the restlessness are side effects of years of taunting by my nasty sibling. If I do not collaborate, she will stitch me up, she avers, with eyes piercing and a tongue almost as sharp.

Accountability is not in her repertoire.

She will not send me away again for her wrongdoings. Admittedly, my time in the unit was not all bad. I made a few friends and gleaned a lot of useful knowledge. Prison, however, is a completely different ball-and-chain game; it will not be up to Betty's exacting standards. She is heading there, not me.

You see, I too have been planning her punishment for years. I will eject her from her plush nest, like a cuckoo. Scarcely anyone knows I exist – apart from my parents, my loathsome twin, her odious so-called boyfriend Seb, and great aunt

Gwynne (who is more gaga than Betty). I will gleefully step into Betty's shoes – she has many pairs for me to try. And guess what? They all fit.

What catches me off guard is her taking me down to the basement and showing me a list of prey and a murder board. Unexpectedly I feel excited for the first time in years.

Nevertheless, I continue to rile her; I relish wheedling and needling her. I know how she hates it. Being a weakling is what she expects and that is not what she gets.

BETTY

'Delay, I beg of you, or scrap your plans to kill those that you perceive to be weak,' Sylvie implored. 'I have a sense of foreboding.'

Understandable, as she was always a wuss.

'Okay, I will delay,' I said to her, and she blissfully sauntered out of my living room.

The bad news: she came back, all smiles, with a box full of vile Moroccan tiles from her recent trip; mainly drab browns (not my favourite colours). She arranged them on my French oak floor and left them there, the bitch.

And then she grinned lopsided at me, teeth aplenty, and eventually informed me she had a few more vials of poison.

After these feeble and futile attempts to disrupt me, I reminded her that I am the one in charge of the gears. To get her out, for she was worse than a skittish cat, I sent her off to plant some knotweed I charily procured from the disused power station by the train station in the dead of night. Naturally I could not walk past without grabbing a handful, taking great care not to touch it. She was to plant them in the ornamental garden of those hideous new builds: one in the oversized planter, and the rest in the surrounding flowerbeds.

SYLVIE

I obey Betty's orders, as always, preferring to lull her into a false sense of security.

Dressed in the garb of a gardener, I plant a species of knotweed that closely mirrors a harmless plant common to our meadows. I mix the two up, as I do. One-dimensional is not my style.

BETTY

I conceded that Sylvie had her uses. The hacking, thieving and scheming: it was all up her street. There was no codependency there, seriously. At least, not on my part.

While she was gone, I broke into her house and rifled through her many belongings. Her recent purchases could come in handy, so I pocketed two packages. She was so dippy. Her mews house, across from mine, was a freaking mess. She wouldn't even notice they were gone.

Alby Fry's death was imminent. I felt momentarily satisfied about my pending use of an untraceable noxious substance. There was not a lot of poisoning about these days, what with all the stabbings and shootings.

CHAPTER 9.

Killing Mr. Vain

BETTY

The deadly potion was ready. It would not be long until prey one had an unpleasant surprise. Alby Fry, the mascara-wearing, big-browed louse with no discernible talent, aka the UK's number one love rat – so said the tabloids – would soon be dead. I know, I know – but I didn't buy them, just checked them out online.

Unfortunately, Sylvie's grating voice made an uninvited entrance.

'You don't do tabloids, yeah right! You used to have a copy of your smut paper of choice in your briefcase; legal briefs rubbing up against lurid headlined tabloids, not forgetting the banana. I hope your ears are burning along with the rest of you, deceiver.'

If she had been in front of me, I would have had the biggest hissy fit ever and slapped her thrice (once for now and twice more because I owed her for her previous snide, but accurate, remarks about my drinking and online gaming). I tried my usual, tralala I am not listening. Insidiously she occupied my headspace.

I shuddered as her parting words swirled and altered; *deceiver, deceiver, deceive her.*

*

Getting back to Alby. It would have been apt, but predictable, to use rat poison; but traceability was not an option.

What's more, he was no Brandon Flowers, Bradley Cooper or Pitt. He had a distorted self-image – fillers, filters, brow brushes and airbrushes had fuelled his vanity.

Yes, to the Insta lot, it was all about looks. But I did not get it; he looked such a fright. OK, he had not jumped on the hipster bandwagon – a meagre point in his favour. Those bearded creepy fucks freaked me out, but his look belonged in the nineties – it had made an unwelcome comeback, thanks to him. He would pay for all his crimes and misdemeanours.

*

Fast forward one caffeine-fuelled week and it was finally the right time to act. The moon was but a sliver hidden by clouds. At Alby's house, I was the night watch. Sylvie was the one who broke in, and I followed.

My plan was in progress.

SYLVIE

I head straight to Alby's seen-better-days bathroom with a cabinet (mirrored, of course) with toothpaste speckles all over it. I open the dental floss casing and add a few droplets of lethal poison. A bit difficult with surgical gloves on, but I manage it. Betty, of course, does not touch a single thing.

'At least he'll have super clean choppers at the very end,' Betty whispers as we leave.

Back at the mews, I throw myself onto my sleigh bed. It hits me like a bullet train that now that our collusion has ended, I feel vexed. The fact that we colluded at all is cause for concern; colliding is more our thing.

Hours later, I look at myself in one of my many mirrors, a pretty sight usually. My face looks fragmented. I have the look of someone who is seconds away from impact; I am about to crash into myself. Something triggers this feeling, the solar eclipse perhaps.

As the solar eclipse makes the day look like the dead of night, something changes; like a light switch, flickering and going out. The car lights are on and streetlights too, lighting the somewhat gloomy London skyline.

I feel our minds, Betty and mine, similarly tune into the enlightened vibration. We are ready, and taking lives is what we are about. My heartbeat quickens. Where sunshine should have given us splendour to remember, clouds hang low and obliterate any opportunity to view the rare event. In the distant past, such happenings were perceived bad omens, acts of the devil and witchcraft. For us, that rings true. But it allows us to see through a murky glass our endless horizons.

The following night I head straight to that tacky XO club. It has maroon plush velvet banquettes; all of them stained and holey. They make it hard for you to get into that sticky-floored nightspot that smells of sick. What a dump, argh! Alby, of course, is not there.

I go home and disinfect myself. If I don't, Betty, with her shark-like sense of smell, will know I have been out.

It occurs to me, my head swimming as I ease it on to my ivory silk pillow, that I did not expect and was not prepared for this surge of emotions after breaking into his house. They start to surface: excitement, fear, ecstasy, the whole lot. Despite years of self-discipline and solitariness, sometimes I have feelings that I do not know how to deal with.

Fuck it; I should be free of all of that.

After protesting much, I practically leap on the bandwagon of deaths with that astringent twisted twin of mine. I am hooked.

CHAPTER 10.

Sometimes Life Is Like a Disastrous Dress Rehearsal

BETTY

I spent years imagining the act of killing, my heart racing at double quick speed in anticipation. Sadly, in reality, nothing happened to slow my fast-beating ticker. I had been waiting forty-eight hours. During that precious swathe of time, Seb had not returned my calls and Alby was not dead. Maybe he rarely flossed his veneered teeth – or maybe he had not been home for days.

Sylvie was back at my house, sitting at my kitchen table, staring right through me, in her unnerving way. She was cupping her mug of tea, black and filmy, no sugar. She badgered me about Alby, I sensed she was ready to crow.

'Soon, Sylvie, soon,' I said, frowning. I did not like her being in my house.

Alby was in the papers again, with an obscene Barbie who, in most lights and from most angles, looked like a manikin in a trance. She was not his regular girlfriend, Mia Higueras. He was cheating again. He had been seen with a pretty, sexy, Crayola-white toothed swimwear model (stick-on veneers, I noted). I disagreed with most of their description of her – apart from the teeth, they were super white. Practically everyone claimed to be a model these days, regardless of his or her size, age or visage.

I flicked through a health magazine aimed, I thought, at hypochondriacs. I was devastated to discover that lead in lipstick caused brain damage; I needed to go lead-free. No wonder my brain was not as sharp as normal – what with swallowing three kilos of lippy in a lifetime, or was it three grams? I did not reapply as often as Sylvie did, I thought gleefully, *quelle dommage*! It took me a few minutes to research and order safe products.

I knew I was just wasting time waiting for Alby Fry to die.

CHAPTER 11.

Hammered

BETTY

It had been a week since we broke into Alby's place. I had not slept well. I did not like it when a plan did not go to plan! I woke, with dry eyes with a song in my head, an earworm. Who thought of that word? It was horrid. The tune? 'If I Had a Hammer.'

I did have a hammer, and I intended to put it to good use.

Knotweed was in my thoughts again too. I had spotted some when I was out jogging in Welling (I did like to get about). It would be an opportune place to hide bodies, I thought, negating the need to dig. The council will spray it with noxious chemicals to boot.

On the way into work, feeling overly tired, I sensed a qualm before the storm. My mind was restless. In the office I told a joke – an old one, but hysterical. 'What's the strongest cheese in the world? Arnold Swartzecheddar.' It went down like a lead balloon. It disturbed me, how my office was filled with humourless suit-wearing morons. It was survival of the wittiest (me) at the office and they were all witless.

SYLVIE

I tell Betty that moaning about work is yawn provoking and that her restlessness is palpable and contagious.

She mentions eyeing some knotweed again recently. 'It will make a brilliant final resting place for someone. You perhaps,' she chillingly adds.

She picks up a hammer, says she wants to use it. I recoil.

'You worry me,' I tell her. 'You have that whole jackhammer-to-crack-a-nut thing going on.

As far as I am concerned, we established days ago that easily identified, non-biodegradable weapons are just not viable and so outdated. I mean, who plays Cluedo anymore? Lead pipe, anyone? I think not; steer well clear. Times have changed, crimes have developed, and murder weapons are far more inconspicuous. A droplet, a spray or pinprick will do the job.'

She is not listening. I am at my wit's end.

'Let me put it simply, Betty; a hammer is not easy to dispose of, and once a murder weapon is discovered, you can kiss goodbye to your opulent life.'

BETTY

The cheek of it. I could have played kill chase for years and never been caught. I was too devious and scheming to be uncovered. I always worked out all the permutations; although at times I could not focus, and that carried big risks. That was only because I was so often stuck in a pram jam in the village. True, when I sat down to drink my coffee, I also had to wear my noise-cancelling headphones as sporadic high-pitched screaming distracted me – decibel hell, it was. One little slap would put a stop to it (never did me any harm).

Sylvie would say that made it worse. I disagreed, I mean, really, could that screaming get any louder. As for the 'naughty step' shite, do not get me started. What sort of punishment was that?

Yet another day had passed. I sat in an artisan café, the coffee was too weak as usual; those stingy, greedy coffee houses. I wondered if Alby Fry had not flossed. Or maybe Sylvie did not put enough drops on it. I really could not rely on her.

*

I was in disarray; I had a timetable to stick to, and I needed to move on to the fat Feeders.

As I ventured out of the village, a bit quicker than when I came in, and as all the prams were now indoors, Sylvie's voice rasped in my now aching head again.

'As for the baby and toddler noise pollution, stop sweating the small stuff, as they say.'

Unsavoury really, as I do not sweat – but, 'whatever' was my unspoken reply.

I heard a screeching noise and with a jolt realised it was coming from me. People gawked, how rude. I attempted a smile and ran as quickly as I could in heels and caught the fast train home.

I went to bed early but ended up checking my phone every time I woke to see if Alby had died. Each time I swiped, a wave of displeasure coursed through my arteries and veins. No news was not good news.

SYLVIE

I have been keeping out of Betty's way for a couple of days, now I am waiting for her. It is nearly midnight, and I am hiding behind her knoll sofa. She gets back from an office do, drunker than several skunks. It never ceases to amaze me that her colleagues invite her out. She is unsteady and is muttering to herself; first she orders me to get out of her head, says I am in it more often than not these days. Calls me a few names too, none that I care to repeat. Then she goes on and on about how no one gets her. Betty is weak. She blabbers when under the influence.

Seems like we disagree on everything; but occasionally our brainwaves merge. For a moment our thoughts, usually discordant, are in accord. She cannot stand me; I cannot abide her. It will not be long until I emerge as the last twin standing. What Betty doesn't know is that I am studying to become a lawyer too. It will take another three years; but, by then, she will be dead, and I will become her. I do not want that flaky wimp Seb; so I will have to kill him too.

I recline, sated; she cannot shut me out, after all.

I wonder what the version of me in her head is like. Worse than the real me, I hope.

CHAPTER 12.

Short Story Long, She Lost Her Mind

BETTY

Sylvie's whining voice resounded in my tender head. Regretfully, I had two too many, last night. I looked at my alarm clock. 6 am. I had had five hours sleep or thereabouts. Fortunately, it was a Saturday. I edged myself up slowly and got a big fright when I saw my odious twin perched on the end of my bed. I removed my earplugs and wished I hadn't. My hangover worsened as my twin lectured me. She was bit over the top, if you ask me.

The first thing I heard was, 'The suggestion that you cannot rely on me to drop poison onto floss properly is offensive.' Then she really got started.

'As for last night… accusing me of getting the dosage wrong and saying that I am useless. The truth is you are the inept one. Your plan intentionally leaves things to chance. Have patience. May I suggest that you let it play out fully instead of undermining my contribution?'

I turned over and buried my head under the pillow, pressing each side over my ears to muffle the sound of her voice, but she continued her rant.

'Face it, you are not a team player! You think you are a lone ranger – or wolf, more like – and that I am annoying, rude and surplus to requirements. You need me far more than I need you. You spend too much time watching shows and playing dumb games and rarely see things through.'

'Are you finished?' I muttered into my mattress.

'No. Worse still is your need to control everything. The reality is that you cannot. Stare into the looking glass, and you'll soon realise that the only thing you can control is yourself. Get a grip.'

Sylvie was the one who needed to get a grip, not me. My skin prickled and I felt nauseous as she said that she had gone out last night. I peeked out from under my crumpled pillow. She was wearing my black, slinky Christopher Kane outfit. She had not even asked to borrow it. Infuriatingly, she was very cattish looking in *my* catsuit, despite her blotchy, gleeful, wide, wild eyes that were staring at me.

To refrain from committing an act of violence, I hauled myself out of bed and strode to the kitchen to make an espresso. At moments like that, ignoring her was the best policy. I grabbed a handful of vitamins and minerals and sat down, only half-listening to Luna 8 Radio. Until the news bulletin. The newsreader had my undivided attention.

NICKY ROWLAND, LUNA 8 RADIO

'The man in his mid-20s found dead in a nightclub toilet in Essex in the early hours of this morning has been named; his agent confirmed that the dead man is reality TV star Alby Fry. Fry had been starring on the Channel 7 series The Real Me. *A cleaner discovered the body at approximately 2 am. Police are not treating his death as suspicious. We will have more for you on this as the story develops.'*

BETTY

Sylvie had followed me into the kitchen and looked like a semi-feral cat that had got the cream, a bird and a mouse too.

'What the fuck?' I asked. 'If Fry had flossed, he would have died in seconds and would not have made it to some grot of a club.'

Sylvie's face clouded over at my uncharacteristically short outburst.

She stitched me up. I could tell. I was seething and wanted to get my hands around her delicate neck.

SYLVIE

I soon recover from Betty's little flare-up.

What a wonderful night… and morning. I love winding her up.

'I went to the XO last night, in Railton,' I breathlessly intone, knowing each word I utter is a bullet. 'Alby was there. I went over to him, and we slow danced some R&B. We kissed; his breath was vile. I am pretty sure he had not flossed.'

Now for the coup de grace.

'Surprisingly, the kiss turned me on, despite the foul taste. I never really fancied him in any way. How could I? For a start, the man goes around with no socks on.'

'We kissed in a dark corner, with intrigue. Tongue over tongue, saliva dribbling from mouth to mouth. Then I dripped something I prepared earlier into his tequila.'

'Stop right there,' Betty hisses, chilling my eardrums and the rest of me. It is the first sign of one of her rages, the hissing.

BETTY

I had to control myself. That much I knew.

I had never liked the thought of receiving and tasting another's saliva – apart from Seb's. I worry that it might interfere with my delicate mouth chemistry.

'You,' I said, prodding Sylvie's clavicle, 'sullied yourself. You're disgusting.'

SYLVIE

I am shaking. She screams in my ear now, another aspect of her rages. She has a go at me for wearing her new designer jumpsuit, then accuses me of murdering Alby on my own, without her permission. Not that she would ever give me permission. She says that she will make me pay.

I tell her I did it for her, so she can move on to her next two prey.

BETTY

The insanity! To say she did it for me!

'Stop acting all altruistic,' I snarled. 'And stop playing with those ruddy tiles as if it was some sort of art installation. If you don't stop, I'll take the hammer to them.'

I glared at her, but she was suddenly a blank. She did not seem at all put out. So I piled on another brutal truth. A few months earlier Sylvie had told me about an unsavoury incident that involved Alby. At the time, it had turned my stomach.

'Alby would never have risked getting within a few centimetres of you,' I told her. 'Not after you bit his tongue and made it bleed, lying bitch'. I knew as soon as the words left my mouth that the first statement was untrue. After all, everyone wants to kiss her; she is the spitting image of me.

That moment I hated her more than ever, but it was my fault for being in a drink-induced coma. I should have been a step ahead, not a billion steps behind.

*

Later reports confirmed that Alby had died of an accidental overdose; however, the police still wanted to interview people who were at the club on Friday night.

'They are coming for you, Sylvie.' I told her as we finished listening to the report. 'Oh, and don't even think for a second that you looked as striking as me in my Saturday best, for fucks sake.'

I was so enraged that she did not give my ingenious dental floss plan a chance, I ranted until my throat was sore. I even called her a fukunt, a word I made up that usually helped me settle. I said it repeatedly in different tones until I started to laugh – manically, I noted. She continued to look defiant. I slammed the door and went for a run, plotting new details of my vengeance every step of the way.

CHAPTER 13.

Anger Mismanagement

BETTY

Fast-forward twenty-four hours.

I conceded that I only had myself to blame; maybe I was accountable after all. It was all my fault for blabbing. I would blab no more. Sylvie had lulled me into a false sense of security, pretending she wanted to stop me whilst planning to outdo me.

To compound it, I was more annoyed than I had ever been about Seb.

'You've been waiting donkeys for him to call,' Sylvie taunted me. *'You'll never hear from him again, not after your juvenile tantrum in Waitrose last month.'*

I let her have the last word. I needed a gin and a few packets of gourmet crisps.

And yet she continued to recount her actions on that fateful Friday night, or rather the early hours of Saturday with Alby. All the while, my blood pressure was climbing, to higher than it had ever been, probably.

SYLVIE

I am compelled to rub it in. I take centre stage. I explain to Betty that the many substances I took in liquid and tablet form the thin-veil of what I remember. Alby's body is barely cold when the forensics wade in, in their polyethylene suits that you can buy for practically nothing on the internet (I know because I have a few).

The XO Club is a blur – I vaguely recall being in the thick of it. But then, as an innocent bystander in the wings, I watch the events unfold. I avoid being caught on camera, but if I was, it would be obscura – mere pinhole images, pixels on badly taken grainy shots by clubbers more out of it than me.'

'Whatever. You will have to deal with that,' Betty says, her voice cold.

She pours herself a triple gin or thereabouts. I tell her to stop over reacting and continue to dredge up details of what happened.

'I eradicated any trace of my DNA with bleach, by baby wiping him,' I assure her (although I did nothing of the sort). 'I did a thoroughly clean sweep,' I tell her. 'Two wannabes were all over him, they left plenty of traces. I saw the entire sordid affair through the keyhole. It was difficult to tell who was doing what. They soon lost interest as he became flaccid. The poisons coursed through his bloodstream, filled his organs, and he started to make a strange rattling noise. I think he had a seizure.'

At this point Betty is clutching the bottle.

BETTY

I suffered stoically as Sylvie told me the whole Alby story and gleefully added unnecessary and unpalatable details of her time at some random man's place. She was unsparing with the more sordid details.

Finally, I said, 'Sis, you're making me sick.'

'Feeling woozy,' she uttered. Disregarding *my* nausea, she grabbed the Alka-Seltzer and codeine tabs. 'Overdid it on the Bacardi and Diet Coke last night and some pills.'

That was all I got out of her for the rest of the day.

SYLVIE

Actually, I save the most fascinating part for later.

'For the press and the law, Alby is the main attraction; for me, he was just the starter. I move on to a delicious main course – a spread better called Jack, who lives nearby.

All you need to know is that roughly about the time of Alby's death, my tongue is in Jack's mouth. I am still close enough to the scene to know that Alby has expired. Jack could have been the first man, or the eleventh, maybe, that I felt I could obsess over. Within seconds though, it all changes and another is in my sights.

As I am about to leave the XO with Jack, I spot the ONE.

Yep, I hate that dumbass term, but he really is.

One furtive glance of his visage and mesmerising grey eyes and I know.

Although I still spend a couple of hours at Jack's flat. Well, you know how it is.'

She tells me to get out of her sight.

BETTY

Hours later, I caught Sylvie watching the latest TV coverage of Alby's untimely and shocking death. Well, shocking to other people, but not her.

I frowned. Clogging the screen were teddy bears of all sizes and colours; candles; an oversized champagne glass; a big, felt heart-shaped cushion; and about thirty bouquets already. All for Alby. The local florists had swelling coffers, I was sure, as well as those gift shops that I hated. The ones that sell soppy, fluffy presents for sappy girlfriends to buy for their boyfriends and the reverse.

It was not even sixteen hours since his demise.

But that was not all.

*

A detective on the TV, identified as DCI Lynch, was summarising the day's events. No mention of Sylvie or anyone fitting her description, just an appeal for witnesses. Lynch looked familiar. He was fresh-faced and striking with trout-grey eyes; he appeared confident too, a potent mix. He did not look tortured or unhinged in any way, like most of the cops I had seen at court over the years.

But then, I remembered him; he hung around in the corridor looking sullen for days on end for a trial that was a tribulation. (Trust me, you do not want the grizzly details.)

Sylvie watched him avidly, sitting on the floor in front of the screen. I felt a plummeting, cold fear. I realised, as Lynch's eyes were a-glittering, he was the ONE she had really obsessed over that night at the XO Club – glanced at, and, in under a second, fell for.

'Shit,' I said to myself.

*

Two days after Alby's death, Sylvie barged her way back into my house. She was going on and on about Lynch – what a fuck up.

'He has enormous,' she rhapsodised, 'hypnotic eyes that remind me of Kaa, the snake from *The Jungle Book* with limbal rings to die for.'

I had to look limbal rings up; I thought they had something to do with outer space.

She knew it all, of course, as always.

She went on about his limbal rings being special, dark and thick. They set off the whites of his eyes in a way that stopped you in your tracks.

She accused me of being jealous, said that I was vain, that I liked to get the entire male or female attention going. She decried that I inexplicably only had eyes for Seb, who didn't even have half way decent limbal rings. I was livid, but I did not let it show.

SYLVIE

To rile Betty, I watch a replay of the recent news. I press pause at the point where I feel Calum Lynch is making eye contact with me. His glittering, glittery, smiling eyes are looking at me and only me. No one else exists. We are crime-crossed lovers, and soon there will be a meeting of bodies and minds.

BETTY

I looked DCI Lynch up. Like Sylvie, he had a high IQ. Alarmingly she relayed that she was thinking of tying the knot.

SYLVIE

'I have changed my mind about till death do us part,' I say to Betty. 'It does not sit well with my views about the outdated institution of marriage or being someone's other half. I would never think of tying a noose around his long unlined neck; this man's eyes are far more appealing alive.'

Besides, I don't want to be tied to her forever.

BETTY

I was livid. Everything that Sylvie had said and done so far was a deviation from my meticulous plan.

'Lynch is not my type,' I told her. 'Well; maybe he is a bit, or maybe a lot. I don't like his odd-looking eyes; one is bigger than the other.'

That was not the case, but my aim was to lessen his pull and to rile her. It did not seem to be working.

I feared I would have to lock her up, so that she could not do any further damage. However, she had never managed to make a relationship last and would probably blow it, ha. If Lynch worked out what she had done, she would be on a new path that would not be to her liking: prison.

After all, it might suit me to get rid of her for good.

Ignorant Sylvie thought that I was OK about her exploits at the XO, but I was seething and full of hate. I would make her pay, I did not know how. I had always had difficulties dealing with spanners in the works, sorting this mess out would be a wrench.

CHAPTER 14.

Wasting the Wasters

BETTY

Infuriatingly, I had not killed anyone yet, so I turned to The Feeders, aka Kevin and Tracy.

The thought of targeting a woman caused some discomfort – after all, everyone else seems to, on TV and on film – when in real life more men meet violent ends than women. Tracy Wilkins was, by exception, dangerous and deserved it. Her obese, languorous, loungewear-wearing other half, Kev (as she calls him) was a waste of space too.

And he took up rather a lot of it.

There were people starving in the world that could live for a month on what they ate in a day, the fat fucks.

Oh, I know, I sound like one of those spineless trolls, but that was not where I was at. I am doing my bit to save the planet's finite resources – it had totally fatted up and dumbed right down!

*

It would be complex and challenging to kill two in one go. I needed the obese duo to ingest poison – sparing the rotund, hapless child. So, it had to happen on a school day, but my freakish colleagues were bound to raise their outlandish brows if I took a day off to travel up to the Midlands, what with my caseload.

I thought of sending The Feeders a hamper, but turning up in person would be more exciting. They would consume whatever I gave them like Scooby-Doo. And there would be no interference from Sylvie this time.

*

I poured my third coffee and listened to Radio 6 Music. The newsreader iced and heated up my innards sequentially. I did not know why I was so worried; I was not at the XO. The cause of Alby Fry's death was a suspected drug overdose, and he was four times over the drink drive limit. I'm not sure what that had to do with anything. It wasn't as if he was going anywhere in his yellow (to match his face!) second-hand Porsche with the vanity plates ALB 1AM.

Later, whilst eating my vegan toast and cashew butter, I thought about DCI Lynch. Sylvie seemed to have gathered scant information, considering she was obsessed with him. I, naturally, knew all there was to know, on the surface anyway. I could not of course read his impenetrable mind.

DCI CALUM LYNCH
When I ponder the death scene at the XO club, all I can think about is the woman I spotted. It was just a glimpse. There was something about her; she was too urbane for that dump.

She was just a blur, reminding me of a swirl of a kingfisher's wings, but she was wearing all black. A glossy crow. I should have approached her and asked her why she was in such a malodourous place.

What the fuck was up with me? Too distracted by the sudden death of that so-called star Alby Fry, perhaps? I would look through the pictures and comments posted on social media on #frydies to see if anyone had posted anything useful. ·

BETTY
As I contemplated Sylvie's imprudent crush on Lynch, my heart thumped alarmingly. I needed to slow it down by removing her from my sphere. I lured her to my basement and locked the door behind her, knowing she would not fall for that one again.

With her out of the way, I flung myself on my bed and gazed at the ceiling. My heart rate slowed until an unwelcome thought permeated: I had a perturbing fault line; I was unable to keep my own secrets.

The night before, I had told Sylvie all about The Feeders. Luckily, I did not spill all. I was cracking under the strain and had had three glasses of wine.

Not a bright idea.

The following morning, I descended the steep steps to the basement door and unlocked it. I expected Sylvie to lunge; but, unpredictable as ever, she walked out, eyes averted from mine. I told her not to interfere with my plans for The Feeders and that I would not drink Gavi again in her presence.

'Gavi de Gavi,' she said, 'you will be on the Lacryma Christi next, then the Chianti. Each one tells a different tale and you will tell many after imbibing them.'

I let her dour remarks go. She acted all contrite and promised that she would not meddle again. She insisted she only did Alby in because I mentioned being fed up with waiting.

Not impressed.

She did it for *me*. Yeah, right.

I slapped her and escorted her out of my house. Then I finally smashed those fricking, unskilfully arranged tiles she had left on my floor. For those interested in the more intimate details, I used Sylvie's hammer, the sage green, cerise and magenta floral handle was aesthetically pleasing.

SYLVIE

The slap hurt, but I do not show it, do not even flinch. I watch her having one of her tantrums and frown as I notice the hammer, it is not the heavy duty clawed one she had before. It is mine; it has been mine for over a decade. When I first crashed back into Betty's life, I remember wrapping it in a pink and yellow silk kimono and hiding it at the bottom of my bag. She must have been treading the boards of my house for weeks to find it. I hide things like that very well.

I remember that incident from my early years. I see it vividly now: as I deliver the first blow of the hammer to a rat, my daisy-patterned dress gets splattered. The blood never does wash off. It is binned along with the viscera of the rat. Truthfully, I do not have much against rodents. The blow is merely practice to find out what it feels like to kill something, again.

Slowly, slowly, catchy Betty. I am playing the long game. Unlike her, I am patient. I will pay her back for everything she has done – and that includes stealing my hammer.

I get a shock as I hear mama's voice echo around the room, '*Sois gentil*, Sylvie,'

Be kind, that's rich. I shake my head to get that irresponsible, uncaring sow out of my head. She often mixed me up with my nasty twin, invariably caused by one too many cognacs for breakfast.

Betty's voice brings me back to the now. She turns on me, snarling, staring deep into my eyes.

'You should have kept that dress pristine. It was mine.'

How does she know I was thinking about the first blow with the hammer and the dress? Have I been talking out loud, or can she read my thoughts the way I read hers?

CHAPTER 15.

A Tuscan Sojourn

BETTY

I awoke with a jolt, hit by the thought that the toilet doors at the XO club are unlikely to have keyholes. Sylvie had been lying again. Did she think my head buttons up at the back and the sides?

I had to send her away again.

When I questioned my twin, she said she stood on the loo seat in the next cubicle and watched the Alby and the wannabes from above. I imagined her peering and leering. If she left any traces, I would kill her. Logic told me there were hundreds of smudged prints, traces of drugs, shit and grime in those cubicles, not to mention other bodily fluids.

I told her to vacate the city.

'A brief sojourn to Italy will do you good. Fuck off to Castagneto Carducci, seeing as you are listing Italian wines like a sommelier on amphetamines, and lie low. No acting up.'

I handed her my passport, the boarding pass and 2000 euros.

'Now go, conniving bitch, I have some cooking to do.

SYLVIE

Naturally, I am suspicious. I suspect Betty is using me as an alibi. However, it feels good to get away from her. Italy is so me, by the way.

Besides, I hate it when she brings up the past and abhor it even more that she has my hammer.

I think back to how everything changed the day I hammered that poor rat. My penchant for eating meat dripping with blood and my offal habit started then too.

Not only do I butcher the rat, but I attack Betty's hideous Turkish Angora cat with an eye of amber and an eye of blue. As Betty is so keen on the past, I launch right in and mention that Minou bit and scratched me; 'I was defending myself.'

Minou is French for kitty – Betty totally lacks imagination.

Whenever I can, I tell her, 'The vet managed to save your precious kitty. What's the problem?'

As for me, at this point in my life, Betty is my prey. I vow to steer clear of animals – it was just a phase anyway.

BETTY

The vet did not save kitty. I remembered clutching the box she had laid Minou in. As soon as I got back to the chateaux, I had a go at Sylvie, but she shrugged it off. I vowed to pay her back, no question, as soon as I had sufficiently honed my killing skills.

When Sylvie dropped back at my house for one last fond farewell, I couldn't resist chiding her.

'Don't do anything I wouldn't do,' I said.

'Oh, I'm way too clever for that,' she replied.

She was asking for one last parting dig.

'For someone so clever,' I said. 'You still took the well-worn path that some other psychos take. The ones who leave a telling trail, risking confinement for life.'

'How dare you?!' Sylvie shrieked. 'Fuck you and fuck you all. Only a sick society can get away with calling the more interesting of us psychopaths or sociopaths. It is not all shower scenes with a bloody knife show, you know.'

SYLVIE

Just for the record, psychopaths have exquisite personalities. They are not all in prison or nearing their last supper. Some are in high security units where they are free to mix with like-minded geniuses and expand their intellects far beyond the limits of the outside 'normal' world. I suggest you set foot inside one of them. Hang out there for a while; get to know the gang, then you can judge.

'You will eat your words,' I tell Betty. 'And if you aren't careful one of them might eat you!'

BETTY

Having thoroughly enjoyed her brief spasm, I, of course, apologised.

'OK, Sylvie dearest, I am just sensationalising, winding you up,' I said.

Without another word, Sylvie skedaddled to Pisa. I had supervised her packing, and all that was left to do was watch her get into a cab to the airport.

I must admit I perked up at her high security tales. On rare occasions, she could be fascinating.

SYLVIE

Despite my warning to Betty, I have yet to meet a cannibal in a high security unit. But I remember Tymington. Standing nearby on Crow's Hill, I think about some of the men inside. Many of them front page news in their day for taking a few too many 'wrong types of lives.' They are harmless now, like muzzled dogs, dribbling down bobbly cardigans, drugged up to the eyeballs.

Memories flood back to me of looking up at the sky above Tymington where the birds do not fly overhead. They move in circular formation around the outside of the buildings. What does that tell you? Maybe it's nature's push and pull, power and force, the pendulum of darkness and light.'

BETTY

Whenever Sylvie reminisced about anything, if I could have switched her off like a light, I would have. I was sure she made most of that stuff up, but I was mesmerised.

Sylvie had only been gone a day, but, as per usual, I was mulling over the nature of good versus evil, me against her.

I concluded I was green with envy because Sylvie could order the best coffee ever up that mountain, in perfect Italian.

My jealousy aside, she needed to learn. I had repeatedly told her to reflect on her irresponsible behaviour, hoping she would return contrite. She embellished every utterance about that night at the XO to the point that she may have put me at risk. Her mendacity meant that the last vestige of trust between us had gone. Her hedonistic streak that night could have brought us both down.

And as soon as she was gone, I suspected she was making some man moan either in pain (more likely) or pleasure even before her first day in Tuscany was over. There would be much drinking of wine from the Bolgheri region, superb for reds. Sadly, I was intolerant to the red grape, but a dry white would go down easily.

At least Sylvie was out of the way, I told myself.

I did hope she was eating; after all, she had to look the same as me. We both had to keep trim. I had been drumming that into her for weeks now; I hated it when she got too thin. Eating is cheating she used to say (same thing the office fucks used to come up with) when preloading with gin before going clubbing and getting up to all sorts of trouble.

Anyway, back to me.

I had finally managed to book a day off. I had to. I needed to wait for a school day, I did not want the child to be in the vicinity. That fukunt Martin Briars-Hedley took my caseload off me. He was making snide comments about me when I crept up behind him. I knew what he was after, he wanted me out; we clashed, he never did take to me. I might set Sylvie on him if he did not pull his Paul Smith socks up. Yes, I noticed those things. I liked a man in decent attire, but not him. I would park him for now but he was 'on my radar' – yet more annoying office speak.

CHAPTER 16.

Feeding the Feeders

BETTY

I could not wait to get started. At dawn on the Monday morning, I got the Suzuki 750 out of the garage, gleaming black of course, and tore up the M1 like a mechanical hare out of its trap. When I got to Walsall, I headed straight to The Feeders preferred fast-food outlet.

I knew their habits and had viewed the grotesque folds of fat close-up. I had also seen them waddle to their maroon mobility scooters.

How did I know all that?

Well, unfortunately I had watched the documentary in which they harped on about it being an illness, an addiction. It would stain my memory for life. They proudly proclaimed that they snaffled ten fried chicken sticks a day each. (Hey, what do you want Feeders? A chocolate medal?)

When they finally exited the food outlet, the chicken sticks disappeared in seconds, their big jaws chomping, chins discernibly moving. Then, they waddled off to the scooters and took off at the speed of what? The speed of mobility scooters on ill-maintained pavements? I would say half a mile an hour.

I followed them, parked my motorbike behind a van, and walked in the shadows behind them. Minutes later I pitched up at the front door of their house, a surprisingly (given their inactivity) well-kept semi-detached 1950s house, with cheerful pot plants flanking the front door, full of pansies and violets.

For a split second I feared for the plants if The Feeders were no more. Fortunately, my rationality quickly passed and I was back on course.

I could hear the talking inside. Tracy's voice was discernible. I rang the bell.

'Get the door, hon,' she bellowed.

'You get it love. I already did my steps for the day.'

'Doctor told me too much walking could get my heart rate up too high. We've got to do this exercise in moderation you know, hon.'

'It's only a couple of steps to the window, Kev. Just peek out, love, see who it is.'

'I dunno. That is fifty-two steps, two over the maximum recommended for me daily. Shouldn't I call the doctor first?'

'They'll be gone by the time you get there! It could be the postie delivering our weekly low-cal order from fat to fab-u.'

'I've got to walk again later to go to bed. I think I've overexerted today already; I can't do it, hon.'

'Oh, I'll go!'

*

'Who are you?' Tracy asked from behind the closed door.

'Not trying to sell you anything,' I said genuinely. The door opened gingerly.

I stepped into their spotless hallway.

I felt repulsed by the size of the woman in front of me and at the onslaught of smells. It was sweat mingled with a toxic combo of curry, fried chicken and beer breath.

Their phone rang loud and shrill, giving me a start.

'Get the phone, Kev love.'

Kev shuffled to the hallway and picked up the receiver.

'Hullo?' There was a five second silence before he shouted to Tracy: 'Oh my god, what channel did you say? You had better talk to my better half. Traaace.'

She waddled to the phone. 'You want us to appear on the telly *again*?'

It was getting quite frustrating: hearing only one-half of the conversation.

'Again; no, we don't want to be on telly again, Trace. Those awful trolls made me turn to more food, and I drank too much of that cheap beer that gives me bad wind, remember?'

I remembered having read the salient points on Twitter at the time, rude! I waited and waited, quite patiently for me, in silence.

'The dirty perverts, remember that one that said my head must disappear up your fanny when we're at it.'

'Ooh, and that one that said I'd get my head trapped in your smelly, grotesque abdominal folds,' she whooped.

'Well, I did wonder if there was a hidden camera in our bedroom,' he added.

She sniggered and snorted and set him off again.

'At least we are getting some. They are such jealous Dylans. And they were just the nice things posted after the programme, weren't they, sweets?'

They looked at each other with what looked like pure love (even I could see it), and I thought of backing out, for the child's sake.

Suddenly Sylvie's voice swirled into my brain, her voice grating as she told me to get on with it.

'Stop pussyfooting,' her disembodied voice said, *'you are a faffer. Hand it over and get out quick. Remember you failed last time with Alby. Your dental floss plan was rubbish.'*

So I got on with it.

I told Kev and Trace that I had accidentally come to the wrong address. Did they want the pizza anyway?

The poison-sprinkled chicken-and-mushroom pizza and a free super-sized bottle of diet coke (heavy, awkward fucker) were no longer in my gloved hands. Tracy was hugging the coke and I handed the now cold, greasy box to Kev, placing it in his mitten-like hands.

They lifted the lid and inhaled the aroma from the box like those snuffling pugs.

I exited sharpish on my shiny Suzuki.

SYLVIE

From afar, I watch Betty do her worst. She looks ridiculous.

How am I able to do this, you wonder?

Six months ago, The Feeders upgraded their set-top box. Intercepting the call is a doddle. The engineer happily takes the afternoon off with the extra few hundred pounds in his pocket. The surprise (undeclared) windfall easily facilitates the installation of a spy cam in their bedroom. Kevin and Tracy make a porno – before you ask, I did not troll them. There are other devices about too, including one near to where they are standing with Betty.

Moments after she has left The Feeders their poison pizzas, I phone her and confess what I have done. She accuses me point-blank of meddling.

'But honestly,' I say in my defence, 'I was only trying to facilitate. You want to see what happens, don't you?'

'I'm not a peeping pervert like you,' she yells.

'Don't accuse and abuse me,' I tell her. 'You know as well as I do that everyone is at it these days, spying that is.' I must admit, I do like to watch. I know Betty agrees, but I have to endure one of her rants again.

BETTY

Yes, I ranted.

'TV nowadays is not what it was,' I said. 'It is crammed with desperate wannabes. The world is a stage and just about everyone is on it, vying for the spotlight. Grasping and gasping for airtime, the fame game. As the late Felix Dennis said, people watch television with "The cold, dead eyes of fish lying in their shallow graves." Wise Dennis, it's even worse these days.

'The same words apply to unsocial media freaks, a drain that has created phone zombies, zombs or is it just zoms? There are so many new words these days, I can't keep up.'

SYLVIE

After Betty finishes, I ask, 'Do you have your laptop with you?'

'Yes,' she says.

'Switch it on then, Betty.'

We could both see and hear it all using the spy cam in The Feeder's bedroom – Betty is grateful now! We wait patiently. It feels like hours but it is only about twenty minutes.

From Italy and Walsall we both witness the moment when Trace nudges Kevin and says, 'I feel sick I think I ate too much.' Kev lays there inert (his usual state) for the last time, his grey T-shirt mushroom and pepper sprayed. She elbows him, and then shakes him, the fat wobbling.

BETTY

All that effort caused Tracy to have a seizure that woke the hapless child: unforeseen collateral damage, dammit.

CHAPTER 17.

Trolling the Trolls

BETTY

When The Feeders mentioned online abuse, it bothered me. Someone like me should have relished it, but I didn't like anything that made people spiral or change their appearance so that they looked fake or ill. Even before I delivered them the pizza, I was going after the haters. I would troll the trolls.

That made me a troll too, I know! They couldn't help it; I couldn't help it. All clever-dick sickos together; outdoing each other until we could not get any further, or could we?

Just before driving up to Walsall, I made a list of the comments added to Kevin (Fat Boy Fat) and Tracy's Big, Fat Blog. Some of them changed their tune after his tragic death. Here's a selection.

BLUEZOO1: *Stick your chicken sticks up your big fat wooooh, woooohs, mr. and mrs. piggy.* Evil smiley emoji times ten.

Like, Like, Like, Like, like 28 times.

SCORPION_RISING5: *being sick right now into my brand-new swing bin imagining THAT. Pity they aren't throwing their load; they could do with losing a few tons. Wan looking emojis times three.*

Like, Like, Like, like 12 times last time I looked – and no I wasn't one of them who thumbed up.

BLUEZOO1: *so sorry your bin is soiled. Trace, if you lost a few tons I'd give you a go.*

LIZARDZX: *sicko.*

I thought it was a bit much, so, I simply typed…

TERMIN8_H8: *I know where you live and I have a paring knife.*

Of course, that is not the best knife to use on a person but it sounds scary.

CHAPTER 18.

The Great Escapade

BETTY

Our next victim, prey three, Terry Baker – would only take *my* death toll to two as Alby does not count for me. Unfortunately, although Kevin is dead, Tracy DID. NOT. DIE.

Suffice to say Tracy was less greedy when it came to pizza than her other half. In a way, that was better. They did a post-mortem, but with no suspicion of foul play there was no need for the police to look too hard. I mean he was a walking dead man; well, he was when he could be arsed to get off his sofa. Watching TV and inertia meant his sofa and his bed were shallow graves. Felix Dennis did tell us so.

I decided to dress up and go to Kevin's funeral. In the brief spate of time I knew him, I found him to be larger than life in more ways than one. Inexplicably I felt some affection for him. Odd for someone like me to feel anything but loathing.

My other motivation? I was desperate to see Kevin and Tracy's daughter. I had saved her life, after all. I also wondered if Tracy had lost any weight yet. The tabloids were full of it: her promise to diet and to be there for her daughter.

I swelled up with pride as they emerged, walking slowly behind the pallbearers. They were still big but marginally thinner than the last images I saw online.

But I couldn't escape Sylvie; she had no respect for the dead. She talked all the way through the service, forcing me to respond.

'You know he'll be wicking by now.'

'What?' I whispered. 'That sounds vile.'

'With all that fat burning in there, his skin is splitting like an over-ripe banana or a fatty sausage, sizzling like pork crackling and then vaporising, pfffff, up the chimney.

I tried not to laugh, but it started when she said pfffff.

'I'm breathing out until I get to the car,' I said. I did not want Kevin's ashes in my lungs or anyone else's for that matter.

'He'll be burning for at least another four hours on Gas Mark 600 to 900 degrees Centigrade. (Sylvie always was good at science.) 'Then that fat feeder fucker will be gone for good. Did you know that a fat body leaves a similar ash mass to a thin one?'

That was not as remotely as interesting as the wicking bit. I suspected that there were a few aching shoulders or slipped discs for some of the taller pallbearers. I walked past Trace, nodding, putting on my sympathetic face – head tilted to the right, then the left. I must have resembled a pendulum. Suddenly I realised that I was looking at her askew.

'Aw, Tracy, that was a lovely service,' I said as I approached her. 'I did not know his favourite song was "Shaddap Your Face" – what's the matter you?' Trace, aw come on give us a hug'. I did not know what had come over me, that was not so not me.

Tracy looked at me, puzzled, trying to work out who I was. She must have thought I was one of those mawkish onlookers.

'Shut up your face,' Sylvie hissed, her voice so clear in my head that she sounded as if she was not far behind me in the throng.

'Do I know you?' Tracy asked me later at the wake.

'No,' I replied. 'But I'm a fan of yours and Kevin's. I saw you on the box.' I emulated to ingratiate.

Thankfully, she did not recognise me from that fateful last day. The pizza was too much of a distraction; and my disguise, unfetching as it was, was just too cunning.

Low fat snacks, carrot batons and slim line tonic were on offer at the wake. Damn, I hated all those things; so I had to drink neat gin on the rocks, not good.

Tracy had taken up Zumba and Spin and joined some weight loss group. Within months, she might even become one of those obsessive fitness freaks that I reviled. Smug fukunts.

Inexplicably, I did have some feelings for her, maybe because she had an open face, not like mine.

We swapped numbers. I was pleased she survived. I was thinking we could be friends; I had never had one of those before.

I sighed as we left the building. I was obviously not as good at the killing game as I thought I would be; going in for the kills was not as I had anticipated. However, practice makes perfect; and, yes, another devastatingly flawless scheme was underway.

I thought my previous plans were perfect, but whatever.

If I included Sylvie's kill with mine, there were two dead and counting.

*

The day after my return from the funeral, Sylvie contacted me to say she was on the road in a low budget hire car.

'I hope you don't pick up a stray on the flight back from Pisa,' I told her.

She ignored me and said she had booked her next break. She was not even back from this one. Fine by me. I only needed her when it suited me anyway.

SYLVIE

It is 6.56 am and unbeknownst to Betty (she thinks I am still on my way back from Pisa), I cut a solitary figure on Bwlch Farm Road near Conwy, North Wales. The sea mist, heavy and low, is obliterating visibility from the feet up.

I pray for weather conditions out of a Victorian novel, and they are delivered. Weather conditions like this are a stupendous backdrop; you could not wish for better cover. I slip on the moist grass and have to feel my way up.

And what am I doing here? you ask. All will be revealed. Of course, Betty is totally clueless.

BETTY

I was simmering, trying to stop myself from boiling over. For I knew where she really was at all times. Ingeniously I had put a tracker in the lining of my new coin purse (one that she predictably stole). Both items cost a lot but was worth it.

What was she doing in Wales? Trepidation coursed through my veins, my arteries, and the whole physiology of me. Was sis jumping ahead of me again? How could she possibly know about my plans for Terry Baker and their culmination in Wales? Baker had fathered a dozen offspring, a heinous crime against the environment. He was resolutely in my telescopic line of sight.

I needed a break, but it dawned on me, what with Sylvie on the scene that I would have to get a rush on even though Kevin was not even cold in his oversized coffin, specially made, cost extra, apparently. Rumour had it they had to employ a few extra pallbearers and keep the fire burning at the crematorium for a very long time. What with all that fat, maybe he was like a big candle. Out, out, fat candle! He would have generated enough power to keep a smallholding in Wales in electricity for a day.

Which was where Sylvie was…

SYLVIE

I'm looking for a suitable place to deal with Terry, Betty's next prey (it pays to be a snoop and she does leave things lying around and doesn't delete her browsing history). I take a rather long detour and head west. Betty mentioned that she wanted to go and visit a purposely long-lost relative in Wales too, not far from where I am now. I know that she has more in mind.

My phone rings shrilly and gives me a fright. She is furious and she tells me that she knows where I am.

She must have put a tracker on me. I throw the contents of my bag onto the passenger seat and gasp when I see a tracker in the lining of my new cerise purse that I stole from her chest of drawers. Wily or what? Later that night, I push it down the back of the seat in a London cab. I have gloves on – do not want to catch anything. Oh no, I am turning into Betty, a germophobe.

CHAPTER 19.

He Can't Keep It In

BETTY

I had to have a six-week break, as work had taken over again. It was a Saturday morning, and I finally had time to focus on prey three, Terry Baker, a 'Serial Dad'. That was what the papers called them. He belonged to a fast-growing number of men who impregnate then go. In his case, he had twelve offspring by nine different women and there was another on the way. According to the latest report. He liked *his* prey young and starry eyed, for he was a star – or so he liked to think.

In fact, he was nothing more than a minor sleb, F List if that. He often fronted low budget TV shows too.

Absentee dad Terry Baker was a weathered, wealthy-enough ex-city trader who had a number one hit in the 80s followed by several failed-to-chart variations. A gimmick mimic, in short.

He exhibited the same repetitive behaviour with women; unhappily for him, he was the wrong side of forty.

I picked him out from a long list of offenders. His head, high above the parapet, made him an obvious and easy target. Serial Dad! Callous philanderer you mean.

SYLVIE

Curled up on her sofa, I try to derail Betty right from the get go.

I am wearing silk and cashmere, looking more comfortable than Betty will ever feel; the thought of it comforts me.

'As Serial Dadding is such a widespread phenomenon,' I say to her, 'rather than kill him, why not teach him a short, sharp lesson. We have the tools.'

BETTY

I lalalalaed trying not to listen. I thought about ensaïmada; that sugary pastry from Mallorca. I so wanted one, filled with creamy custard. Soon I was salivating. I could almost taste the melting lard: problematic for a vegan (lard, that is).

SYLVIE

Sensing Betty's lack of focus on my plans for Serial Dad, I walk over to her chaise longue where she is reclining and shout in her ear. 'Teach him a lesson, sis, one he will never forget!'

BETTY

I didn't need to listen to Sylvie to know what sort of lesson she had in mind. She had already shown me, on her flashy new laptop, a clip of a vasectomy being performed. She did not need notes, but recited the whole procedure, including what was bound to be perfect enunciation of the medical terms.

She even listed the medical equipment she needed to procure.

My head swam deliciously at the thought, but I couldn't dwell on that; I had to get to work. Sylvie looked so gleeful for a change that I just said 'bye,' exited my house, bought a double espresso from my local, overpriced artisan café and gulped it down.

I needed time to think, I thought.

SYLVIE

We know a lot about Terry – or Tel as he likes to be known. I have been stalking him, at Betty's request, of course. A sorry state of affairs: she wants to do it, but she can't. She has a day job – scuppered again. The benefits to us (or should I say, 'me') are obvious. Knowledge is power, unless you do something stupid with it, which some people do.

The lowdown is that Terry Baker spends much of his time with Lottie Turner, a round-eyed brown-eyed blonde; less than half his age, naturally.

I expertly break into her flat and leave motion-sensor state-of-the-art spy stuff in every room. We watch and listen from afar, at Betty's place or mine. I watch in person when he is on the move. After all, I don't have much else to do.

BETTY

As we shared the motion sensor videos, Sylvie picked out key highlights.

'Oh, looky here, sis! Serial Dad is talking to Lottie, the latest woman he has impregnated,' she said. We listened together.

'Lottie, it is not an illness,' he says. 'Just cut down on the booze, love.'

'You shit face,' Lottie replies.

'You should be happy you've got someone to support you.'

We surmised that Terry wasn't referring to himself but to Lottie's mother, for he was already on the hunt for his next target.

Sylvie gleaned that he was after a weather girl, just his type. He first saw her on the oversized (so vulgar and passé) flat screen television when having a postcoital lie-in after Lottie had left for work. He had a quick play with himself under her white Egyptian cotton duvet and finished what he started in the shower.

How did I know, you ask, about his interest in a synoptic meteorology expert?

Because Sylvie had followed him from Lottie's flat the previous morning.

SYLVIE

I see him pitch up outside the central London studio the weather girl works. I see him bump into her, making it look as if it is accidental. Bizarrely, his tactic works. He is so predictable.

The weather is not so – I get thoroughly drenched.

CHAPTER 20.

A Night to (Mis)Remember

BETTY

Her voice resounds with echoes of yesterday.

'While we sleep here, we are awake elsewhere and that in this way every man is two men.'

Fess up Sylvie. Where did you read that?

'Jorge Luis Borges in The Garden of Forking Paths.*'*

I did not bother saying anything.

'And every woman is two women.'

Sylvie being in my head made me two women, and that other woman was driving me cra-cra. To erase her from my thoughts, I turned my mind to something more exciting. It was going be our birthday soon.

We would be twenty-eight on Friday-week and I was having a party. I know, it was not like me to draw attention to myself, but going out of character keeps people on their tippy-toes. Naturally, Sylvie was not on my exclusive invite list, way too risky.

I always preferred even numbers – the year would be *'Red in claw and tooth',* all hammers and nails, I thought. Then I caught myself. I was getting all intellectual, quoting from 'In Memoriam' A.H.H. Alfred, Lord Tennyson, no less. *'You misquoted,'* Sylvie said, deflating me in seconds. *'One thing I have learned is that people never learn.'*

That remark made me bristle. To calm down, I ran a bath and filled it with essential oils. I tried to relax inhaling the gorgeous aromas of geranium, rose and neroli, but I could not settle.

That she-devil never gave me a minute of peace. I reflected on how she had been scaring the living bejeezus out of me with her vasectomy obsession. I told her about my trepidation the following morning.

SYLVIE

Scaring Betty? Now really. All I do is show her a relatively straightforward, snip-snip procedure. But I can tell it vexes her by the way she runs out of her own house without making me leave first. Highly unusual behaviour.

'How can you even think of it?' she says (actually, she shouts). 'You are so obviously not a highly trained surgeon.'

But then again, I have always been good at sewing. No worries on that score.

BETTY

I was going to kill Terry Baker anyway. I could not let my erratic twin outdo me again.

Consequently, I made another attempt to distract her until she forgot about both Lynch and MY next victim. And nothing succeeds in distraction, I told myself, as much as a sordid and painful past.

In a sisterly way, I tried to get Sylvie to talk about her time in the unit. I had persisted on a sporadic basis with trying to get her to 'open up' (as they say; bleurch). It was a sore subject, but (I told her) I was trying to get round to making amends, in the hope that she might not want to murder me in my sleep (or when wide awake even). I suspected Sylvie preferred the former, but I had several locks on my bedroom door, so no chance there.

However, strangely enough, I found myself also drifting back to that time of turmoil – that time of whirling and swirling thoughts, when my moods were not only swinging but also swaying and doing about turns. That was before I learnt the importance of order. Since that time, I also found I could sometimes quell my wrath by inhaling deeply and exhaling until you have to gasp for air.

'Do you remember,' I said to Sylvie, 'two pivotal events that happened in lightning quick succession before we turned thirteen?'

SYLVIE

Of course, I remember, but I let her talk in pretend shrink mode. She was dreadful at it.

BETTY

This was what I said, or at least started to say, whilst I could get a word in edgeways.

'The first event entailed you and the boy next door, well down the road from our chateaux, in Aix-en-Provence, one of those run-down ones, some might describe it is shabby chic.'

Only, I mentally removed the word 'chic'.

SYLVIE

I have to interrupt her at the very start.

'Okay, it's a sweltering August day,' I tell her. 'I made an acquaintance, a boy, the same age as us, but he looks and acts younger. I use him as an excuse to get away from you and our fusty domicile. That is all there is to it, *finis*!'

BETTY

I could not let her get off that easily.

'I remember the atrocious mess you made,' I said. 'Repugnant it was. The blood-filled syringe and splatters on the floor we saw before the rest of the scene allayed no fears. He, Gerard, was not hurt physically (much).'

'We were just playing "quacks and nurses",' Sylvie said.

Whatever you called it, the sight still made me queasy. The other witness, his mother, skipped nausea and flew straight into a rage, like a vertical take-off. She grabbed you roughly by the arm and dragged you out onto the street and back to our home. Mama sorted it out, or so I thought, in her own indomitable way. An envelope was handed over, full of cash; she uttered something – a threat, no doubt – then she waved the bewildered mother and her protestations off and slammed the door.

Gossip was rife in the village that evening over pastis and cognacs; there was talk of little else. I heard a man say with vehemence that the boy's mother should have called the Gendarme. 'Too late, her words against mine,' mama said when I told her. '*Déni plausible*,' she added.

I remember looking that up. Plausible deniability, denying all knowledge. I liked the sound of it.

Papa fled to his room; mama spent the rest of the evening pacing up and down, pausing only to stare at Sylvie and then me, and trying to work out which one of us had committed quack-gate as I called it.

And fifteen years later in my kitchen I glared at Sylvie again. 'What I observed that day was irrefutable evidence of your inability to read people's emotions, despite pretending otherwise.'

She looked bemused at my accusation, not at all helpful. I noted that the puzzlement she felt, as I questioned her was fronted by a suitable expression – learned behaviour. Another one of her flaws she had tried to overcome. She had many more than me.

SYLVIE

'Now let me tell a tale about you, dear sis,' I say. 'When you were at school, you could not abide Cecile Berger.'

BETTY

How dare she mention that name. 'I never took to anyone prettier, wittier or brighter than me,' I said. 'That is not my fault, I was born that way.'

SYLVIE

'Don't interrupt,' I say. I could see I had unnerved her.

And then I proceed to parade the details, to the forefront of my brain. A faint recollection that had been swept beneath the folds begins to rattle along with metronomic timing, until it is so vivid and I am there, once again.

On the first day back at that mind-numbing school after a six-week break, Betty gets up early and takes newly laid wasp traps (with the toxic killing solution removed) down from our wild garden. She furtively walks to one of the school outbuildings, sticks tape over a small hole in the window and lets a score or more wasps out. She retreats quickly closing the creaky door behind her.

'Lair, lair!' Betty shouts, rudely interrupting me, I continue. Although more accurately, she yells it in French, '*Repaire, repaire!*'

During playtime on that day, she tells petite Cecile she has a surprise for her. Cecile is apprehensive but follows Betty nonetheless. As they near the shed, Betty waits patiently for her to catch up. When she grips Cecile's ponytail and pulls it, the rest of her naturally followed.

BETTY

At that point of her little macabre fantasy, I screamed at her, 'Must I listen to this?!'

Her answer was blunt and I felt overwhelmed and unable to stop her.

'Yes,' she said as she went on.

SYLVIE

I continue.

'With her other hand, innocent Betty opens the door and shoves Cecile in. Dismally for Betty, a few wasps escape, but many stay behind.

'Betty bolts the door and runs back to the playground. She beckons me over and says, someone is locked in the shed. "Do you want to help?" she asks. Naturally, I run. I hear a scream. Others hear it too, including Madame Lousteau. They arrive in time to see me unlocking the door and Cecile careering out, gasping and glazed. "Bee stung lips," Betty says to me under her breath. "Some people pay a lot to look like that."'

BETTY

What a relief her story was over or so I thought. She gave me one last withering look. 'That is when they took me away,' she said.

For someone who lived so much in the present, Sylvie had a maddingly persistent memory for painful moments, especially those associated with me. Hence, some fifteen years later, we were in my kitchen still arguing about it.

But I was patient and persisted in trying to both explain and placate.

'Since that day,' I said to Sylvie, who was unable to maintain her wrathful look. 'I have become more aware. I may have gone a bit far, although you had gone further by killing my cat. Driven by my wants and needs I had not thought about the consequences.'

The crux of the matter, the truth, was that I did not want and did not need Sylvie, until I realised that I did. Maybe I would have to start being pleasant.

I continued to explain to her about Cecile, who had been shaken up and scared but not scarred after the incident; 'wasp-gate' I called it. I felt an apology was in order, not to the captivating victim, but to my twin. I was not sure the right words would come out. I need not have bothered. Sylvie quickly stepped in and began to annoy me with more of her new age drivel. The words 'new' and 'age' together especially riled me. I made a supreme effort to listen to her nonsense for a change.

'As I repeatedly say,' Sylvie concluded, 'we shouldn't live in a past that is long gone. No good can come of it. My mindfulness podcasts advise me to live in the moment, to be here now.'

Argh! I screamed inwardly; they mouthed those irksome 'be here now' words in the office too.

At that point, she switched to talking about her main flaw as if it was mine.

SYLVIE

'Yes,' I tell Betty, 'I do have an inherent inability to empathise and to understand and respond appropriately. However, as you keep pointing out, I mask it well. You can stop getting all high horsey though; that Lady Gaga song "Poker Face" could be about you too, not just me. You sporadically bluster that the fukunts at work say you cannot stay away from the needle. They think you have had Botox; the bloody cheeks of it, you say!'

BETTY

Sylvie's comment was partially true, so I tried to smile, with my eyes and with my mouth, but I ended up looking like a spider monkey. My default expression was impassive. Anger the one emotion I could not easily veil.

I was not so keen on our similarities and often thought more about our differences instead – so does Sylvie. I let her go on.

SYLVIE

'You know that we will never be one and the same,' I tell her. 'Noughts, crosses, evens, odds. You like the Even Stevens; I prefer the odd numbers. The odds have more potential, don't you think? Evens are just too goody-two-shoes, too damned predictable. Not for me.'

BETTY

So she went back to her numbers game. But I had enough of her dominating play and going from pillar to post and off to another random pillar. I had important things to say.

I changed the subject abruptly to Lynch.

'*He* could put us in the frame,' I said. She knew who I was talking about. 'He could "like us" for our past crimes.'

In my defence, I was *not* overreacting. The reality TV star's drugs-death shocker still made the news, with lurid stories in the tabloids, variations on a well-worn theme:

'My sexy, fun night with Alby.'

'Alby kept me up all night, my drugs-fuelled threesome with reality star.'

'Alby and the selfie-stick!'

(I made that last one up.)

Kevin Wilkin's death made the papers too and the regional news. After that dicky program they were on, some of the trolls had a field day. Tracy had become a sleb all over again. All of it meant that I could not rest. I knew I was devious and careful and clever, but still.

'Lynch is as clean as a whistle,' Sylvie said, 'and hasn't put one and one together.'

'A whistle isn't clean if it has been blown,' I answered. 'In fact, it can be quite dirty, full of germs.'

I did have an aversion to dirt; instead of the glass being half-empty or half-full, I always looked to see if it was clean. No lipstick, fingerprints, spittle or marks from the dishwasher (might be clean, but I had an aversion to marks and specks).

Sylvie, on the other hand, was not averse to a bit of filth.

The differences didn't end there: what with her preference for rum and my partiality for gin. Her red-wine-and-red-meat thing the opposite of my penchant for champagne, Chablis and veganism. Well, I was not averse to firecracker shrimp on occasions and pork scratchings, whatever.

Lastly, with the exception of the number one, which oddly appealed, I could not abide odd numbers; they made my heartbeat quicken.

SYLVIE

'Let's skip Lynch for the moment, dear sister,' I tell her. 'You are going down a path that belongs to me. Let's focus your plan, why don't we. Your next prey, Terry dearest.'

One thing we agree on, for all our talk, is that we are not happy about this entire Serial Dad mass-repro thing. What happens to the progeny; do they get a timeshare on the father? No matter how hard I try, I cannot work out how it will work. It is impossible to see all the offspring in a fortnight, what with them being in so many disparate locations (he had spread his seed so far and wide).

Saying that, I am fine with single parents. And Betty agrees.

BETTY

Yes, I admit we had to put up with a bit of that ourselves after the incident with Cecile and the wasps. Papa upped sticks and moved northwards out of Aix-en-Provence to Vendome for several months. To cope, mama took up baking when he left. She also spent the next five years visiting Sylvie once a month, handing over her unpalatable culinary efforts at security.

Anyway, enough of our – sob, sob, cries crocodile tears – sob stories.

I was determined to deactivate the fecund fukunt Terry, but my careful planning was on hold. I insisted that Sylvie tell me the truth about what was going on with Lynch.

'Nothing,' she said.

Then she went on about how we needed to focus on that spurting prick, Terry Baker, foetus maker.

SYLVIE

He brags about his on-target spurts: big freaking spunk hoorays. His golfing mates call him a tart in a jealous, jokey way – and he loves it. He goes wherever his dick takes him; no doubt, it has led him to the hot weather girl. She has been making him sweat. He has moved in with her by the looks of it.

BETTY

Sylvie knew this because she tailed him on and off for days. He did not venture far out of a southwest London postcode so she never had to go too far on *my* motorbike.

It was late and my brain was overloaded with thoughts of the past. Was it really what it was? What did it matter? I would rather think about the future. I had a lot to reflect on, so I ejected Sylvie and slept as well as a teething baby.

CHAPTER 21.

At the Gin Palace

BETTY

I shelved Terry Baker for the moment because I was planning my birthday party at that new Gin Palace in Palmers Green.

Sylvie, of course, was not invited.

Still, she insisted. She would like a rum palace, she said. I said, 'I'd like a Palais de Champagne.' She was not welcome there either.

Anyway, I invited Martin from work and a few of the other fukunts. Yes, the one who made me so mad on my first day back after my trip up North when he complained, 'Your out-of-office is still on,' in a whinging, whiny voice. I wanted to strangle him, slowly with his salmon pink tie.

Despite his annoying voice and his general limpness, I decided to be sweet for a change; he had his uses. 'Oh, Martin Briars-Hedley, you handled my work so well, you're almost as good as me.' I was so all flattery and buttery-upper with him that he agreed to come to my party.

Bit over the top. I did not blame him for the sideways glances and subsequent huddles with the others that night.

I even invited Shelley, who always got drunk and dribbled when eating the finger food, then inevitably put her grotesque, diaphanous fingers back into the bowl.

*

As the party began, Sylvie made another unwelcome entry into my tiara-topped head. I had left her counterpart sulking at her mews house an hour before. Alarmingly before I set off, she said, 'Huh, like you can have a birthday party without me, dream on!'

Just as I was beginning to enjoy myself at my do (imbibing a double gin and tonic helped), I heard her familiar nagging voice in my mellowing brain: *'Whether you want us to lead separate lives and keep me hidden is irrelevant; you cannot have it your way all the time. We are perpetually bonded. To use your favourite word; now who is the fekunt?'*

'It is "fukunt", you id!' I replied.

I had done as much as humanly possible to keep Sylvie from crashing my party. I left her behind, double-locking her front door. I had taken her two sets of keys and her window keys as well, but conceded her being her; she would somehow manage to break out.

Her voice went blessedly silent in my head, and I forgot about her for a while. The Gin Palace was intriguing. There were a few hundred different brands of gin on offer, all tasted different. I liked variety and I was excited about trying a few that I hadn't sampled before.

I was wearing an eye-alluring, canary-yellow froufrou dress. There I was neck to toe in lemon sumptuousness on my fifth type of gin, 50mls a time with soda and lime.

Then I spotted Sylvie's reflection in the mirror above the art deco fireplace. The real Sylvie, not the annoying voice in my head. She was in the distance and in semi-darkness. It looked like she was wearing the same outfit as me.

'Are we five years old?' I mouthed, not sure, if she had seen me, or my reflection. I was livid but resigned to the fact that I expected nothing less. I would have to eject her, even though she was in disguise and skulking out of sight, almost. With a red wig atop her head and ringlets aplenty, she was a bit too eye-catching for my liking. I felt jealous, the wig was one of my favourites.

I saw her head to the toilets and was about to follow when the next thing I encountered was DCI Lynch handing me a birthday card and a book-shaped package.

'Do I know you?' I asked. Of course, I knew who he was.

He gave me a strange look, like really, odd.

'Calum Lynch,' he said. The next moment his cold, dry, large, soft hand was in my hand. 'I've seen you in court.'

'Oh yes, I'm law and you're order. Although right now, I'm disorder,' I joked. Actually, I said 'dish order,' the shame. He did not even crack a smirk; lips didn't even twitch. Obviously, he had no sense of humour. There was something deeply wrong with him.

'Are you going to open your present?' he asked.

'No.'

That thwarted him. I was desperate to know what it was, but also thought it must be a trick. He wasn't getting one over on me. I felt apprehensive; I knew why he was here. I just did not think he would be that clever or that I could be that stupid.

'How do you know Tracy Wilkins?' he asked, looking at Tracy who was flirting with a group of wannabes that had ignored the 'Closed for Private Party' sign.

Silent gulp. 'Excuse me,' I said, 'I need to go to the toilet.'

*

Yes, I invited Tracy; against Sylvie's advice. She made the long journey – I was her bezzie mate, after all, or so she said a few times over, a bit slurred, only minutes into the party.

She was now twelve kilos lighter, with natural curls and cheekbones that no one knew existed, even Tracy ('Always been a bit on the heavy side,' she said). She was still in mourning. She looked quite stunning in black, it had to be said.

Lynch stared at her, eyes gleaming, while I made my exit.

Sitting down in the cubicle, carefully covering the seat with toilet roll, I ripped open the packaging of Lynch's present.

The Poisoner's Handbook.

Freaking, fucking, fuck. Of course, I had read it many a time.

I bunged it in my bag, but before I could properly get up and make my way unsteadily back to the table, there was a knock on the cubicle door. It was Sylvie, and she asked me to let her in. Luckily, it was not one of those cramped toilets, the ones where you can just about squeeze yourself in through the door. There was room for both of us.

Naturally, I scolded her. Then she surprised me by grabbing and twisting my wrist and having a good rant, culminating with, 'That bitch Tracy should not even be here. You mucked up the pizza topping, Betty. Did not sprinkle it evenly as I instructed. You fucked up big time.'

'Is your teeny, tiny rant over sis, I need another drink,' I said, digging my nails into her hand.

SYLVIE

A rant, really? I am always open and honest and frank.

About my wearing the same dress: 'Same outfit?' I begin. 'As if, Betty!'

Anyone worth their salt on the fashion scene nowadays knows the dress I am wearing, unlike her outfit, has Christopher Kane's stamp all over it. OK, the light was dim; you probably could not see from the distance. Up close, you can see my dress is transparent and suits me down to the ground. On the surface, it looks classy; underneath you see there is more to it, a bit like me with my hidden depths. I conclude by saying, 'Stuff that filthy look into your miniature clutch bag, why don't you, Betty, and stop scowling; it is so unbecoming.'

She tells me to leave immediately and that my presence at her party is another thing that she will add to the very long list of my trespasses against her.

My outburst is far from over (ooh, perhaps it was an outburst. Am I becoming like her?). I tell her that only one person fleetingly experienced the full effect and joy of the transparency and that is Calum, my favourite private dick at the XO on the night of Alby's death. My image is etched on his retinas, without a doubt.

I tell her that the present-giving ceremony didn't miss my attention. I have my eye on you two, I explain. I also clock the enlargement of his already large pupils when he eyes Trace.

'Yeah,' I admit, 'she's not bad looking, but her fat suit isn't far behind her. I would tell him that, if I didn't have to hide all night.' Plus, that is the sort of nasty, wide of the mark remark that Betty makes. I find that one I start I cannot help but spill.

'And another thing about Tracy,' I say. 'There must be plenty of spare flesh beneath the designer clothes she receives from sponsors. It will only be a matter of time before a scalpel hovers over it. What a pathetic plastic world we live in. How I hate it.'

At that point, Betty tells me that I am rude and glares at me. I look away, I can't take her beady eyes anymore.

BETTY

My heart was going at 200 beats per minute. I was sure my heart strings were about to snap.

If Lynch ever discovered that we were two, I swore, right then and there, I would kill her.

I had given Sylvie strict instructions earlier before I locked her in her own house and took her keys, including her spare set, I took her window keys too. Of course, she was one of those people who kept a spare set of the spare keys.

I clearly told her she had to leave the premises, but I knew she wouldn't even as I left the toilet to re-join my party.

Everything Sylvie said angered me. What's more, she was such a hypocrite.

Hates plastic, indeed; she would have done anything to stay looking like she did that night.

Poor Tracy, you could not begrudge her getting her overhanging folds removed. Me, I was scared stiff of knives, needles and any other sharp items pointing in the direction of any part of my body. It would be non-invasive all the way – it would be face peeling, burnt-car-crash-face blotchiness for me. In the meantime, you would be amazed what you can do with makeup, Burberry shades and wigs; they hide everything.

Anyway, I was on my sixth gin when Sylvie swerved past me and ensconced herself in an alcove one level above. She was surveying all she saw, in semi-darkness again. I could tell, even from a distance that she was getting more incensed by the second as she watched Lynch and 'Tracy, the survivor'.

SYLVIE

Flirty, flirty, Lynch, do STOPPIT! I am getting… what am I getting? Jealous? A new feeling; I am not sure how to process it. My ears are getting quite hot. They might even have been sweating. Repulsive. I am livid; I am thinking Calum is fast and I am furious.

BETTY

Meanwhile I was earwigging.

'Was Kev buried or cremated, Trace?' Lynch asked.

'Cremated, we had a little ceremony,' Trace explains. 'Scattered them in that little pond down the road from his favourite takeaway, where we used to get our chicken sticks. Of course, I couldn't eat one now. Got to look after my figure, like.' Wiggle, wiggle.

'Touching,' he said. 'Who was there?'

I don't bother listening to the rest of their conversation.

Tracy and Lynch's noxious tête-à-tête jolted me back to the past. I savoured the smugness I felt that Kevin's ashes were no more. The fishes in that fetid manmade pond were sated. The pond with the shopping trolley sticking out blighted an already blighted sight. Although, I wasn't sure if ashes were good for fishes or if there were any in there in the first place.

I thought about Lynch being on a road to nowhere. He had no evidence for we left no traces. The fact that he was at my party was cause for concern. I had to accept that he was one of those annoying dicks who have hunches. Dangerous.

I felt assured he would not find any forensic evidence from the ashes. I knew forensics had moved on; Kevin's ashes were in a pond. Examining them, even with the latest methods, was a stretch too far. As for Alby, well, the poison from Sylvie's pipette was untraceable, what with all the other stuff he'd ingested (for Sylvie fed him a few drugs beginning with e, f, GBH, h and whatever else they are called these days).

Three jeers for looking, DCI Lynch, but you will not find a thing, nada. The verdicts would be death by misadventure and heart failure in that order.

SYLVIE

I am still loitering in the shadows, so Betty won't see me again, or anyone else at her lame party for that matter. She is out of control with so much repressed anger and seven gins, or thereabouts. Her outfit looks absurd. She bears a passing resemblance to Big Bird from Sesame Street. I bet her colleagues are laughing behind her plumy back.

I look down from the alcove, watching, amazed at my self-control. One day I will lose it entirely. I am desperate to get on the dance floor and cause mayhem. I watch Tracy, despising her for making moves on Calum, but I envy her carefree attitude and the way she tantalises with her body and moves her hips.

He is lapping up the attention. I am inert with jealousy, and I can barely think. Oh, see if I care. I will tearlessly and fearlessly ditch him. Not that he is mine to ditch yet; but after I finish with him, he will crawl back, naked on all fours. Just you watch.

Now though the needle pricks of jealousy are too much for me. He must feel the wave of possessiveness and jealousy emanating from me. That wave, more forceful than an ocean, takes me by surprise, I want to be above all that wanting and needing.

He slowly turns, looks up and spots me leaning over the balustrade. I retreat acknowledging that Calum does not recognise me from the XO, I can tell. That night, I had coloured contact lenses on and a different wig and latex face, but even so he seems a bit slow. Oh, how you disappoint me; you head straight to voluptuous Tracy and my less interesting klutz of a sister, Betty, whilst I skulk in the semi-darkness.

Talking of the she-fiend, I know Betty sees all of this. Out of the far corner of my left eye I catch a fleeting death stare. I get the message. I decry being the uninvited guest; it is my birthday too. One day I will access all areas, after I kill her and dispose of her body. That is the only thing that keeps me going. I could take her out now. I could easily lure her up to my hidey-hole and push her over the balcony, she is that drunk. But she intrigues me too much, and it is gratifying to toy with her.

I exit the so-called Gin Palace. It really is just a glorified bar with trendy décor and some big light bulbs. I wait for my Calum to leave and stalk him. More of that later; suffice to say I do not like what I see. I decide not to trail him any further. Plans are formulating to capture him and lock him in my basement.

That can wait, for it is late and I need a drink. Oblivion is what I seek to numb the pain of knowing what he has been up to, with Tracy. I scream inwardly as I head to a late-night drinking club in Soho. I order my third double rum and coke and catch the glare of a shady character. Our eyes almost meet as we take sideways glances at each other. Within seconds, he introduces himself.

His name is Carlos; things are looking up methinks. I take his card. It is time to bring in another. It is a no brainer. For a start he bears a passing resemblance to James Franco in a 1950s gangster suit, with an obligatory fedora. What's more, Betty will spin off her axis when I tell her that I am bringing him in!

BETTY

The next morning, I clutched my head, expecting a hangover and was surprised not to feel the usual pounding behind irritated dry eyes. What I did feel was dread as I remembered that bloodhound Lynch's unsettling words last night. At some point he raised a tenuous link – three reality stars had died in the past few months, I overheard him telling Tracy purposively, as they danced around her ocean-clogging, non-sustainable sequined handbag. He said he did not believe in coincidences. Tracy frowned and asked to speak to him about it somewhere quieter. I followed them.

Lynch furtively said that he believed that the death of a middle-aged man who had appeared on a TV talent show was suspicious. The public loves a trier and he, Todd Dickson, was notable because he managed to hit nearly all the right notes. Like most wannabes on those shows, he had a sob story that made him blub, all for a place in the final and a few more votes from the wet-eyed public. He died in a motorbike accident.

As he relayed this to Tracy, I wanted to shout at Lynch. Todd Dickson's death had nothing to do with me; it had to be an accident. Lynch was seeing something that was not there. Clearly, he liked to make connections, bah. Still, Lynch's ability to see the big picture, even though he had not put all the right people in the frame, perturbed me.

Which reminded me of my current prey.

Terry Baker presented a banal show too – though not as excruciating as the ones Alby and Kevin starred in. It was about upcycling furniture in people's houses; they did a whole living room or bedroom at a time. He seemed to have a talent for it or maybe the skilled professionals that do all the hard work behind the scenes did, more like.

At that moment I considered refraining from murdering Mr. Terry Baker for a while longer at least to keep Lynch off the scent. Another 'sleb' on the slab would draw too much attention. It would really be careless.

However, I also knew the DCI would be diverted by other crimes in the capital; his obsessive nature would keep him occupied on whatever case he was on until arrests were made. What's more plans were plans, breaking them was flaky, and I was impatient to kill again.

CHAPTER 22.

Normality

BETTY

Although I hesitated, I still went out to see a band.

I don't mean to freak you out, but yes, I did have a normal life for a femme fatale. I could be sitting beside you right now, if you too went to grossly overpriced gigs. Just saying!

It wasn't a good idea. All night I thought of making like Louie the Lilac from Batman and using my deadly spray on the god awful 'singers' around me.

At one point I shouted, 'Hey, you, tuneless twat twerp over there, go learn how to sing.'

With the booking fee hefty enough without the ticket price, I did not want to hear their whiny sharp or flat attempts to hit the note or even gets the lyrics right, shitheads.

I even turned on the other people there, although, they couldn't hear me over the din. 'You tuneless, shouty irritants,' I yelled, we are not on the football terraces, shut it, shut it, shut it!'

Then, I went completely off my now formerly favourite band as they encouraged this vulgar offence. I swore it was my last gig ever!

In short, I was in a right bad mood. I needed to channel it and escalate dealing with Terry, my latest prey. I could no longer put it off. It was dangerous to my health.

*

This time, I also realised, we would need help to keep Lynch off the trail. And we would get it from Sylvie's latest acquisition, 'A young man of extraordinary personal beauty.' That was how

Carlos described himself. I had to agree. He was to be our facilitator, enabling us to get more things done.

Sylvie met him in a bar in Soho after she left my birthday party at the Gin Palace. She fell for him; no surprise there, she seemed to fall for everyone. She gave him the job title of 'facilitator'. We needed one if we were to get to the end of my long list of prey, she said.

I video called him the following day, obscuring my face with a spider plant. As an extra precaution, I donned the red wig and a pair of oversized sunglasses. I liked what I saw. He would naturally be under the illusion that I was Sylvie. I already knew a lot about him as she had told me much.

Carlos, was over two metres tall and a natty dresser. He had the build of a rugby player although he never played; he didn't fancy the mud and all of the grabbing and yanking. Sylvie thought he would be good for transportation and cleaning tasks. For someone of his size he was adept, light on his feet and could, like us, fade into the background when required.

Ray-bans, hair sleeked back with gel, he was striking. The preoccupation and importance placed on looks these days helped detract from his nefarious activities. He had a chequered past – I did a background check. Passers-by focused on the indisputable fact that he was hot, attractive to all sexes.

Sylvie was excited, as she was when she first eyed Lynch. To me it was a no-brainer getting Carlos onboard. For some reason, my willingness to do so disconcerted Sylvie. I liked the look and sound of him; plus, it appeared Sylvie was losing interest in Lynch, what with the way she was on about her new find. I was wary but knew I could put him to good use.

Then Sylvie ruined my burgeoning optimism. I had been ecstatic when she told me that she had lost interest in Lynch. I plummeted back down to earth when she informed me what the DCI had gotten up to with Tracy after he left my party.

SYLVIE

This is what I tell Betty.

'To my satisfaction, I discover that, for Lynch, Tracy is just a fling, or at least it appears so. He goes to her new apartment after the gin palace, but he leaves much earlier than Tracy must have anticipated. Probably cannot stand the mood swings: morose to bubbly and back, I bet.

'There is no mucking round trying to switch the complicated-looking set-top box on. No pretence – on either part – of being there to watch something or maybe getting to know one another less intimately to start with. They get straight to it, and then he disappears into the night.'

BETTY

Even so, I knew that Sylvie was insanely jealous of Tracy. She said she had to stop herself throwing the binoculars down and storming into the apartment block. 'It will not be long, until I exact revenge,' she said.

That last bit startled me for I had become fond of my newfound friend Tracy.

'Do not cross me, again,' I warned her. 'Tracy is off-limits.'

I tried to catch a glimpse of her reaction, but Sylvie had left my kitchen without a word.

SYLVIE

Right now, I desire Lynch so much so that I pay a trip to Agent Provocateur to get some fancy pants. Tracy will be but a distant memory once he sees what I have in store for him. There will be no sweetness; there will just be salt, sharpness, sour and smoke. Betty turns me to fags, she is so uppity, she stresses me so.

Betty is still obsessing over needing to kill Terry, when surgery would be more fitting. I will deal with her later.

BETTY

Frustratingly, days later, Terry Baker remained a work in progress; the sharps were sharp and scrupulously spotless. Naturally, I would rather have dealt with him myself. However, when Sylvie put her mind to it, she could outperform everyone, and she was so excited about it.

'I have practiced incisions before,' Sylvie said proudly.

'Yes, and your stitching is rather neat, as you like to say,' I replied.

'Good enough to work for Chanel,' she added. How conceited.

'I do not think Terry will tell anyone about his ordeal,' I predicted. 'He is not the type to learn and evangelise. What's more, he is unlikely to squeal to the pigs. Oh, I am so funny today, sis.'

'But he might squeal during the operation.' Sylvie's unpleasant high-pitched laughter rang in my ears.

This was my reasoning: even if he did tell, he could not identify us. Surgical masks, goggles and those surgical caps would ensure we left no trace of our handiwork. Besides, he would be so woozy he would not remember what we knew would be the theatrical performance of the year.

'Doctor, doctor,' I said.

'Yes,' Sylvie replied.

'It is nearly time,' I murmured.

What I really meant was that it was nearly time to get even with her.

SYLVIE

There will be more than enough time for doctoring later.

While Betty focuses on Terry, I have something new to report. It turns out that a tragedy has befallen Tracy.

Back up; back up, before you start to finger me for the crime! I had absolutely nothing to do with it (that is my story and I am sticking to it).

By my watch, Calum (my Calum) was with her from 21.59 until precisely 23.43. I even have digital images recording the exact time they enter the building, arms like spaghetti all over each other. Not even two hours later, he leaves the building, notably alone.

You can escape but you cannot hide, Tracy. If the Grim Reaper wants you, he will find you, although the Reaper has sadly not reaped yet. The next day the front-page headline reads:

Reality TV star's latest tragedy: slimming pills the likely cause.

With an insert: **'Reality TV Star Tragedy'** above a flattering picture of her and one less so, plus a recap of Kevin's tragic demise too, all so dreadful.

The townies are out in droves, flowers, balloons and teddy bears in hand and a few chicken sticks scattered about willy-nilly outside the hospital.

And the real tragedy? She isn't even dead. Argh!

Anyway, the report suggests that looker Tracy, who had lost over ten kilos since her husband's tragic death, is in a coma after ingesting something beginning with D that I cannot pronounce. (Between you and me, it was pills purchased online.) I have to read the article twice to fully comprehend how such a heart-wrenching event has occurred without me having anything to do with it (I am superglued to that story).

At least Calum cannot succumb to the unsubtle promise of newly ripened, curvaceous fruit – unless she wakes up. Oh, maybe he will feel guilty and ask her out if she comes out of her coma; I do not like to think of that.

BETTY

After another unpleasant day at work, I returned to the mews. Sylvie is in my house – gleeful, excited, she positively quivered. She read the entire tragic story aloud, each word enunciated deliciously in her pouty mouth, whilst I sat in my favourite armchair, (teal velvet) devastated.

Tracy was MY friend. OK, I had only met her three times, once when I was going to kill her, but she ended up being the only friend I had ever had; I needed to go and visit her.

Sylvie denied having anything to do with the latest turn of events. Her eyes shifted from side to side as she forgot which side denoted that she was telling the truth (the right, of course). I laughed out of nervousness, sceptical. Sylvie fed her those pills somehow at my birthday party; I would bet her life on it.

My twin had a habit of making things up just like mama. Most things mama said you could add a naught to or divide it by ten.

'Your papa lost 10,000 euros at the races, ("Yes ma") and he blew a million on that dreadful Picasso titty jug back in the seventies ("sure mama").

'I broke both legs in a terrible skiing accident in Maribel and was back on the slopes within weeks.' In fact, mama had only scraped and bruised her knees.

Baron von Munchausen and Walther Mitty were veracious in comparison.

*

And now, for a few words about grief and revenge.

After a long, hard day at work, I took a deep breath and realised with a jolt that I was feeling something inexplicable, just a tiny bit of warmth and uneasiness in my abdomen.

When Sylvie wasn't around, I found myself saying aloud, 'Tracy, I miss you, please wake up.' I did not know if the feeling was real or a figment, but for a few seconds I felt something. Frozen cold-to-the-bones me was thawing at the rate of a melting polar icecap. I was actually afraid bits of me would start breaking off. Help! My eyes were inexplicably watering, odd for someone who did not do tears unless I wanted something.

I took Tracy's absence in my life badly. She had shown an interest in me, confided in me even. I should have been able to proclaim that Seb was a friend, but he was the total opposite – an 'un-friend', a total let down.

Despite her wide-eyed protestations, I had an unshakeable belief that Sylvie had something to do with Tracy's plight. My sister's death might be sooner than anticipated, the way she was going. She hissed in my ear that a lie detector would prove her innocence and continued to protest too much that she had nothing to do with it.

'If you dare to take a test, I'll set it up to kill you,' I said out loud by mistake, my brain whirring. Faulty wiring, an electric chair. I'd be down in the basement later, screwdriver in hand, amongst other deadly items to make her fry. She informed me that she would pass the test, she had done it before.

'You are over fond of bragging and making spectacular claims,' I told her and headed down the creaky stairs to my basement to cool down.

CHAPTER 23.

Theatrics

BETTY

Enough of panties-on-fire liars and grief; it was curtains up show time for Mr Terry Baker. The operating theatre set was ready and even smelled like a real one. A week before the scheduled event, Carlos spent half a day, last week, getting it right; I did like authenticity.

You would not believe how easy it was to find a derelict hospital ready to be demolished to make way for eyesore flats and rubbish shops. This one had minimal security. All the good stuff had been disposed of, sold or stolen. Carlos, our new facilitator, purloined and pilfered scalpels, a suction contraption device and retractors. He was meticulous, getting the place looking spick and span.

Dressing up in scrubs was a scream. I loved those clogs; always liked them and those dinky blue plastic overshoes. We expected a bit of spillage and did not want to ruin the clogs. I told myself I could wear them again, but would have to store them in my hiding place, my next-door neighbour's attic where they would never be found. There were plenty of rubber gloves, swabs, dressings and tape at the ready. Oh, and analgesia; I was not cruel, not intentionally so.

Spurt prevention was what I was about.

Up until the day before his unscheduled appointment, Sylvie continued to track Terry. It was easy, he was still sniffing around seducing and bed dazzling. Gossip sites were useful for discovering celebrity haunts and habits. Stalking was a breeze in London too, so long as you didn't lose sight of the prey on the crowded street. Sylvie sported the geriatric look again, with a bit of swagger (she couldn't help it). She had worked that walking stick, steel-tipped, retractable poison-filled (only joking). Then Terry finally looked round. Did not see her, of course not.

Over 50s were invisible to spunk-spurting addicts, I said.

*

There were two plans in play for serial offender Terry. I veered one way then another and back again, till I felt rather dizzy.

Originally, I was going to send Sylvie to abduct him. He would not be able to resist. But Carlos had other ideas. He wanted to dress up and lure him into a van, and he was proving to be very persuasive.

'I want to be a fat, bald postie,' he said. (He did like a uniform, who doesn't?)

Like middle-aged women and beyond, no one noticed fat, bald men in uniform invisible, and it gave us an alibi of sorts and more prep and recovery time.

Cons? None that I could think of.

'Zshoooop,' Carlos made the noise of the syringe plunging into his neck, sedative filled.

Decision made.

Except that I had second thoughts again, third thoughts, in fact. Carlos had permeated our closed group because Sylvie recruited him. I knew he was no security risk; we knew more about him than he knew about us, but still. Sylvie's voice followed me to the basement. *'Bit part players carry risk. I hear you. The thing is, we have plenty of dirt on him should the need arise. You know exactly what I am referring too. He will take the vow of silence if we need him to – the threat of a slice and a chop usually does it.'*

I was not totally assured, but hey-ho.

*

The morning after her stalking escapade, Sylvie went off the radar again. I needed someone that was focused. She met a footballer that night in a top London hotel, after she had shed part of her disguise.

Now all thighs, not just Lynch's, mesmerised her. It seemed like she had started to compare his to any passer-by. She denied it and had a go.

SYLVIE

'Thigh eying – as if I do not have better things to do, really.'

I have a full-time job keeping Betty in check. Disguising Carlos is a ridiculous idea; his size counts against him for a start. Although a private dress rehearsal might excite. I look forward to peeling off his uniform, layer by layer, a strip tease by one eager to please.

For life is like an onion; all of our layers can be peeled off, with inescapable tears and a few toddler-like tantrums along the way. I can be profound (sometimes).

BETTY

I reflected on Sylvie's unprofessional attitude – as usual, Sylvie could not help herself, hanging around in the West London hotel bar that Terry frequented with his ovine hangers-on. She was only supposed to watch him from a distance.

Bah, why couldn't she behave?

Her 'stalking' outfit consisted of a big floppy hat (bit hot for it), enormous shades, a flame-coloured wig and a walking stick, drawing attention BIG TIME. Onlookers, she informed me, squinted, wondering if she was someone famous.

She came back very late (2.13 am), most of her disguise had been ditched. She was flushed and muttering about binning Carlos's already agreed plan.

'Dumpster for Carlos,' she said. 'He leers excessively.'

Sylvie, calling the teakettle black, had caught him eyeing up other women, sneakily glancing through those Ray-bans while he played at watching the watcher at the hotel. 'The eyebrow raises give it away,' she said. 'And there was him thinking I couldn't spot it. One look is the same as spending the night.'

Yep, rationality out of the window, but I did not bother arguing with her. His furtive staring provided a glimpse into his one-tracked, side-tracked mind. *Ay caramba*, charismatic Carlos simply could not be trusted.

SYLVIE

His brown eyes put Carlos at a distinct disadvantage over Lynch's mysterious grey, tinged with green flecks, making his dark limbal rings appear bigger.

BETTY

As usual, Sylvie was delusional; Carlos's eyes were dazzling, Lynch's were weird, his irises were like miniature distressed mirrors with one eye socket higher than the other. At least I thought so at my birthday party; although, I was looking at him askance after my gin guzzling session.

'I know you prefer tall, dark and impossibly handsome,' Sylvie added. 'But for some reason you go out with Seb – you can keep him.'

My blood boiled to overflowing; 'Seb is the most striking man in the whole wide world.'

SYLVIE

Betty is still besotted by wan Seb, how irritating. I only engage in conversation with her about Carlos to punish him for planting a device in my bag. I find it on the night I first met him in Soho and make a mental note to use it at a later date. Leaving it in my cupboard is no hardship. I have as many handbags as I have wigs, I prefer to go out without a handbag, instead stuffing things into pockets.

I start toying with Carlos via the device, he must have heard every word I said. I have fun – insulting his plan and his eyes, ha.

Next I hammer the device repeatedly until it is sparkly dust.

CARLOS

I was listening in. My earpiece felt like a furnace in my ear.

I wanted to run a mile; no, ten miles. I raged against Sylvie's casual dismissal of my alluring eyes and my ingenuous plan to kidnap Terry. It was frustrating that I could only hear one voice. Was she talking to herself? Or maybe she was on the phone to someone in the small hours of the morning. She was not from this planet or any other for that matter.

'That Sylvie is despicable,' I found myself saying. 'I would like to lock her in a cupboard.'

But no, I would never hurt a woman, even her. When it comes to maiming and occasionally killing, it is strictly men only for me.

Being into surveillance and countersurveillance, I placed a device in Sylvie's bag, on the night I first met her. Just for kicks, now I wish I had not. I did not hear much of note till today, silence most of the time, in fact. I wondered if she was one of those women who changed their handbag every day. Bet she was.

BETTY

Later that evening, I found I could not let my foreboding lie – her comment about Lynch's eyes made me anxious. She was still into him, in spite of picking up Carlos in a bar, she seems to have gone off him already.

'Be wary of Lynch, sis,' I told her. 'He wants to send you down. Moreover, I mean to the nick – and not where you might be thinking. My plans for Terry had stalled because of HER Lynch obsession and HER visit to the Hotel. We could not proceed, yet. I poured myself a gin and called Carlos, pretending to be Sylvie again and told him to forget about the postman gig. He was off out anyway with his ivory-handled garrotte to play some games. He had his own gripes and prey – his side-hustle.

Despite what Sylvie said about our facilitator lately, I recommended that she 'Date Carlos and bin Lynch, madam.' (She bristled when I called her that.) Let us see.

*

Later, I sat up in my king-size wrought-iron bed thinking of the next steps in the Terry Baker clip-clip caper, when I heard, '*So, how are you going to get him to the North Wales Asylum?*'

But my Sylvie already had an answer…

'Easy peas like squeezing lemons. Beckoned by the verdant grass of home and by whispered promises, Terry will oblige. I entice him in lambing season and administer a mind-altering substance. Exotic mushrooms are all the rage. Addled and beyond, he carries out an unspeakable act. Sacrificing sheep, letting them bleed out and pinning them to trees won't go down well, especially with the local farmers. The local press will report that a "Former popstar has been caught with the blood of Welsh lambs on his hands" and he will be caught red-handed.'

'Mr. Terry Baker would not be hung for a lamb,' I told her.

'Your bloody-fur-fetish freakshow went to the dumpster too, along with all your other idiot ideas.'

And I had only just gotten over Carlos's strange love of ivory.

'You two cruel fucks are a good match for each other,' I said aloud. 'Do not deny it, Sylvie. Remember, no animals will be hurt again. Leave no traces; sloppiness is not an option.'

There was no answer. Sylvie-in-my-head was totally silent.

*

The next morning, I called Sylvie on the phone and said, 'Hey sis, change of plan; we are going to Welshpool instead, you and I, to visit Great-Aunt Gwynne. In the unlikely event the DCI gets a sniff of a trail, she will make sure he leaves with brain ache.'

What I didn't tell her was that I had private business to take care of first. I was removing Sylvie from the picture; she was not going to go anywhere near my next prey. That meant I had to get our new facilitator back on the case.

Two days later Carlos bundled a rather sloshed Terry from a dimly lit side street in South West London. He manhandled him into the back of a stolen van, tied him up and drove.

Hours later he arrived and manhandled him once again whilst I waited patiently. Carlos watched over Terry, who was strapped to a gurney, while I prepared for the operation.

CARLOS

Let me explain what happened with me and Terry.

'Where am I?' Terry asked, slowly coming around.

'Don't worry' I said. ''We will take good care of you.'

'There was a bird with me earlier,' he said. Little did he know it was me in drag, rather fetching if I say so myself. I was affronted that he called me a bird. If I *was* one, I would have to be an ostrich, what with my stature, or maybe a cassowary and I would peck his stupid head.

Terry rambled on, with a cocky, faux-cockney accent. 'I turned around and she had gone. I have never had that effect on a bird before; they are usually like putty in my hands.'

'Don't worry,' I mumbled, thinking: who is the putty now?

I was enjoying myself. This was far better than the breaking and entering, spying and eavesdropping people usually asked me to do. What's more, this person was famous. And I thought, maybe I could enter the world of fame by proxy just by hanging out with him for a few days, after he recovered from his pending operation.

As I tightened the straps pinning down all limbs, I had another stray thought. A lightbulb moment, one of those oversized bulbs with thick filaments. I could become famous by rescuing the famous Terry Baker from the crazed pretend surgeon.

I imagined myself saying to the police: 'I heard a scream from afar ran towards the disused building to investigate.'

I could end up on a reality TV show. Maybe I could go on that bollock eating show in Oz. The sky was no limit; a limit was no limit. Just for the pleasure of it, I puffed up my gigantic chest.

I had more to gain than lose by helping him.

OK, I could lose Sylvie, but that was no biggie. Nah, nothing worth holding onto.

I still couldn't quite work out if there was just one woman and she was a good mimic or if there were two playing with my addled head. Since meeting Sylvie, my mind had gone into overdrive. I had to tread carefully around her, or them, even. I couldn't keep up with the transformations.

CHAPTER 24.

Who's the Daddy Now?

BETTY

The operation on Terry Baker was a backslapping, high-fiving, running-man-dance, runaway success. It took a few minutes longer than anticipated; but once I got started, it was like, I imagined, watching Damian Hirst at work, sterilising fluid and sponge on a stick thing, suction, scalpel and Prolene stitches.

Oh, I should have been a surgeon and not a staid paralegal. I kept my scrubs and mask on, and surgical glasses on too; you couldn't be too careful. Carlos could never pick me out at a line-up. Not that it would come to that.

Terry's head was lolling, groaning a lot.

'What is that song?' he said. 'I have heard it before, cannot even remember who sings it.'

It was Kid Creole, but I did not reply, a good one for someone who does not want to be anyone's daddy.

OK, he did not say that first. He struggled against the restraints, he screamed and pleaded rather pathetically. What have you done to my? Scream, scream, piercing scream. I stuck another roofie to him and gave him a quick drink of water that he almost choked on as he tried to spit the tablet out. Disgusting. Anyway, I bunged it in and waited for him to stop writhing. I spent a few minutes longer there, and then skedaddled out, leaving my motionless patient behind.

Carlos, Carrrrrloss?'

There was no sign of him or his van. I got into the hire car and exited the scene.

*

I had another place to be – Welshpool for a fleeting visit to Great-Aunt Gwynne. The day before Carlos delivered Terry, I handed Sylvie a wad of cash and told her I would meet her at eight o'clock in a bar in Powys. I did not turn up; I was otherwise occupied – killing Terry and then burning my scrubs and all before tea time. In the unlikely event that a question about my alibi came up, I was in Powys that night (nearly an hour away). I could prove it, look at the CCTV.

Unsurprisingly, Sylvie turned up at 10.15 pm at Gwynne's. I had already had a cup of tea and some delicious homemade crumpets. I ate all the cakes too. She glared at the empty plates and sulked and skulked in the living room. We had left clothes there, having decided to disguise ourselves heavily as refined old people. She was sullen and glared at me again.

As planned, Sylvie drove back, the next morning in a hire car. I returned to London on the 6.35 am train, leaving my bike hidden behind the undergrowth that is my aunt's back garden.

Six hours later, I was inserting the key in MY front door, when Sylvie swung it open, ushered me in and slammed the door. I heard the radio blaring in my kitchen.

RACHEL CARR – LUNA 8 RADIO
'Terry Baker, the former 80s popstar and father of twelve, has been found dead in a disused hospital in North Wales. A passing motorcyclist discovered him in the early hours of this morning and reported that he heard screams. The passer-by called the ambulance. Reports are unconfirmed that Baker died before the paramedics arrived. He was at a nightclub in South West London in the early hours of Tuesday morning. It is not known at this stage why he was in Wales or how he got there.'

Sylvie had a right go. First because I had stood her up at the bar and gone ahead without her. Second because, last night at Great-Aunt Gwynne's, I assured her that Baker was fine and dandy – granted, a tad sticky, bloody and whimpering when I left him, but very much alive and kicking.

Yes, I told her that, even though I knew that was not the case.

SYLVIE

'Wrong path, reverse,' I scream at her. 'We were only going to teach him a lesson. Lo and behold, the balls-up has gone tits-up. I am raging. The stitch up was a stitch up, and you went ahead without me.'

And then Betty has the audacity to reply.

BETTY

'So what, I never liked your stupid plan, sis.'

Sylvie was just a passing distraction, with her uncalled-for ranting. I had bigger problems.

I hoped the 'passing motorcyclist' mentioned on the radio was not amateur-hour Carlos. I soon found out that it was. He called me over a burner phone and relayed breathlessly what he had said to the first cop on the scene.

CARLOS

'This was what I said to the cops…

'On hearing the cries (that sounded like foxes yelping in the London night), I ran to the slaughterhouse just as the poor man took his last breath. It looked as if a blind butcher had been at him with a meat cleaver. There was no sign of skill.'

BETTY

Lies! Well, mostly lies. Carlos was a blatant liar. I remembered thinking at the time: 'He will fit right in.'

Consequently, he had left multiple big paw and footprints behind, on the body, on the floor.

I had not joined the print party and wore plastic blue covers over my clogs – the ones they make people wear when they walk round swimming pools in trainers. Oh, and like the ones Forensics wear. I could have left them a pair or two.

To be fair to Carlos, he did dispose of the van: set fire to it and prodded it over a precipice. Then he went back and tried to resuscitate the dead man.

It was a stupendous way to sully the rather magnificent and gory scene.

DCI CALUM LYNCH

I duly noted that a striking man called Carlos Smith showed a blatant disregard for the crime scene (which was not well received) even before I arrived on the scene.

And what was his explanation?

'So sorry, DCI Lynch, I thought I could save him,' he said, working his big flirty eyes.

His narcissism and hero complex disorder prevented him from being a prime-sized prime suspect. I bug-eyed him, thinking that his story did not add up.

'Any imbecile could see Baker was dead,' I told the Welsh detective who was eyeballing me, looking rather annoyed that the swaggering figure in front of him was on his territory, treading on his phalanges. 'As for the noise he heard when passing,' I said. 'Well, maybe there was a fox about. I'll give him that.'

BETTY

That evening, my ears were prickling again as I listened to the radio. I turned the volume up to hear more from the reporter on the scene.

RACHELLE SLEDGE – LUNA 8 RADIO

'Tonight, Welsh police cordoned off an area surrounding a former asylum. They have not disclosed details of the forty-six-year-old's death but have confirmed that a murder investigation is underway. The victim, Terry Baker had a hit with 'Funky Party' *in the 90s. He has starred on several reality shows. His most recent TV appearance was on the Channel 7 show* Me Actually. *Mr. Baker was due to replace Alby Fry who died of an accidental overdose earlier this year.'*

BETTY

Replacing Alby Fry? I did not know about that. Oh dear, that was another connection for Lynch to make.

Meanwhile, back at my house, Sylvie barged her way in again. She was lecturing me, big time; she sounded like mama, whining, opining.

'Betty, you should have controlled your foul temper. You said you were going to let him go.'

'Yes, Sylvie'

She went on and on, la, la, la, lalalala. And one more la for luck: la. I was not listening.

'And let's get another thing straight,' she said.

'Whatever,' I replied. That goaded her further.

'You totally disregarded my faultless surgical skills,' she said. 'Jealous, I bet. You did not even give me a freaking chance to operate; you used me, bitch. You sent me to Powys to provide you with an alibi, just in case there is a whiff of a trail.'

Sylvie gesticulated, rather a lot. Luckily, she had no sharp objects in either hand or my soft furnishings would have been slashed to ribbons. I did not hesitate to caution her of that.

'Knives and I go back a long way,' she added, unnecessarily. She forgot I knew her history inside and out, most of it anyway.

'Well, he wouldn't be dead, if you'd pitched up in the first place,' I said rather cruelly.

All credit to me for that one. I should have been more patient, taken the higher ground. I could have let her make an appearance.

I exited, stage left – out my front door, that is – sharpish and sheepish.

*

I went out for a coffee, giving me time to reflect that Sylvie always had an unhealthy fascination with weapons. That was why I was surprised that it was me who practically hacked Terry into thirteen pieces. Of course, he was not screeching as Carlos testified, he was way beyond that.

I was also annoyed about it being an odd number. One for each offspring (including the unborn one) was in my head as I struck him.

I found that even when I switched Sylvie off, she managed to get in through the back of my mind, sometimes at the front. That night at the asylum, I channelled her knife fetish; it was not like me to create such a mess. I blamed her. I told her as much.

The Sylvie-in-my-head did not answer.

SYLVIE

As for her emergent knife fascination: well, she has to go and ape me again! It all starts in childhood. Mama does not allow me anywhere near the kitchen knives; she locks them away. However, to me, orders not to play with things are anathema, a blood red rag.

After fleeing France and all of my bad memories, I excitedly pitched up in Japan. What an amazing country. My visa allows me to teach English but I immediately enrol at a martial arts school in Kyoto. I brandish deadly objects and prey on those who prey, but I do not act on it until I am about to leave. In Japan, they only ask at customs on the way into the country if you carry swords. Oh, it is nothing serious, just my attempt to copy something I had seen on *Kill Bill* that summer.

If you do not believe me, look it up. I left a trace, but they never caught me.

I create quite a splash. I also learn how to clean up, though not as meticulously as I should have. I get away with the slashing by veiling my face with my black mesh-fencing mask – oh, and by using another fake passport to get out of the country niftily.

It is amazing what mama's money can buy.

Aside from that aside, I vow never to let Betty get one over me again, I am the brighter, shrewder one, not her. There will be insufferable consequences for my odious twin.

BETTY

When I got back to my house, sufficiently fuelled with coffee, Sylvie continued to rage – but to herself. This time it was about Carlos as if he were right in front of her, which was a bit odd. I could hear every word; she didn't even notice that I was back.

'As for Carlos, pussy man, if you cannot stand the heat, get out the kitchen, wimp. Bromancing with Calum and trying to deflect suspicion: it will never work. You will end up with a new address: perhaps the delightful-sounding Belmarsh for a spell.'

Talking to oneself is not the first sign of madness,' I thought. It is perfectly normal in this lonely, snarling beast of a city.

Nevertheless, ranting down a meandering, nonsensical path, now that was mad.

Much as I hated to agree with Sylvie, she was right about one thing: whatever happened, we had to keep Carlos away from any more interactions with Lynch.

We had reason to fear. Although we (actually, I) left no traces, he could still blab. We were always vigilant and took steps to ensure that neither of us were ever followed to the mews, but if Carlos ever found out where Sylvie lived, he could easily find me living in the house opposite, gulp. What's more, what if the weird hypnotic eyes of DCI Lynch caught him unawares. Sylvie relayed that Carlos already expressed an interest in the un-fairer sex. He claimed to have had a relationship and mentioned a game that went wrong.

*

Sylvie's rant having subsided some; I poked my timid head into my kitchen.

'You're not seeing the whole shebang,' I said. 'We discussed the many possible outcomes of Carlos clod hopping on the scene – not once but twice. Your impeccable, got-it-all-planned-out-minutely cerebellum is ha-ha out of sync,' I told her. 'You are skewed, Sylvie. You are letting what is in your scanty panties do that thinking and not your brain!' Her pants were way too skimpy. Thongs should be banned – they are a health hazard.

Sylvie scowled. She could not deny that Lynch was all-consuming, inhabiting too much of her headspace.

'We will get away with it. Carlos will too,' I assured her.

At that moment, I decided to apologise, a placatory measure. I stared right at her and lied through my picture-perfect teeth (they had to be – the veneers cost enough).

'Touché,' I said. 'You've got me on the cutting and hacking and a distinct lack of darning skills. I did try to copy what I saw on that snip-snip clip you played. Saying that, there really is no need to slag off my efforts, bitch! Itty, bitty, pity that I nicked that artery; it really was just a slip of the scalpel.

Sylvie was unmoved. '*Uno, dos, tres*, victims down. Happy?' she asked.

I wasn't really, but I did not bother replying.

Carlos might not be a prime suspect, but I doubted he was off the hook. As for his blab ability, I knew an easy way to stop that, but it would be quite messy. It might attract attention and possibly be more hassle than it was worth. Carlos had secrets that only we knew – Sylvie had a talent for extracting deep and dark secrets. The faintest sniff of weakness and/or betrayal, and Sylvie would enact the painful plan to shut him up for good. And he knew it.

A Digression on Lovers and Other Strangers

CHAPTER 25.

Off the (Ghost Train) Rails

BETTY

For three and a half months I kept a low profile and put my whole being into work, simultaneously trying to avoid speaking to my colleagues. Finally, there came a Monday evening when I badly needed to let off steam. At my kitchen table, I sipped a large gin at a slow but steady pace; Sylvie was opposite me, not drinking. I recounted the conversation I had that morning with Martin, the office fucktwit.

'He was whining at me again, sis. Said I wasn't a team player. He said there was no "I" in team, I said "But there is in prick and dick" Not original, I know, but neither was he and it seemed appropriate at the time. He skulked off, uttering that he was going to speak to the boss.'

'Your life is temporarily blocked,' Sylvie declared in an effort to placate me. Her words resounded caustically in my frazzled head. 'You need to keep focusing on work before Martin ousts you. He's super snide and a snitch.'

She was right; I reluctantly had to ask my twin for help. She was like a jackdaw anyway – always watching. Unfortunately, her mind remained mainly on Lynch. Still, when she agreed to help, her eagerness unsettled me. Maybe she had forgiven me I thought (yep, irrational, I know). As a habitual user, I felt compelled to use her. Besides, she had ample spare time and was *almost* competent at tracking. She proved that with Carlos. He thought he found all of the devices Sylvie ensconced in his flat. He had found all but three.

There was an upside to my nefarious activities being on hold. I liked the idea of resting between killings; full stop was advisable sometimes. Even better than a rest though was a change – I was due a night out.

I headed to the Black Bar.

*

I sat in a quiet corner and perused my new file. It contained the lowdown on Benjamin Dacres, prey four. Dacres was a judge with ropey judgement. Inappropriate sentencing was the least of his failings. Too long, too short, suspended or community. He made not only a pig's ear of it, he threw the trotters in and the snout too.

A year-old debacle put Dacres more firmly in my sights. Dacres summarised the charges against a 37-year-old groper of teenage girls as if they were a series of mischiefs and hijinks finishing with: 'They all look so much older these days.'

I was too incensed to talk.

I was moody anyway because, despite the months that had passed, the Terry fallout had not come to a halt. There was no new news, so the old news was doing the rounds. I could not wait for nascent salacious breaking news. The fourth 'celeb' death in a year they said. The idiots! That motorbike victim had nothing to do with us, but it made things look worse than they were. Another good reason to prolong this break. If I killed someone, it would light up social media and the papers. Lynch was bound to link it to the other deaths.

I let a few days go by before I picked the Dacres file up again, only to put it back down. I was so bored that I called Seb again. Let me be clear, I was not desperate for him; killing, planning killings and a full-time job left little time to think. Besides, I was losing interest in him; that's what I kept telling myself anyway.

On the subject of men, disconcertingly, I ran into Lynch at court twice in the same week and was starting to see what Sylvie saw in him. Dangerous! Was he following me or did he have a legitimate reason to be there? I had precious little time to check; it was time to put him under surveillance.

I contacted Seb for a second time in minutes; a force of habit, what else could it be? Still no answer, I just got his curt 'leave a message' voicemail. Where was he? He said he was going away on business to New York, but that was three weeks ago.

Seb, my lover (okay, maybe I was lying earlier about losing interest), always came running back, eventually. But I was worried.

SYLVIE

My dear murderous twin Betty, Seb is in the basement of my mews house. He has been there for thirteen days, seven hours and nine minutes. Seb, once built like a rugby winger looks more like a puny teenager.

I'm keeping it to myself for now, as my sister bemoans Seb's absence. I feel somewhat guilty keeping such a big secret from her, but he has to change. She is too desperate for his approval. It annoys me.

No two lessons have been the same for Seb. Latex masked up, I am training him, like you would train a dog, to be obedient. I reward him when he is good with the odd treat. Not saying what that is, but he enjoys it all right.

From the pet store, I buy all manner of paraphernalia to get him in the mood so that he could get into a dog's psyche. I am now a dog walker; that way I get to bring a different dog in each day for him to interact with. They don't pay much attention to him, apart from a cocker spaniel who tries to mount him. The Labrador just stares at him adoringly.

Seb cries. As emotions aren't my strong point, I can't tell whether the tears are born out of humiliation or sadness or any emotion for that matter. This is his thirteenth night sleeping in a kennel, eating a mixture of dog food and rare steak. The photographic evidence is hilarious, and I am sure one day my sis will see the funny side of it and thank me for the valuable lessons I taught him.

The master and subservient theme I take further. I keep him chained up and whip him. I begin to see what Betty sees in him: his playful glittering eyes and that charming smile, oozing sex appeal. He starts enjoying the punishment a bit too much, so I change tack.

I decide to go back to basics, treat him like a baby and retrain him. I dry breastfeed him, give him a dummy when I have to go out (so he will not cry) and keep him in nappies. It starts to work; he is becoming quite respectful and dependent on me. It will soon be time to start reintroducing him back to adult life.

Trouble is, he now finds it difficult to speak without crying for no apparent reason. He says it has affected him psychologically and begs me to not to make him go back to his old life. I hadn't quite banked on that happening. Surely, he is messing with my mind.

The baby idea I got from the file on the judge: Dacres frequents illicit sex parties. He has a penchant for dressing up as a baby and attending an adult nursery school, led by a dominatrix with punishment for naughty toddlers. It inspired me and got me thinking.

I planned to release Seb after forty days and forty nights, but I am bored and will let him out sooner, methinks.

BETTY

I was in the most tedious meeting with the fuddy-duddies when I got the call. The return of the Seb; he was back at last and wanted to meet. I suggested the Black Bar. I should have made him stew in his own juices like one of those formerly fluffy rabbits Sylvie occasionally cooked. He said he had been tied up. He muttered something about Sylvie, and I was sure I could hear a dog whining.

I turned up at the bar a few minutes late, seething and ready with my well-rehearsed-in-the-theatre-that-is-my-head 'where the fuck it's over this time' speech, when I stopped in my tracks. What had happened to him?

He looked ravenous, nothing like his usual ravishing self. He clung to me and whispered that Sylvie needed to be committed. His eyes were glassy; he got hard in a second like he was having a Pavlovian reaction at the mention of her name.

'Sylvie, he is mine, bitch,' I thought to myself. 'Wait until I get home.'

I could not look at him in his ill-fitting trousers; he looked ridic.

Instead of dealing with Seb, I thought about going clubbing. Why waste my black leather Gucci dress – retro, but it still did the trick – on him.

SYLVIE

Standing across the street from the Black Bar, I can see Seb pressing against Betty. She is not beaming like she usually does after being reunited with the emotionally unavailable prick. The binoculars give me a clear view of a slither of action through the almost-closed purple velvet curtains. He is acting weird and she is backing off.

Hmm, I think to myself, maybe he needs a bit more orienteering. Still, he might get his fix there. There is a secret room at the Black Bar where you can engage in a little '*je ne sais quoi*', probably why she chose it as a rendezvous. Also explains the leather.

Since living with the dogs that are permanently active, Seb has become more physical. In hindsight, my crime (the kidnapping, that is) and punishments (too many to mention) might have turned him into a sex addict.

You never know, Betty might be grateful. It could take her mind off Lynch; she has been reacting to his pheromones at court, even though he is not her type. I do not blame her for falling for him. He is so alluring.

*

I get a shock when I hear a deep, hoarse voice behind me.

'Can I help you, madam?'

I quickly drop the binoculars into my bag and make like I am hunting for something. I look up to see DCI Lynch. I scream silently; he just called me madam!

'Can I help you?' I ask.

'You haven't seen a stray Shar-Pei about this high, have you?' He asks, pointing to knee height.

That is totally made up, I know that he doesn't have any pets. I feel uneasy; it is a bit odd that he mentions a dog. He could not possibly know about Seb and his special training; this has to be about something else.

I shake my head carefully so as not to disturb my awful wig. His eyes fleetingly glance towards the Black Bar. He must be following Betty, I realise. I feel a modicum of fear (I am afraid he will see through my disguise with his laser eyes) mixed with a lot of glee. My twin bought this on herself – she should never have invited Tracy to her excruciatingly abysmal birthday do. That can be the only explanation. *He* is the stray dog scenting a long-interred bone.

I swear his stare penetrates right through my oversized Prada sunglasses. He takes a step back. 'Haven't I seen you somewhere before?'

'No,' I reply, 'I do not get out often.' After a pause, I say, 'I am a carer, full time job.' My voice is croaky.

On the way home, I laugh so hard I almost cry. Life's little ironies; I want Calum, I will have him one day, but what with my latex face, Great-Aunt Gwynne's cast-offs, grey wig and walking stick – well, no chance! Note to self: Never say never – positive thoughts.

I go home, pour a large measure of dark rum, and lie in my claw-footed bath, drinking.

BETTY

All right, let me confess: letting Seb know I had a sibling was stupid. It was uncharacteristic of me to make mistakes; but, in the early days, he wanted to know all about me. After downing a few glasses of Chablis, I let it slip. I did not spill the fact that she was my identical twin; I was not that dim.

Now she had gone and ruined him, irreversibly I feared, I was determined to make her pay for whatever she did to him to make him so repellent. I could barely bear to look at him. I told myself I would have to get rid of him. As for her, if I wanted to continue to use her as an alibi and sometime helper, I would have to stop short of murder.

My success hinged on no one else discovering that I had a rotten, flawed twin. Obviously, our parents knew, but they were in France. Seb had to disappear for good. That was my plan. It would be painful for me when the time came; maybe just as painful for him.

Fortunately, that meant that my list of prey went up to eight as Tracy was no longer on the list.

My head was swimming – well, floundering and almost drowning whilst attempting the butterfly stroke. That was how it felt. I went to bed knowing that sleep would evade me.

CHAPTER 26.

Woe for Woeful Sebastian

SEBASTIAN SPIERS

My miserable life had taken a turn. For. The. Worst.

I had supposedly been absent from work with a bad back and got a knowing look or two. Besides I really did have a bad back after my ordeal. Actually I had several stress related illnesses.

I could never tell the truth to anyone. After everything I had been through, I was convinced I might never be able to work again. Sylvie went too far. I should have called the police or paid someone to take her out, but I didn't 'know' people like she did. Not knowing her address or what she looked like did not help either. Plus, I had to admit that I was complicit. Plenty of men would be willing to pay for what I had to endure – and they would go back for more.

I was fleetingly going out with Betty again, Sylvie's so-called better half. She upped her game but not enough. You never saw them together though, which was lucky. Phew, there would be one locking me up, abusing me and feeding me dog chow, and the other boring me to death about her work whilst I am at it.

I would have ditched Betty, but every time I rehearsed the words and envisaged her reaction, my train of thought hit the buffers violently. I felt a stirring as I envisaged her skewering me with her rose gold corkscrew – twisting and twisting until my heart beat no more. Although she was too much of a clean freak to go down that route. That made me feel marginally at ease, so much so that my heartbeat slowed to 100 beats per minute.

*

The morning after I met Betty at the Black Bar, she called me from work and went on and on ad nauseam. I would never be nausea free again after all that Sylvie put me through. Betty gabbed and blabbed.

'B999 boss emergency,' she shrieked, 'that awful woman asked me to write my own objectives. 'She went on about output and execution, the freaking cheek of it. Making me do forward planning and working on KPIs.'

'What is a freaking KPI?'

'Metrics.' I said to unhearing ears.

'That fukunt Martin Briars-Hedley squealed after he caught me doing my Ocado order last week. It was a necessity; I needed gin and fizz. You know how much I hate to lug it. Get in the car, park the car, get out of the car, load the car, get in the car again, drive home, park the car again, get out again, unload. Why would I, why would anyone?'

I put the phone on speaker and sat there dazed. My trousers were loose; that total headache of a woman Sylvie had made me look about ten years older. I was surprised my hair had not fallen out from the fallout.

I staggered to bed and slept for twenty-two hours. I woke up feeling even thinner.

CHAPTER 27.

Betty Does Outcomes and Execution, just as the Boss Requested

BETTY

I was on the phone to Seb again, because for once he was taking my calls. Those fukunts at work should be careful what they wish for, I told him. It was all about output; I could do the work of two or three of those prickunts, and my boss knew it. I did the least interesting stuff first; delayed gratification it was called. Then I tackled the other marginally more interesting shit. The key was to be a finisher-completer; I worked fast so I had more time to play – and shop.

SEBASTIAN SPIERS

I was Sobbing Seb that day. I had my phone near my ear. Betty started up again, where she left off, just when I thought she was about to end her diatribe. I didn't understand what she was on about half the time – more like all the time.

'Did you get the feeling we were being watched the other night at the Black Bar?' she asked. To which I replied, 'Well, I was questioned by that odd-looking cop. His eyes were quite alluring, but, saying that, he looked a bit stoned. He asked me if I had seen a stray dog.'

She did not respond for once, so I got a few more words in.

'It turned out he is with the murder squad. Very odd I thought, so I went home quite addled.'

I ended the call without a bye. I was wary of dogs now after the entire creepy dog, patting petting thing Sylvie put me through.

I went back to bed after eating a whole cos lettuce.

SYLVIE

I have been listening in and spy-eying Seb for days now. I am seething. Stress-related illness, my ass; he does not know what stress is! If he thinks fourteen days of raw meat and diapers is stress, he should spend some time in my past. The things I have had to endure.

It is character building, Seb. I guess he might not ask for a 'bleu or saignant steak' again. It is all he ever used to eat, according to Betty, with a raw egg atop it. She ordered it once, probably to impress him.

Betty is a vegan now, so it's all changed.

BETTY

I was raging after my call with Seb. It appeared Lynch was following me. I would have to lie lower than usual. I could not fathom why. I had done nothing to rouse suspicion, which made me worry what Sylvie might have done.

OK, inviting Tracy to my birthday-do was foolish, but that was months ago. It had to be for some other reason. Maybe he fancied me or maybe Sylvie did not disguise herself well enough at the XO Club when she killed Alby.

I have had a bad feeling about that since it happened. I felt waves of anger and unease. I grabbed Sylvie by the neck and categorically told her not to go out, in disguise or otherwise.

I let her get a word in and wished I hadn't.

'You are not the boss of me; you are not even the boss of yourself,' she said and left abruptly.

SYLVIE

I return to my house and make a call. I hate to admit it, but I need help. I cannot stalk more than one person successfully, and my current tally is unmanageable. I need to keep my eyes and ears out for not only Betty but Lynch, Seb and Carlos; for I like to know what's going on with all my men and prey four, the judge, of course. That is practically and literally impossible. Betty hates it when I say literally, so I have literally taken to saying it all the time now.

CARLOS

So I got this call and immediately recognised the voice, it was Sylvie.

'Carlos, darling, how are you?'

I answered with a monosyllabic: 'OK, I guess.'

'Can you do me a favour, baba? There'll be cash or payment in kind.'

I made an odd sound. I had no idea where it came from, and it wasn't a yay or nay.

'What exactly do you want me to do?' I asked.

'Track a man called Benjamin Dacres, out of hours only. And can you keep an ear on Sebastian Spiers? There is a tracker on his mobile; I'll send you the details.'

'Sure,' I said, 'leave the cash in the usual place, no payment in kind, please.'

My mind drifted to that hideous, perverse and rather frightening previous payment-in-kind encounter; quite painful, it was.

SYLVIE

I realise from his reaction that Carlos is not yet over the twenty-three minutes we spent together at his place a few weeks ago. Me masked and leather gloved too – couldn't risk leaving fingerprints.

I throw my burner phone in the river and walk home, taking a protracted route. I go in and out of shops, hop into a bar, change my jacket, and wig. It is tiring doing all that, but essential.

I feel satisfied; I will bypass Betty again.

I am not going to be outwitted or used by her, ever again. She really is not up to meticulous planning – or the aesthetics of death.

CHAPTER 28.

Lynch Gets Up Close and Impersonal

BETTY

At court, my latest case had come to a successful conclusion. I was ready for the off – well (the off-licence, actually), when Lynch slinked by and started to fiddle about in his pockets. Looked like he was searching for something in his carefully ripped-up jeans (makes him look a Colombo-scruff mess).

'Recognise this woman?' he asked, whisking out his battered-looking phone. It was Sylvie at XO, taken on the night of Alby's death. My heart and guts sank. I examined the grainy image, a side profile, eyes downcast as if she had seen something shiny on the floor. She wore a long dark brown wig. Although my hair is a mousy tone and chin length, there was a fleeting resemblance, namely the stance and the cheekbones.

'Never seen her before. Why do you ask?'

'Because it is you,' he replied.

I burned within and gave him one of my stares. We held one another's gaze for what felt like hours, until we both looked down at the picture again. If we hadn't, we would have been there all day.

'That is not me,' was all I managed to say.

He shrugged (somewhat sullenly, I thought), and we went our separate ways. I returned to the office. Who knows where he went, to the cop shop, I imagine. I got the distinct feeling that weirdo fancied me, and it was best not to tell Sylvie.

I picked up one of the four phones from my significantly oversized 'oversized' bag (possibly the biggest handbag in the world, I think, and very handy). I needed help, so I called Carlos.

'Carlos baby, I need you to set up some spyware on that detective you met in Wales. And be very careful.'

He sounded confused: 'But I am already watching Seb and the judge,' he said.

At that point, I was the one who was confused. 'You gargantuan freak, you had better not go anywhere near my Seb. He is not well. I want you to watch Lynch tonight, on the usual extortionate rate. Put it on my tab. And whoever else you've been told to follow, don't.' I said in a menacing way (at least I hoped it was).

I hung up.

CARLOS

I put the phone down, puzzled but pleased. Double pay, I laughed. Frowning (but not for long as it ruined my good looks), I pondered: she asked me to bug Seb last month, now she was having a go. On the other hand, I had a sneaking suspicion there could be two of them, sisters maybe. They sounded similar on the phone.

I could not think straight.

Oh well, I told myself, it had been a few days since I have been out spying. My leathers strained uncomfortably. I will tail this detective, take a few snaps, might keep some for me. More straining of leather; I didn't bother releasing it; I liked the discomfort. I did a little dance in front of the mirror getting more excited; time to go out and play.

And so I snuck out, straining at the bits, into the alleyway at the back of my terraced house.

BETTY

I was reclining at home when I sensed scurrying, before I could turn round, Sylvie grabbed me by the hair and said she had seen me with Lynch. She must have lurked somewhere in the recesses. She hissed in my ear as I watched *Criminal Minds*.

'You are a flirt, a tease.' I poured myself another gin and told her to make herself scarce or a dog walker might find her in little pieces somewhere.

That shut her up. She knew what my knife skills were like. Yep, erratic and not aesthetically pleasing. I took that small window of opportunity to remind her that she had put me in jeopardy by going to the XO Club to kill Alby.

She launched a rant.

'Remember, it is me that keeps you safe; for you are reckless,' she said, winding me up – that was a big fat lie.

I told her that our focus was Judge Dacres and Doctor Woolf. Lynch, Carlos and Seb had to be removed from her repertoire.

'You have an unhealthy interest in all three,' I told her. 'You have gone dick crazy when, like me, you should be raging to take out the trash and the egomaniacs. Pull yourself together.'

To which she said, 'Dick crazy, what the freak? Who do you think you are? Do not reply or we will be here for days.'

I did not take that remark well. Even though Sylvie left my house of her own accord, I needed to get away from her – far away, for I was reeling. I slipped an emerald green Chanel cocktail dress on and killer, car-to-bar heels and headed to the Black Bar. On the way, I called Carlos and asked for an update on Lynch.

'Last night DCI Lynch,' Carlos said, 'was at an exclusive underground club, a rich man's pussy and arse playground.' Yep, that's right, female and boytoys. He had a tip-off about people traffickers; at least, from what I heard, that is what he told his colleagues. Lynch didn't hang around to see the raised eyebrows and knowing looks.' He assured me.

I concluded that Carlos, even after I told him to tread carefully, had gotten a lot closer than I anticipated. I asked no questions. Whatever happened to Carlos, there would be no evidential trail to me.

CHAPTER 29.

Doctor, Doctor! I'm Self-Combusting

SYLVIE

I'm relieved that Betty is out and not watching over me or going all didactic. I think about Lynch; it has been months since our eyes did not meet at the XO. They did not quite meet at the Gin Palace either, but now it is time to act. I have restrained myself; but playing the long game is hard. I am astir: time is ripe to get even with one monkey (Betty) and catchy another one (Lynch).

When I earwig in on Carlos's call to Betty, I discover that my beloved Calum is working undercover. Masked and clad in red leather, I enter the underground club, ignoring multiple stares. I stop at his table, give him a look and lure him back to his flat; there is no need for words.

I need to satiate my all-consuming wants.

BETTY

That evening, when I knocked on Sylvie's door, I had not spoken to her for twenty-four hours. I wish I had not knocked. She told me that she had been using imagery to understand the situation with Lynch. It was obvious guff and stuff. Puppets?

SYLVIE

I see Calum picking me up and putting me down. He is the puppeteer holding the puppet, dangling, helpless; it is always him pulling the strings. Seconds later, the puppet is lying face down in the bin. Lynch picks up all the other puppets and begins playing with them. I feel dejected

Oh, fuck that for a game of toy soldiers. I know what it really means – I will cut the strings, hide the puppet and make sure the other puppets in the Lynch show disappear.

'That's sounds a bit tame,' Betty says, so I recount the final image: the puppet with a knife, attacking the puppet master and blood trickling down, in aesthetically pleasing straight lines.

BETTY

She only mentioned straight lines to placate me, but it did not work.

At that stage, I was puzzled as to why she told me about her stupid dream.

Her eyes went all vacant as she told me that, against my express wishes, she had spent much of the night with Lynch. What an obscene mess. She insisted that he had no idea who she was. She had her latex mask on; and, for some of the night, another mask on top, like the ones from those Viennese balls. I demanded to know what happened at his place, but she was in a glazed daze. I expected her to be aglow, not dull and listless. I felt a wave of schadenfreude as I realised that her interaction with the DCI might not have been up to scratch.

That feeling was short lived. I felt a chill, a rather nasty filleting knife was gleaming on her kitchen table.

I glowered at her.

'The knife was for a sole,' she said, 'a fish I mean, not a person, obviously.' Her eyes opened a tad too widely as she said that she loved Lynch. My soppy sap of a sister was lying. I could see right through her beady fish eyes, her expectations and reality were unmet.

My heart, that had swelled (albeit momentarily) at the thought of working with Sylvie as a team without sabotage or subterfuge, sunk like one of my soufflé fuck-ups. I should have known she was my enemy; after all, she was the Riddler and the Joker in the same body.

*

I set off for work, feeling murderous and thinking I would have to lock Sylvie up again. The feelings surged and soon turned into a hate-fuelled rage against her. Someone came and sat right next to me on the bus when there were six other empty seats (I had counted). I felt like giving some styling advice. 'Hey, you should never wear trainers with leggings. Your feet look massive, you big-footed fuck.'

After the next stop the bus was rammed. A sly-eyed school fuck rang the bell repeatedly – ding, ding, ding. When the driver asked him to stop it, the horsey-headed, horse-haired mother said, 'Ooh, someone got out of bed the wrong side,' causing a flare up in my already overheated head.

But I needed to keep my profile low. Still, I couldn't resist.

I heard an audible, satisfying and gratifying sound of very small foot bones crushed under my three-inch heel. There followed all of two seconds of respite, bell-less silence; then came a scream worse than the fricking ding fucking ding. His small grubby accusatory podgy finger pointed at me. Too late; I was out of there – pronto.

My day was looking up. I Cheshire-catted it all the way to the coffee van. Yes! I would rather have pierced the little fukunt's mother's happy bubble with my pearl hatpin, the one I got from Portobello market that Sylvie kindly sharpened. It was a thing of beauty. Right through the carotid twisty-turny. I could have found it, easily. Unfortunately, I had to make do with acting it out in my head and doing the hand movements – that really was not much cop. I would never act on it, harming women was a no-no.

Speaking of women, I called my mutinous twin and said, 'We need to talk about Lynch.'

CHAPTER 30.

There's Nobody at the Door

BETTY

Sylvie was trying to ingratiate, it grated. She sat opposite, her hands cupping a mug of extra strong tea. 'My heart thumped last night,' she said.

She thought someone was outside, she exited her house to investigate and shouted, 'Hello?' Foolishly and needlessly drawing attention to herself, I thought, shaking my head.

'It makes me laugh,' she went on to explain, 'when a psycho is on the loose, and the prey gives itself away by uttering, "Hello, is anyone there?" Might as well say, "Hey, here I am, come and kill me." It happens so often on films. I want to scream at them, run or hide or do both. But look who just did it. I did; yes, me.'

'Are you hearing things again, Sylvie?' I asked faux sympathetically.

I wondered whether those auditory hallucinations that blighted her early years had returned. There clearly was no one there. We really were secure as our mews houses, I assured her.

I distracted her by switching the channel to Lynch's streaming feed. Since Carlos had installed spyware in Lynch's apartment, we could see what he was up to in real-time.

We watched him reading a case file (very tedious). He then spent hours on his laptop. Keystroke monitoring indicated he was so off-track from our activities, he seemed to be on someone else's tail.

Sylvie got bored. Strange, I thought, after all that obsessing. Being Sylvie, she finally spilled the beans.

"I have mixed feelings,' she admitted. 'I loved the kiss-chase last night. Now that it is over, well, I'm not so enthralled.'

She was always like that, only wanted new things. I severely chastised her for putting us at risk.

'He will get your DNA, if he hasn't already while you were sleeping. Safety-first sis,' I told her.

'Sully me one more time, just one more time,' she jeered. 'And I will stick that fucking hatpin where it really will hurt you. You know how careful I am – I even stripped the bed when he was in the shower, sis, put all the bedding in the machine and selected a very high temperature wash.'

I told her to get out of my sight. But when she was gone, I could not help feeling fondness towards her. She had been honest about her loss of interest in Lynch. I should have stopped her there.

SYLVIE

I omit something from my account of my night with Calum. I leave him one of my burner phone numbers. Scratch it on his back with my hatpin. Just kidding – I write it on his blackboard. Despite me loving the chase almost more than the two-sided capitulation, I would like another encounter with him. Of course, I have not told my nosy, interfering sister. In fact, I make her think the opposite. I pretend to be sincere, as if.

For Betty, there has been little catch-the-mouse, meow action for some time. The frustration is killing her. She longs for one of Seb's short texts, even a few words: 'how about it?' or 'my place' or any lazy bait to that effect. That is all it takes for her to hot foot it to his side; it works every time, she is a spaniel. And we know how fond Seb is of dogs these days.

Instead, I tell Betty that hearing noises outside my house takes me back to my time in that dire unit, a decade or so ago. I can see the laurel green walls in that austere building so clearly, the high ceilings and long drain pipes. I see myself lying there and focusing on the ceiling rather than the steel poker (or rather 'curette') on the sterilised instrument tray with a kidney dish spooning next to it. 'That is where the biological debris will go, the nurse tells me.' I expected a cackle but silence ensued.

I remember feeling numb, not knowing what will happen, glancing sporadically at the long metal instrument with a French name and a loop at one end. The nurse closest to me grabs my hand and squeezes it tightly.

'Don't worry, sweetheart, you won't feel it. Just focus on breathing,' she says, lying through her overlapping teeth. What she means is, 'If you can take this, giving birth will be a walk in the park.'

She meant well; but really, much as I like sex, a poker up one's ass is no pleasure. I scream 'Stop it, you fuckers' at them all. I suck hard on the gas and air, but it doesn't alleviate the pain. Although the pain subsides, the experience sticks like superglue. I try to bury it as deep as possible in the repository of my mind, but every now and again something happens that brings that pain flooding back.

BETTY

I thought she would have gotten over it by now. A week after she left the unit, I moved to England and took on a new identity. Reinvention was cathartic. If anyone asked me about my family, I said that I was an orphan and only child. That shut them up.

I told Sylvie that I was sorry for her pain, whilst not owning up to the fact that it was my fault that she went into the unit in the first place.

SYLVIE

No one needs to feel sorry for me. The steel poker from the operating theatre is now in my collection. One day soon, I'll have an entire set of instruments. I am missing a bone cutter, chisel, and Cottle cartilage crusher. The trephine and trocar (both delightfully named cutting instruments) look like they might be useful too, now that I come to think about it.

I manage to get to sleep by reciting the names of surgical implements in alphabetical order. I usually get as far as 'surgical hook'.

BETTY

She was always too much of a show-off. That was why I ushered her out swiftly that night.

I spent the night at Sebastian's place. I was giving him not so much a second chance but a twelfth or twentieth, maybe (I'd lost count). I felt uncomfortable, Seb eyed me up and down. In fact, he was blatantly scrutinising me. I glared back at him. He still looked a bit thin, but better than he had at the Black Bar

At dawn before he awoke, I went back home and knocked on Sylvie's door. I wanted to wake her up for a change. She was up and looked present and almost correct. She was playing with strange looking implements, practising on a cow's heart, as if she were a surgeon. I felt nauseous.

She would have been flawless if I had let her try out her skills on Terry Baker. Still, I had no regrets about tricking her that night; at least not until she said, with a sideways glance, 'Maybe I will perform an operation one day.' My face felt hot at the thought.

To compound matters, she returned to the previous night's sore subject and recounted another time they stuck it to her at the unit with implements in hand. It was totally uncalled for. There was no need to go on about something that happened years ago. I knew there was a cover-up; I could see and feel it festering. Tendrils of blame gripped at my throat and constricted my lungs.

'Sylvie, leave it out,' implored her. 'Your self-obsession is so unbecoming.'

'You're a one to talk,' she said.

'Ooh, get you,' was all I could manage.

*

The next day, I got changed at mine and went to work. It was so uneventful; I'm not going to waste time or space on it. That night I meet Seb again at an East End gin bar. I tried Monkey 47, a curious, refreshing gin.

Seb was back at work and seemed to have gotten over that whiny canine phase. He even asked about Sylvie. I couldn't stand the fact that he knew about her. I should never have told him – a momentary weakness on my part. That made him dangerous; he'd had a reprieve or ten already, and one day he would be gone like the others.

He would have been the love of my life if either of us were capable, but we were damaged goods.

For once Sylvie's voice in my head was supportive, but she ended it with a stern lecture.

> *'Damaged goods you are and are not; you are just over compensating for Seb's failings. Your sense of morality and reason has warped because you are complicit in his frustrating games, waiting games usually. Calm and chaos both appeal to you, sis. His erratic personality disrupts the mundane and breaks those rules you work so hard to enforce.*
>
> *'We should kill him. He does not care for you, Betty; he never did.'*

*

Once her voice faded, I remembered the first time I saw Seb. Our eyes met across a crowded courtroom. I really do not know why I was attracted to him. He was pale; tall, but pallid. Anyway, we ended up chatting outside the toilets (how salubrious). He was at a protracted fraud case (are not they always) against the bank he worked for. He told me later how he had imagined silk stockings and suspenders under my suit. How like the rest of the herd he was, he got a surprise when he saw what lies beneath – yep, thick tights and big pants that held me in.

SYLVIE

Let *me* tell it how it is, sis. It turns out that Seb is worth millions, and he could keep you in the Christopher Kane style that you have become accustomed to. You do protest too much: 'I have my own money,' you say. However, his money is hush money aimed at stopping you from giving him a hard time for disappearing for weeks at a time. Of course, we prefer generosity to those miserly new rich dicks and fat-of-the-land fucks that get all Silas Marner. Moreover, they pay their 'help' a pitiful pittance: deplorable.

BETTY

I was so relieved that Seb didn't have a mean bone in his lean body.

We both hated pinchpennies so much that we were apoplectic when we heard about a Black Bar member who had shopped around for the cheapest funeral he could find for his mama. You would not want to be seen dead in many a thing; including an eye-ruining laminated coffin.

'Why waste money on items you will only see on one day, like a wedding dress, wedding flowers or a coffin?' Sylvie protested.

For once, I didn't argue with her.

CHAPTER 31.

Strife at the Office

BETTY

It was time to get back to my weekend and night-job, killing. I showed Sylvie the website I had been eyeing and she whispered, 'Him?'

'Yes, him, Professor Grave – remember, he stuck a label on you and ruined your life.'

She lay on the floor and curled up into a ball. 'We can't,' she said, barely audible.

'I thought that was what you wanted,' I said.

I remembered mama telling the misguided quack on the day they took her away that Sylvie was clever, a genius, that she didn't have a personality disorder or anything ending in 'path', that he had it all wrong. He turned his back, gripped his desk and exhaled loudly, turned and looked right at me and frowned.

I wondered why, for years. Did he sense something? I've always wanted to go back and ask him, hammer, cleaver and hatpin in hand.

'OK, not him, not yet,' I said.

SYLVIE

I talk Betty round to going after one of those year-round, tanned, hair-dyed, veneered teeth plastic surgeons instead. You know the ones. They transform haggard-looking mothers to the point that they are unrecognisable to their offspring. We have all seen the shows, I am sure. The alarm on the children's faces is most disturbing: wail, wail. You can almost feel their distress. His name is Dr Woolf.

'He is irritating, especially his put-on accent, and his glow in the dark teeth,' Betty says. 'I am sold.'

I manipulate her so easily.

BETTY

The next day I gave Sylvie my new file on Dr Hans Woolf, Botox addict and pusher. A complete solipsist. He ruined faces that could tell stories in seconds, replacing them with blank canvasses.

Cases in point: Two former models, their careers ruined; catalogues, once beneath them, were now their bread and butter. Not that they ate bread – or butter, for that matter. Once they were pretty; now one looked permanently displeased, the other perpetually smirked. Of course, some people like that sort of thing.

I felt the need to celebrate being on two murderous paths simultaneously. I headed out to the Black Bar, two nights in a row, get me.

I felt reckless and took a French man called Pascal up to the roof where we necked, long and hard-tongued. A thought crashed into my foreground and took the high ground. Seb was obsessed with me; he did not say so but I knew he was. It would destroy him if he found out about the sultry male that sat aside, then astride me. I came to my senses and ran off before it went too far.

Ten minutes later, I rang the buzzer of Seb's penthouse apartment. He looked rough and unshaven; I half regretted my impulsiveness with Pascal.

*

We needed to lock in (as the fukunts say at work, yeurk) our plans. I told Sylvie. The judge I would handle on my own. As for her Dr Woolf, I suggested administering enough Botox to paralyse the dear doctor's facial muscles forever.

'Shall we give ourselves a couple of pricks before you do it, might as well take advantage,' Sylvie suggested.

'Unbelievable! I was beginning to think that you were serious about our work, and now you are more concerned with yourself and your looks.'

She sulked. 'Typical, you are just jealous that I am much more attractive than you and younger.'

I screamed at her, 'You are not! We're fucking identical twins!' – although I knew she was. Younger than me that is, but only by a few minutes.

Soon women of a certain age will be the least expressive group of people. When I said a certain age, I meant in our late 20s, like us, I told her, and they'd have lips like duckbills too. 'Let that be a warning to you.'

Furtively, I thought Botox was tempting.

*

Another week passed, but Woolf and Dacres were still going about their contemptible daily business. I was determined to soon put a stop to that, as soon as I got a window of opportunity (apt office jargon for once).

I was foul tempered again. That snitch Martin was stealing my work and taking the credit for it. He really did not want to mess with me. I may go around all coffee and sympathy all day, but that was just me getting the lowdown from my learned and not-so-learned colleagues.

'Credit where credit is due,' I told him, 'and it is not due to you.'

To which I added, 'I will pay you back for stealing my thunder, prickunt, with lightning, barbed and dangerous.'

I did not say that last bit aloud of course, or he would go crying to the boss again, wimp.

I so wanted to turn him into a lightning conductor and give him a big fright. There were plenty of storms forecast for later that month. He could have been our next victim after the judge and the quack.

By the time I got home, I felt dizzy; my thoughts were befuddled. I suspected Sylvie of spiking my food or drinks. I suffered from an unmade head. I drank two glasses of wine I was sure had not been tampered with, staggered to my bed, and plonked the now half-empty bottle on my bedside table.

At 7 am, Sylvie appeared with two almond croissants and a wide-mouthed, genuine-looking smile. Just in case, I took the one she was about to bite into and made her eat the one she had intended for me. It was delicious.

I could not help myself. I told her about my plans for Martin and why.

SYLVIE

Thunder and lightning, very, very frightening, sis. Let it go, fucking let it go. What happens in the office should stay in your mundane office. Anyway, if Martin does not step up to the mark, you can always make him suffer once you finish with your list of prey. As for your stupid idea to kill the judge and the plastic surgeon in quick succession in an effort to make up for lost time. Head my words: overambition will trip you up, arse over tits, if you are not careful.

BETTY

I told her it was '*Heed* my words.' I ignored the rest of her annoying comments. I am clinging to my 'two prey in a day' plan like a limpet.

She promised me that she would stay away from Lynch in return for me ditching my dumb plan to electrocute Martin. She laughed in my face. 'You cannot control where lightning strikes thicko,' she said. But I was sure I could.

'It is the most stupid thing you have ever thought of,' she said. 'We would get soaked too; you know the wet look does nothing for our hair.'

We argued. Me not well after imbibing the remainder of the white wine the previous night in bed. I had felt nauseated and fractious before then anyway. I knew I should have abstained, but wine usually helped me sleep.

Nausea took over again – I swayed to the bathroom.

'Never again,' I gulped. 'I mean it this time.'

'Yadi yadi, haha,' Sylvie said, laughing.

*

A few days later, I recovered from my hangover, or having been spiked with mind-addling drugs by Sylvie, whatever it was. I was spoiling for a fight. I brought up the picture of her that Lynch showed me in court again, told her how careless she had been. Sylvie had turned her head to the camera, putting us both at risk.

'Lynch is the only person to have ever unsettled me, apart from disruptive, despicable you. Keep your nose out,' she threatened. Sylvie's default setting was and always will be Lynch. So she was lying about losing interest in him earlier.

She was in such disarray about him that she overshared again. 'To be able to deal with how I am feeling,' she admitted, 'would be something! But I'm not equipped, my emotional gauge is off.'

'You are incapable of love,' I told her. 'You are permanently unfeeling.' I put my headphones over my smarting ears and left before she could reply.

SYLVIE

Betty is as cruel as Professor Grave. I shake with anger as I remember the words he uttered in my presence to quacks-in-training over the years – personality disorder, on the spectrum, dissociative disorder and narcissistic tendencies. He is a liar, none of his erroneous labels apply to me.

Now that Betty has raked up the past, like she is clearing leaves from the path, I realise I must deal with that malign professor on my own. He will readily agree to meet up. His ego will not be able to resist revisiting the past and seeing how it behaves in the future after a prolonged press of the switch. I will tell him that I need help. I long for the two of us to be alone.

Oh, not just me, but me and my tools!

Betty's husky voice brings me back to the here and now.

'By the way, I've been wondering about getting a taser,' she declares, determined, as always to have the last word. 'It will be an excellent substitute given, as you so wrongly say, I cannot harness lightning.' 'Faulty electrics are a fall back – what about an electrified bed for the plastic surgeon?' she suggests. 'The shiny, tight faced quack, Dr Woolf, who quacks louder than a miffed Donald Duck, will be like Tom from Tom and Jerry when he lands in the frying pan on the hob. On the other hand, we could fill his face with so much Botox that his face implodes or explodes.'

Betty looks at me waiting for a response. Her plans are absurd. She mistakes my silence for consent.

'Sylvie, what wonderful times to look forward to,' she says as she grimaces. She probably thinks she is smiling. I half smile back.

BETTY

How wonderful, I finally felt that Sylvie might work with me, at least for a day, and stop being the enemy within. I suggested a way to kill the judge: how about sprinkling poison in his short bench wig or stiff collar, or both? She did not respond; she was mesmerised by the television.

I watched her as she watched Lynch. He was on the television after the conclusion of a triple murder case: the man killed his wife and children in a fit of jealous rage; she had told her family that she was going to leave him. It happens too often.

Unlike Judge Dacres, he meted out a life sentence.

CHAPTER 32.

Judgement Day

BETTY

Now, back to prey four, Judge Dacres. I followed him to the funfair on Blackheath. It was a Saturday and there was a bank holiday Monday coming up again, hurray. I liked the fun of the fair in my youth. Opportunity had often knocked for a quick feel up by a fit, tattooed ride turner. Faster, faster, faster, ah!

As I trailed him, I thought about using a gavel. It was a poor relative to my hammer, but I wouldn't mind hitting Dacres with one.

Marking Judge Dacres in any way was out of the question; it needed to look like death by natural causes.

I should mention something curious about that day. Judge Dacres was with the progeny of his sister's progeny. They really were relatives; there was no dirty old man pretext. I inexplicably warmed to the children; they were so small. I almost wanted to remove him from my list when I saw them laughing with their great-uncle.

It was too late; I was not the sort to go around crossing names off the list before they were dead (much). Afterwards only, rules were rules.

*

The ovine 'follow, follow, follow, like, like, like' herd thing was really getting on my nerves. I couldn't stop looking at tweets and retweets and Insta posts. Stop it already, already, already.

Anyway, back to my like, like, like topic – murder. As I reclined, gin in hand, my thoughts took me back to that day in court, in the case against Mr [redacted] charged with seven counts of theft and attempted murder. I switched off; I knew the verdict well in advance, knew it before the case even started. It was in my boss's client's favour. Of course, it was – easy when so many files go missing half way through the case. The judge (not the one we are about to take off the circuit) came down on me like a ton of breezeblocks, but whatever. My paw prints couldn't be traced.

For Judge Dacres, I needed to make it look like death by natural causes, as I could not have Lynch turning up and questioning me in court again.

I waited for the judge's clerk to go to the toilet. She was a mousy character, slight, slim build, hunched in a painfully shy, librarian kind of way. She wore childish hair accessories in hair that was already thinning and greying. I used a pipette and dropped some harmful bacteria on the roast chicken in his sandwich. A weakening dose only.

Before I knew it, I was standing outside court, feeling the cool London breeze on my face. A short hop and a skip across the road and I would soon be eating a gourmet sandwich myself. That was, after washing my hands thoroughly, of course.

'Wash your 'ands Georgie,' I enjoyed telling myself that whenever my hands needed a good wash, and they did. Through the years, I had enjoyed playing out all the parts in *The Cook, the Thief, His Wife and Her Lover*. Some might say that film had warped my ways somewhat.

I washed my hands like a surgeon: between the fingers too, not like those work fukunts that rubbed their hands together quickly under the tap and made a cursory effort at drying them, the dirty fucks. Worse still those that left the loo and walked out without even glancing at the sinks.

When I got home, I felt in an expansive mood and shared with Sylvie the finer details of hand washing and the intricacies of the human appendage.

'Did you know,' I concluded, 'that the bit between the thumb and index finger was called the thenar space, sis? Bad area to get a paper cut. Hey, why are you running away? I thought you loved learning new facts?'

*

The next morning the judge's assistant relayed that he had a bug and would not be sitting. 'It could not possibly have been food poisoning,' the assistant declared, 'for he makes his own sandwiches.'

Unfortunately, the day after that, due to other forces in my life, I was on the fast train to Glasgow. Seb had enraged me by taking back his power base; he was incommunicado again. I also had enough of Sylvie; both of them were sulking babies. I needed some 'me time', as they call it. Odd, all my time is me time, methinks.

A small boat on a calm sea took me to Fingal's Cave, a dark alluring place surrounded by green-blue sea. When the sporadic dazzling rays of light hit it, the sea was the colour of Seb's eyes. Nevertheless, it was only a short break to think and re-charge.

*

Upon my return from the North, I went down to the basement and inspected a dead leg pipe. It was rife with legionella, a theory that I hoped was a fact. Carlos took it from the disused asylum. After his food poisoning, Dacres would be weak; legionnaire's disease would likely fell the scrawny, heinous judge. It was nearly time. All it required was for the pipe to be operational. The judge's demise would appear to be death by natural causes. That was bound to keep Lynch's weird prying eyes out of it. Only three people would know any different, or four if you counted the judge.

*

Three days later, Judge Dacres received an invite to a special event that same evening. The whiff of a party – his sort of dressing up party – was all that was required for him to feel better.

I was the advance party. Carlos and the judge arrived on time at an empty house in South West London where the water had not run for years. Carlos had replaced the existing pipe with the even older one from the asylum. Up to no good in a disused building; been there, paved the way, sis.

Carlos lifted and shifted the judge out of the car, under cover of darkness. His spindly legs were sticking out. I wore a surgical gown and a gas mask. Carlos wore a boilersuit and toolbelt. My heartbeat quickened at the sight. He had procured just enough sedatives to render Dacres semi-conscious. Carlos donned his gas mask and awkwardly bundled Dacres into the dank shower and turned it on.

Before he was plonked in the cubicle I said, 'Take a shower, dirty boy,' I had rehearsed my line until I was pleased with the intonation. Although I don't think the judge heard it through my gas mask.

For a brief moment, I was beside myself with happiness. Unfortunately, seconds later, doubts started to niggle and wriggle. Maybe the judge did not inhale the bacteria; his breathing was very shallow and the water pressure was weak. On the other hand, there was enough steam to disperse the legionella, surely?

Oh blast it. You know what they say about the best-laid plans of mice and men? I always wondered why mice needed to make plans? Even if they made them, Sylvie and her sharp instruments probably were not in their risk assessments. I told Sylvie as much. She didn't seem to appreciate it.

SYLVIE

'Mice are not my friends,' I inform her, after listening to her odd pondering about said rodents, the next day.

I distinctly remember a snouted, rotund, tailed creature lurking in the corner of my kitchen one night. At first sight, it takes the appearance of a shadow. But closer inspection reveals a creature, a mouse. It scarpers under the oven when I approach. Had a knife been in my hand I would have plunged it into its chubby body without hesitation.

I also feel the need to tell Betty that she is driving me cra-cra by focusing on two prey at once.

'It is sticking in ma craw! Lynch is bound to be on your tail,' I say. 'You have made some brusque comments about Dacres in the past, sis.'

'That is why it needs to look like death by natural causes, silly!' Betty replies, then she swears at me using worse language than usual. I feel relief as she departs.

BETTY

I woke up scowling the next morning, fretful. Killing was not making me feel as calm as I thought it would.

Worse still, Sylvie was in my house again. I must bolt my front door in future. Her eyes were out of kilter. I told her that she looked like a scaredy cat.

SYLVIE

Perhaps I do look like a cat. In that case, so does she.

'Speaking of cats,' I say to her, 'one followed me the other night back to my house.'

BETTY

'It must have caught the scent of mouse,' I callously told her. 'Given that your kitchen and basement are laden with them. All down to your nefarious culinary efforts and poor hygiene, I am sure.'

Unable to come up with a suitable response, Sylvie departed swiftly, slamming two doors behind her on the way.

SYLVIE

In my need to get away from my overbearing twin, I spend all day getting ready. I exit my house looking mirror perfect. Betty goes out like that too; perfect at the start. But by the end of the night, she ends up all smudged and washed out. I put on a pixie wig and head to the East End. I might even pick up a hipster; I laugh at the thought. The next thing I sense is someone staring at me; he is clocking my every move. I side-eye him; he is hot, but I am hotter.

I escape to the uber-trendy unisex restrooms and look at my reflection, mesmerised by the stunner looking back at me. Sometimes I forget what I look like; the other me jumps in and out of my life, a sudden portrait of someone else entirely. I grab my flesh to pinch myself. The high cheekbones, feline eyes to fall into, perfect size ten with curves. I could go on, but I get the feeling I am boring you.

OK, hardly anyone likes a narcissist; perhaps I will desist. My self-esteem is sky-high tonight. I want to take the mirror home, but the oily bearded hipster behind me and is now looking at me. I can feel his lustful eyes from behind. Eventually I move away and escape.

I would have stayed to find out more, but he really is more Betty's type.

BETTY

At dawn, Sylvie was in my house again recounting her AWOL night out. She only looked drop dead striking because she borrowed my clothes again. She rabbited on, eyes a glittering, of what had happened. Starting with how attractive she was!

'You can stop it already with the solipsism,' I shouted. 'It is not about you right now; it is about me, the quack and the judge. Order, order.'

She laughed, but I knew she hated me.

*

You know I really could not wait to see the quack Dr Woolf's face after umpteen pricks of Botox. I shooed my disobedient sibling back to her place. I would lock her away for a few weeks in my basement; but that would be impossible, unless I got a gun or drugged her and dragged her there. My head reeled and spun as I thought it through. I would send her away again. I booked a flight and took stock…

I had, as planned, evaded capture. OK Lynch had his suspicions, but a facade of normality and a respectable job helped keep me off his prime or subprime suspect list. Executing plans and leaving no trace were my talents. Latex faces, surgical masks in case you sneeze, and wigs were necessary. DNA betrays, and what lies within, and on the surface, can be your enemy.

I had already decided to have a few months break from my deadly pursuits after the doctor and the judge were dead. Any trail the DCI was on would be long forgotten and all overgrown with weeds by then. Besides Lynch had been up to his swan-like neck in murders and had his head down.

This time I was at Sylvie's place – I'd had it with her coming into my house uninvited.

'I think we need to get out of here for a few days,' I said. 'How about New York?' "BA flight 437 to JFK NOW BOARDING".' I mimicked the pilot as I handed her a boarding pass for the red eye.

It may surprise you, but I had never been to the Big Apple. I did not like heights but would take a bite. One day maybe.

More pressing was the fact that I needed to get Sylvie away from that pesky bloodhound Lynch. Why did he keep sniffing around? He would have to watch out, I told her. 'You know what happens to curious cats,' I said. 'Their names are added to my half-full notebook.'

No one would be on our trail if we killed Lynch, but where was the excitement in that?

'High ten, New York,' I said to Sylvie and pointed to the cab that was outside. Mine was due ten minutes later, I would see her at the gate, I told her.

*

Having arrived at the airport, Sylvie called and asked if I was playing her *F/X – Murder by Illusion* game. I disguised myself so well that, despite scanning every face at the airport, she could not pick me out. That was how good I was, *Face/Off* convincing.

'For all I know you could be in the cockpit,' she said. 'God forbid, we are in for a bumpy ride. If I hear "Buckle up, buckle up," I will know it's you.'

I thanked her for her sky-high praise and asked her what she was after, or more to the point what had she taken already?

'I should have supervised your swift, furtive packing,' I said. Then I thought: probably my new Prada top.' I ran up the stairs to check. Yup, the top was gone. I must put a padlock on the door of my walk-in wardrobe, I told myself, though I knew that wouldn't stop her either. She unpicks everything, including locks.

By the way, I was a no-show at the airport.

'You are on your own, Sylvie,' I muttered to myself, laughing.

As a quick aside, I should let you know that I purchased the latest generation 3D printer for Sylvie to play with when she was back from New York. You could make guns, prosthetic hands, prosthetic anything ooh err. But best of all was how it made the moulds for our many faces. This new device was a step up from the one housed in the basement; it would keep her occupied when she came back.

SYLVIE

Betty suggests that we go to New York and I jump, eyes wide open. I could go home to irritate her, but instead I board the plane. I am not one for turning down a free holiday.

I will leave her to her own shaky devices.

BETTY

I was forward planning and that required downtime.

Sylvie always got mad when I shut her in or shut her out. Now that she was at liberty, I didn't know or care what she was up to.

I am not going to lie, as everyone annoyingly says these days – a sure indicator a lie has just been birthed and another one is about to be (not in my case though). The truth was that I had not gotten over Sylvie killing Alby; I never would. I took my anger out on Terry Baker, but it only assuaged it for a few minutes. I loved hacking at his limbs, although I was subdued. Just like a real doctor, I had to be careful that my brow did not sweat.

Ever since then, I have felt a bit queasy every time I go past the meat counter.

I know I brought it on myself.

*

I had a dreamless night; guzzling a couple of sleeping tablets pilfered from Seb's medicine cabinet helped. I woke up in the early afternoon. I felt stiff of limb and jet lagged, attuned to Sylvie no doubt.

*

With Sylvie gone, my plan for another murder, the one I'd given to her to lead, coalesced perfectly. I made an appointment for Sylvie to see Dr Hans Woolf when she got back. Her false name would be Antonia da Lala.

Odd as it may seem, I missed my odious twin. I even called her.

'Hey, Sylvie, I hope you are having a NICE DAY in nice-day-land whilst I am working,' I began. I did not allow her to get a word in and launched straight into telling her about my day – it had not been anywhere near nice. She had time to enjoy hers still.

I was livid at a man on the train, I told her. He was tapping away furiously on this laptop. I wanted to do some eye poking. My blood pressure went through the freaking roof of the carriage, and it was me that ended up in pain with a blinding headache and a pressure cooker brain. I swear there was steam coming out of the top of my head.

Although that never literally happened, my brain did feel full of dry ice and ready to blow – I could have killed someone right there and then! That would have alleviated my stress-related pain. The over-the-counter drugs didn't work for me – but my clearance of nuisances might have helped. I so wanted to lure him to the toilet and kill him. I always carried a hatpin, in case of emergencies; I haven't used it yet, but one day...

Instead of doing the dirty but more satisfying deed, I closed my eyes and meditated. I had no happy place to go to, so I imagined a cold glass of gin with tonic, just the right amount of ice and some bitters. I could almost taste it.

It was not a good thing for a representative of the court to be thinking about it on the way to visit a client.

SYLVIE

I tell Betty my own story. For seven and a half hours, children on the flight to New York inflict fast-paced kicking on the back of my seat! The jolting is at such a pace that a pianist could keep perfect time without the need of a metronome. I get through it by imagining stuffing stale candy into their faces. They only escape punishment because of their tender age and the fact that they aren't old enough to know better, yet. Am I a softie, or what?

BETTY

'I share your frustrations' I told Sylvie. 'Ooh, the seat banging thing! Seat bangers should be put in the hold or airlines should have family-only flights.'

I made that suggestion every time I flew. I suspected the poor crews on those flights might need to be committed after only a few transatlantic crossings.

SYLVIE

Self-help books are quite on point when they say you attract what you focus on, I tell Betty over the phone, even though I honestly feel too tired to speak. On the train to Long Island, I am treated to a high-pitched public lecture delivered by a mother to a blank-eyed brat under her nose. I wouldn't mind, but it is so loud, and the content causes quite the stink:

'"Who would have done a thing like that," asked the farmer.'

'It has to be the fishmonger.'

'"The fishmonger.'

Betty is not impressed. 'Maybe you have to be there,' I tell her, 'to really get the true annoyance of the statements and the intonation, pitch and volume of the repetitive "fishmonger".'

Fortunately, my headphones enable me to block out most of the sound. Next thing I hear is "The bear went up the stairs". Oh, please.'

'I can hear you from way over here,' I say to the woman in a neutral accented tone – despite the many countries mama and papa dragged us up in. 'Loud, I say, your voice is very loud.'

Pursing of lips: 'No, it's not,' one decibel down.

'Not now it isn't, ha,' I get the last word in, always.

BETTY

Sylvie often withered and reduced irritants like that annoying woman (it did not always work, and words often got exchanged in a crossfire, bad ones). She turned her music up to the max to try to block everything out.

'Careful, sis, mind your delicate ears,' I advised.

At that point she told me to 'Butt out, man.' Sylvie had gone all-American on me.

'You are twisting my titties man, I'm only trying to help,' I said. 'You don't want to have that awful ringing in your ears again do you?'

For a moment that made me flash back to that fateful day and the ball twisting that I did to Terry Baker. His short-lived screams ringing in my ears, I had an overwhelming urge to recount the operation in graphic detail to my twin, but she suddenly had to go.

When her side of the phone went mute, the other Sylvie screeched in my head, giving me quite a start. *'That balls up of a cock up was entirely your fault, and you know it. He should have lived to tell the tale as we planned.* She could not let it go.

I switched my phone off and found myself thinking about Seb. Days had passed, and he had not contacted me. He promised much, and I must make him deliver. But he had become flakier than a catering-sized-pack of cornflakes sat on by Kevin the Feeder before he departed his big, fat, mad, mad world.

I tried to make myself feel better by telling myself that I had no time to spare for Seb. Killing was almost a full-time side-hustle, what with stalking and staking consuming a lot of my time. Carlos and Sylvie were assets, of course, but I was the one in charge. Work was the downside – a pretence of normality with everything else that was going on. I hoped my migraines could be my way out; doctor's orders I could tell them and I would take two weeks off.

Talking of which, I still needed to set up the appointment with Dr Woolf. Botox can also be used to treat headaches, genius. I sipped a gin mare, full of rosemary, meant to be good for you.

All was fine until I awoke.

I could not even utter a word or emit a soft moan in any language. My head was done in again, a mix of neat gin and rage. Dehydration compounded by ten packs of very salty crisps, or it seemed like I snaffled that many.

And what was the cause of that rage? A call from Great-Aunt Gwynne.

'Hello dear,' she said, 'I thought you'd like to know a young detective called Finch just paid me a visit. Funny eyes, dear. Always nice to have guests, dear. I gave him a brew and some biscuits. Handsome young man he was. Did I mention that he had funny eyes? He only had one question, love, 'When did I last see Sylvia?' I told him that I didn't know who he was talking about, dear.'

It transpired that the dear, deaf, old, not-so-daft aunt soon saw him off. As anticipated, she gave nothing away and confused him big time – well and truly, melon-twisted-and-twirled him so much so that he left sharpish, by her account.

Finch, Lynch? What treachery. Another reason to desist from killing for a while.

At that moment I desperately needed to get hold that liability of a sister. Where was she? She must be back from the USA – she was due back that morning. I texted her and braced myself for her appearance.

CHAPTER 33.

Cop Out

DCI CALUM LYNCH

The morning after my visit with that queer old lady, I woke at 5:24 with a fuzzy head. The fuzz gone fuzzy, I thought, frowning; that was a strange brew yesterday. I had a feeling that old bat Gwynne had slipped me something. I wasn't yet back in charge of my faculties, but I had moved forward a pigeon step at least. I was on to something, but I didn't know what. It felt as though several woodpeckers had been let loose in my head.

My thoughts drifted to hot, but prim, Betty who had that party and the other woman in my life who was even hotter: the masked woman who came back to my flat months ago. I tried to remove her mask that night, but she slapped me rather viciously. I didn't dare try again. Called herself Silwia or Sylvia, or something like that. I couldn't quite read her scrawl on my blackboard; I assumed it was a made-up name.

Maybe Betty and that crazy masked woman were relatives. They smelt similar; that's what they have in common. They have different hair, although maybe Sylvia wore a wig. They were the same height and build. Not that I'd seen Betty undressed, but my imagination didn't usually lie.

Betty said she was an only child of only children and claimed that she had no living relatives. I was no town clown; I knew I'd get to the bottom of it soon enough. But not that morning; I was too Coco after imbibing the bizzaro Gwynne Jarot's tea and eating too many bourbon creams. I'd written the day off.

Fortunately, the night the mystery woman was at my flat, I'd put a tracker on her bag (a routine precaution). She did some pleasant and several not so pleasant things. I traced her as far as the address in South Wales of the Miss Gwynne Jarot before the trail went cold. The elusive Sylvia or Sylwia must have found the tracker.

Still, my mystery woman was close enough to where Terry Baker was hacked into thirteen pieces (albeit at least twenty minutes' drive away) to be a person of interest. On the other hand, maybe I was kidding myself – being obsessive, compulsive and disordered. Another tenuous link was that still image from the XO, but it would never hold up in court.

My colleagues thought I was wasting my time – seeing things, they argued, that were not there. Probably the scent of a woman involved too, they said, or a man; no one was entirely sure. I liked to keep them guessing. What else did they say? They said I was anyone's if they were attractive and even when they were not. I was up for anyone, apparently, that's what they said. I beg not to differ.

BETTY

Our DCI Lynch had pulled a sickie – first one ever in his twelve years on the force, I discovered. He dialled the number that Sylvie stupidly chalked on his blackboard (another reason I would like to lock her up for good), but he got me instead. Awkward. I picked up the wrong freaking phone and had to pretend to be Sylvie. In other words, act coquettish and change my voice. Not a problem.

Our conversation went like this:

'Would you like to go for a drink? I know you like a martini, a dirty one,' he said.

By that time Sylvie was right next to me, flapping her arms furiously, which sent me off-track.

'I have a boyfriend now,' I said.

Sylvie quickly grabbed the phone and finished my sentence, 'but I guess one drink would not do any harm, just a single.'

'What the frick! Here goes everything,' I mouthed to her.

'I look forward to MY date,' she said.

Our discussion, if you can call it that, culminated in her saying 'Oh sis, do not let your thoughts pinball in that hot little head of yours. I will disguise myself again. Sunday school teacher may go down well, all flagrant and floral.' Fragrant I said, not flagrant. She gave me a look; I gave her one back.

Sylvie was not impressed with how easily Calum succumbed to my primness at my birthday party before he sniffed Tracy, the cheek. I couldn't help if I was a glamour puss-puss that night. She said she would pounce if I went anywhere near him again.

'Maybe he wants something from you' I suggested.' Have you thought about that?'

'Yes, he does – it is called sex,' Sylvie said.

'No, I am not talking about "that". He is on our trail – tenuous, circumstantial links only – and he is clutching at wet paper straws.'

'Worst still, he thinks you are called Sylvia. What the freak? That is too close for comfort. Beware, sis,' I told her and watched her seethe.

Sylvie called me a monumental Mickey Mouse character! Then she made a welcome exit. As she stormed off, I shouted, 'Come back, Sylvie. Nothing is forgiven. Oh, and about my drinking, you are one to blabber'.

In fact, Sylvie's recent penchant for a martini with briny olives rubbed off on me. I took to drinking it neat, potent and addictive. I especially enjoyed drinking it when listening to loud music.

*

A few hours later, I threw myself on my bed and slept. I don't know how long I spent in la-la land before I was rudely awakened by clattering. I went downstairs only to see my bone-boiling bitch of a sister in my kitchen cooking some kind of onion-based soup like mama, marrow and fat floating on the surface. Give me a plate of pimento de Padron instead, *s'il te plait*, any day of the week, but not that.

It made me feel nauseous. It was evocative of our early years in the Chartreuse-coloured kitchen in Provence when she assigned us our chores, usually chopping vegetables, skinning rabbits or plucking chickens.

'Onion sliced, diced, spliced, whatever way you want it, mama,' I said, obediently one day.

'Are you crying, Sylvie? How weak! Peel and slice the fucking onion, imbecile,' she said mockingly.

Mama was a bit harsh like that. She never could tell us apart.

Anyway, that night I crept up on Sylvie in my kitchen. 'What the frick are you doing, sis?'

She jumped out of her perfect skin.

'I'm stressed,' was all she could manage. I also caught the word 'Lynch.' She was looking forward to meeting him. At least I thought she was, but I had scared her and she was on edge.

'Cancel the date or go kiss-chase him, bitch, see if I care,' I said. But I did care.

She told me she did not fancy him that much anyway; she had others on the go. Sylvie changed her mind as often as she stole my clothes.

*

Sylvie waking me up in the middle of the night last night and rendering me sleepless, had done wonders for my imagination. I finally hatched a rather nasty plan. I looked in the mirror and smirked, what else could I do?

More of that later.

I am pleased to report that I did not look like a marionette that morning despite being up half the night. More like a man with a plan. I put on a Saville Row suit and the face of a geeky dweeb. The thick black-framed glasses made me look brainy, like Brains from *Thunderbirds*. There were so many that looked like me around, not so well attired, but I blended in so well. Oh, I was not up to anything bad, just trying out a new disguise.

I walked along thinking about how our sisterly row had erupted the previous night.

If I remember correctly, we argued about what cheese to grate on the bone and onion concoction she was poking at. In France, it is not called French onion soup. Why would it be? They tended to drop Swiss cheese on its fatty filmed surface, bread drowning. I preferred the Oaxaca variant myself. Hard to get.

It was academic nonetheless: you wouldn't get me anywhere near that diaphanous brown liquid or anything else made by my sister's unfair hands. As the soup simmered, Sylvie went all philosophical on me.

SYLVIE

I confess to Betty that I feel a spine-tingling warmth at the shadow in the mirror. I do a double-take but tell myself that it is just my imagination, a figment of it. We all have that sixth sense. We recognise it from time to time and promptly forget it when we live the pleasures and pains of love and hate, those contacts with the Sebs and Calums of this world. Each of us has the same story; different characters, that's all.

'I know you hate my soliloquising, Betty,' I say, 'but it's for your own good. Wake up and smell the bones. Why do you think we find it so easy to do what we do? For us, there is a certainty of life on the other side of physical death. Each of those wasters will have another chance next time around, another chance to do good or bad. So, let's cook these bones and get every bit of goodness out of them.'

And I think to myself, but don't say it out loud: You are angry about the smell, but don't you wonder what kind of bones I am boiling? You should. The strong smell of onions and sage can disguise foul smells. Ditch the Padron peppers and embrace the goodness of the bones. A natural antibiotic.

BETTY

I immediately started to worry, but the alarm bells were even shriller when Sylvie added that she was cooking for her doll's tea party.

'You know I don't have any "real" friends, besides you,' she said. 'So I like to dress friends the way I want them to look. The best friends are the silent ones. Insults aren't an issue with my friends; their lips are permanently sealed. Talking is overrated, outdated, especially loud mouths, what with us living in the shouty era.'

'What the freak, freak?' I muttered and stormed off.

My sister was displaying behaviour that was more unhinged than usual.

*

It was Sunday, five in the morning. I had a long soak in my bath and rested, lying in boiling hot water, just how I liked it. The next day was Monday, the start of another dreary workweek. I had to do the work of two people (and sometimes three, they were all so useless, my fukunt colleagues). Putting in a lot of effort at the start of the week freed me up to focus on meaningful activities at the end of the week, like the plan for my victims. I was often so tired, I almost felt I might not be up to it.

Sylvie's all-night cooking had to stop; it was exhausting. I couldn't stand the heat anymore; she was going to be ejected permanently from my now fetid kitchen. The smell of frying onions lingered, not to mention the stench of putrid animal flesh.

I had no idea who she had dispatched and boiled up into a bony broth. I began to suspect human flesh. Carlos hadn't been about for a few days. 'Oh, bitch, it better not be him,' I said to myself, grabbing my phone (not a wise thing to do when in the bath), texting, texting, fast as anything. I received a reply in three seconds; not him, I sighed a relieved sigh.

Later than night, I questioned Sylvie about the contents of her vile soup.

'Was it that pug ugly bull terrier I'd seen you goading from up the road?' I asked. It belonged to that strutting, lanky poser Hayley who set her barking, gnashing canine on Sylvie. Although in Hayley's favour, her dog was very obedient when called to heel.

'That pig dog?' Sylvie asked.

'Oh, stop making me laugh,' I said. 'Pig dog, pig dog. Is it him? No, who or what is it?'

SYLVIE

Fished in! Betty is so damned easy to beguile. So fricking gullible. Does she really think I would have the time or the patience to get a chainsaw and shorten the bones sufficiently to fit into a rather fetching looking pan? That is hilarious! Funniest thing in months.

I just love how easy it is for me to pull one over on her. She doesn't even know it when I am joking about joking, my humour is couched in such mastery and trickery. I can just feel her fume… not noxious fumes from a pot of bones (haha, ha) but fumes of anger, red with rage!

All I say to her is, 'I love it when you get like that. You are mad!'

And Betty comes back with, 'Takes one to know one, or two.'

BETTY

That Monday, I still wondered about the bones whilst I was on the bus at 7:03 am. But I was soon distracted.

There was a creepy looking character sitting in my favourite seat; hood up, face down, could not see the face at all, gloves on. The stench was worse than Sylvie's cooking. No one went anywhere near him, everyone without fail pulled a face.

I was sure the poor man just needed some sleep – and, with me used to *mal* odours now, I sat down beside him. Everyone gave me looks, I mean the whole bus – but for once I thought I felt a bit of empathy. I knew what no sleep did to a person. Just look at me for a start, I thought. Less shuteye equalled another dead guy; soon, the bodies would be piling up even faster. When you can't sleep, what else can you do but think about killing?

By the way, I tried to wake him up at the last stop. He did not stir. I was such a thoughtful person, letting him rest like that on MY seat! I did a wonderful thing. I left a tenner in his pocket. He had given me an idea on how to get about without being noticed; I would just carry a bag around containing

Sylvie's leftover bones and wear some of mama's old clothes. Although, now that I think back on it, I don't think she ever had a hoodie, not even a Chanel leisurewear one.

*

That evening I was thinking about sharing my bus journey story with Sylvie, but she went all judgmental in my head. *'Moving onto more serious matters, your new friend on the bus, the down and out with the threadbare clothes and let's not forget those grubby gloves. You make it seem like it is philanthropy and charity towards the poor soul, but really isn't it just to stroke your own ego? That people will say, "Look at mother Theresa there helping the poor, such a kind and caring soul".*

'I know you. You don't get involved in anything unless you can get something from it. What looks like charity is only about you and how you feel about it. The vulnerable are just a means to an end – the end being stoking and stroking your ego. Altruism does not suit you; give it up.'

I did need to get rid of my awful twin. The one in my head even more than the other one. She was a worse annoyance than Jiminy Cricket.

Tuesday was no better. I decided to tell Sylvie about an unpleasant encounter I'd had that day, as I poured a big glass of wine for myself. There was none for her. She could bring her own if she was going to practically move in.

Anyway, I told Sylvie I ran into an old school acquaintance, Amanda Lines, during my 200-metre dash from the office to the nearest cafe. Yes, lunch was for wimps, but I was partial to a hummus and carrot sandwich – with maybe a tub of quinoa or bulgur wheat thrown in and obviously a double espresso. If I didn't have that I could barely function.

Well, in regard to Amanda, I would not use the word 'friend'. She was someone that I used to know at that dreadful boarding institution in the South of England that mama sent me too. This was after Sylvie went to the unit – at a time when I was weak (a very short phase I have to say).

163

At any rate, Amanda interrupted my dash to apologise for her atrocities against me.

'If it is any consolation,' she said, 'bad things have been happening since I was horrid to you.'

'I don't think that has anything to do with me,' I said. Although I was immediately suspicious that Sylvie had been out to play again. She was, after all, all about vengeance. She knew all about Amanda as she was on the back page of my book containing the list of people I would like to kill. Martin from work was on it too. But I dismissed any thought of Sylvie being involved in foul play against Amanda. She was never one to have my back.

Amanda asked for my phone number. Steam out of the ears time again! I could see my hydrangea-shaped cranium getting ready to explode, the petal-shaped fragments going sky-high and plummeting back down again. Why the fuck would I want to hear from her? Bad enough to be recognised when I was going about my business.

Of course, I couldn't tell her about my name change. I gave her a false number anyway – all the time thinking one day I would prey on this guilt-laden ex-bully. I was full of glee that she hadn't aged well – a bit chub with deep lines, wearing cheap, drab clothes. The high street was useful for buying the latest trends, I told her, but only if you go to the right shops (and her so young, to look so withered). She had turned into an inverted version of her nasty former self, the useless creature. Amanda's modus operandi consisted of launching a charmless charm offensive. Rude.

I remembered mangy Mandy and what she said to me when I was just thirteen – she told me I had a sly face.

The only slyness to ever cross my face was when I had to pretend to be friends with her. More fiend than friend. There were many things I would tolerate, but bullies I would not. May they fry in hell.

When I told Sylvie about my Mandy meet, she disarmingly applauded me for thinking about extending the kill list.

'I have other plans for her though, Sylvie; you will see,' I told her.

*

We had so many lessons from the bitch maestro, our very own ma. She was raised (by grand-mama) to belittle, disarm and wither her opponents to the point that they could not think, rendering them ineffective and reinforcing her dominance. As children, we soon learnt that her nasty remarks were too close to the bones. One day she came home muttering about the daughter of one of the villagers.

'Did you see the way that Violeta's progeny looked at me?' she said. 'It was a blank-eyed evil looking thing.'

Not like me, I thought, acknowledging that mama was right. Rumour has it Violeta still lives in the village and gives mama a wide berth to this day.

*

As we were having a reasonably civil conversation, I updated Sylvie about the judge too. This is what I told her, maybe not word for word, but close.

'Carlos and I cajoled him from the limo into that awful house. All masked and gowned up, we stripped him, sat him in a chair and turned the shower on; the water was hot to start with. We left him tied to a chair in that mouldy shower for over an hour with a large bowl of steaming (the vapour was essential) bacilli and legionella from the dead leg pipe on his lap. Eventually after two cups of tea, Carlos led him out of the shower, picked him up, covered him in a sheet, practically threw him in the back of the car, and dropped him off back at his place.

The judge shouldn't remember anything after the collection of prescription and non-prescription pills we gave him. He might wonder why his threadbare hair was wet and why his skin felt like a soggy, wrinkled, crinkle-cut crisp (well, it looked like it anyway, yuck), but I am sure it wasn't the first lost night of his life. I had seen him comatose before: in the Black Bar for a start. Drink spiking had been known to happen there, but don't look at me!

I finished briefing her, saying, "By the way, Sylvie, it did pollute my eyes – the sight of him – but if you want to do good and make a difference, you must make some sacrifices. The only thing troubling me was that his breathing was shallow and that he might not have inhaled enough of the toxic steam.'

Sylvie said that was very careless of me and showed lack of foresight. I let it go for once.

By pretending to be a concerned relative (I knew their names, obviously), I got updates from the hospital. He wasn't dead, but his condition was serious. I said I was sorry to hear that. Not long now, I told myself, and it would be time to focus on Dr Woolf.

*

That was Tuesday. Wednesday did not start well. I was livid again.

My coffee was so weak even though I asked for a double shot, I felt like throwing it back in the barista's face! I could not even smell the coffee! I could see the headlines: barmy wannabe barrister burns barista.

Breaking news, sis, ding-dong. Dacres took a turn for the worst and was critically ill – lying in his final bed – in a hospital and not in his own home or in one of those vice dens he frequently frequented. The shower scene worked, Sylvie. He was in the hospital fighting for every breath.

I did love it when a plan came to fruition, joy! I was as happy as Carrie before the prom. I looked like a million dollars, and I felt like a billion. Some people couldn't look that good with upwards of that sum.

*

When I got back from work, I was restless. I needed more distractions from all the heinous lunacy around me. Maybe I could work on lengthening my kill list and add the names of those on the back-burner page or look for more prey?

It was so easy to find prey– local papers were a good reference. It was better in Ireland where they sometimes provided the addresses of the perps, but you can't have it all. I was researching clear up rates and trying to keep out of nosey Lynch's reach; although he did get about poking that snout in inappropriate places. I switched my phone onto flight mode so that social media (fuel to keep the ire burning) or online games did not hook me.

I know, I did protest too much before saying that it was not for me. I'm a liar, and I did change my spots. I recently discovered that I liked to scroll and to even swipe – one must keep up with the times.

CHAPTER 34.

Does It Hurt When I Do This?

BETTY

I needed Sylvie to focus on someone other than Lynch, so I handed her a morsel: to dispatch Dr Hans Woolf. My success hinged on her help, I grudgingly admitted. I had been very tired of late; lack of sleep took its toll. I should stop it with the coffee and the drinking, but I couldn't. Maybe, I told myself, I would at some point, but not this year. The lingering judge, kept me awake too.

*

Dr Woolf was on a mission to turn the masses into doppelgängers. The taut cupid's bow covered veneered that teeth looked like a row of blank Scrabble tiles. That disturbed me much. And he was to blame for eyes and mouths that scarcely closed, along with a few digital influencers that will remain nameless.

He was the hushed utterance on the lips of all the wealthy and the wannabes. When the needle was effective and applied more times than lipstick in a week, you knew you would be counting fewer lines. Whether you would be able to express that was another matter; but in a society obsessed with looking ripe at a ripe old age, it was the number one priority. Crow's feet, whether barely there or deeply creviced, marionette lines and any other perceived affronts meant countless thousands took the plunge and tried out the sharp end of a plunger. Dr Woolf cured all tribulations and ills, even if you did not need it.

The business had become so balm pots that Dr Woolf was a daytime TV star. Yes, indeed, his show even crossed the Atlantic. The coy British demeanour of the doctor appealed to the Park

Avenue set who wanted that '*je ne sais quoi*' with a Dick Van Dyke accent and a Germanic twist. They craved a face as expressionless as his and crossed the Atlantic to achieve it. Well, how grandiose was that. The absence overseas, a long vacation in Europe, was much easier to explain away than recoup time behind closed doors in Manhattan. One's absence would be noted; tongues would wag and the platypus like lips would go into overdrive.

What better way than to say that the youthfulness was down to a good old sojourn in Europe; the fresh air, change of scene, takes years off you! Ha, if only!

*

Once a month Dr Woolf held a 'Botolotto.' You guessed it: a raffle to win a life-changing session with him and his hypodermics. An annoying pop-up advertised the coveted prize: him sitting behind a desk in his practice on Harley Street, surrounded by teak bookcases full of unread medical journals. The learned image enticed millions of viewers to purchase the dream of the winning ticket every month.

Botolotto created such a storm that it surpassed all of his expectations of a profit margin. The profits easily enabled him to pay the rent and accumulate wealth like nobody's business.

Unexpectedly for Dr Woolf, puncturing skin so often started to make him both uneasy and queasy.

*

It was shaping up to be a usual Friday from the top floor of his Harley Street practice.

'You look at least fifteen years younger, already,' he exclaimed proudly. 'Not that you need it,' he told the needy forty-six-year-old in front of him. Most were no doubt happy with 'You look as if you are in your 20s.' Even though their hands and necks told different tales.

'Thank you doctor' said the almost expressionless woman.

Little did he know that that needle would be the last needle he would ever use.

He was set to fly off to New York on Monday for an appearance on some cruddy chat show, advertised as 'An interview with the King of Botox' to entice a larger US audience, with a view to a future permanent residence on 5th Avenue for all those central Manhattan clients. In his wildest dreams, he had not banked on that kind of notoriety, or return on his money. He lived in a bubble of first-class travel and a suite at the Waldorf Astoria. Last time he was there, he shared a lift with a famous fashion designer and had to pinch himself as the lift descended. He slipped a business card into her Luis Vuitton bag which her miniscule dog immediately started to chew.

The good doctor's overinflated bubble was about to burst. The needle he held so still would not be the only needle he would see that evening. The next one would be a lot bigger and would enter the skin with far less attention and skill – and with a lot more force.

SYLVIE

I'll tell it now.

It is just minutes before five o'clock. Dr Woolf's eyes are bloodshot, tired probably, although his neutral face tells a different story. He stands up feeling relieved. Last customer of the day, he thinks as he glances at *moi* in the waiting room.

His receptionist, eager to leave for the evening, has already logged out.

'Ms. Van der Merder?' he calls out.

Something makes him do a double take. Does he recognise my face? He must meet thousands of women; they have started to blur together, no doubt, like one homogenous mass.

Dr Woolf grabs my hand. He has a surprisingly strong handshake and tilts his head slightly.

With a slight intonation suggesting that I am Dutch, I acknowledge that I am indeed. 'der Merder'. I did not like Betty's suggestion, Antonia de Tralala or whatever it was, ridiculous.

'Ms. Van der Merder,' he says, consulting his files, 'you have requested Botox and dermal fillers.' I nod as I watch him as he carefully lays everything out.

BETTY

We had carefully planned the whole shebang with malice aforethought. All Sylvie had to do was get to the point where he was leaning over her. As he lunged toward her, needle ready, she would pull him down towards her so that he was on top of her, then she would wriggle around so that she was on top. That way she would have more control to jab him with the needle tucked up her right sleeve.

SYLVIE

Let me tell it, please!

And that is exactly how it plays out: quickly, almost noiselessly, the doctor slumps in the patient's seat, motionless, expressionless, staring at the locked door.

My escape is quick. The sun is setting, but the fire escape at the back of the old Georgian building backs onto a vacant property. A month prior, a fire had rendered the building uninhabitable. They have yet to find the arsonist.

And so Hans Woolf slowly slips from semi-consciousness to being no more. I have to check his pulse as his face could not slacken.

His eyes are another matter.

BETTY

From my cramped position under the reception desk at the doctor's office, I heard Sylvie leave. I entered the room and surveyed the scene. I looked at his face. His eyes looked more enraged than mine when I am set off. I decided to add a few finishing touches – that always made a difference; a scatter cushion here, a candle there.

I used my paring knife. I was tempted to spike/spell out a few words on his face – to let others know why he was being punished, a la Kafka. His crime was being a pusher of an obnoxiously bland type of perfection: straight fluorescent teeth, lid lift, brow lift, tit lift, face lift, filler; and, hey presto, a lineless, wind-tunnel face. With the end product being that people bear little resemblance to their former, character-full self.

As I worked on him, I reflected that I hadn't seen any interesting teeth lately; everyone had invisible braces, dazzling dazzlers that you needed snow glasses to view. People should embrace the gaps and overlaps please – unless their teeth were a total horror show. Stop it already with the copying and the homogeneity; it was all wrong.

*

In the aftermath, the police (as I expected) wanted to interview Dr Woolf's last few clients. The last one had, of course, registered with a false name and date of birth. I relished the thought that Lynch and his team would have to track everyone down in the appointment book – and all paths were a dead-end.

Thwarting, conniving Sylvie had hacked into the database and entered so many false trails it would take him weeks.

To sum up. The bad news: Judge Dacres was still gasping and rasping. The good: Dr Woolf took the death toll to four, not bad for a few months' work. It was time for the break I planned. But, as always, catching a break was hard.

I congratulated Sylvie after she told me that she hacked into Woolf's bank account and transferred all of his money into an offshore account.

'Well, that is fab,' I added. 'Shall we go shopping? Taxi to Bond Street, pronto.'

No one would ever know how much of a killing we made from that killing.

*

The next morning, I ran into Lynch outside court and got a full download a few hours later over a coffee. I put a few droplets of truth serum in his black coffee when he went to the toilet. He soon mentioned Dr Woolf and how they suspected a new, money-grabbing doctor at the practice who had only been there a week. Apparently, suspicions were high, he was making enquiries about the lotto funds. How serendipitous, I thought. Although I was still guarded; he might have been lulling me into a false sense of security.

CHAPTER 35.

Risky but Doable

BETTY

Nineteen hours later Sylvie bounded into my kitchen.

'Now who is next, sis?' she asked, grinning, happy – probably because I was inexplicably altruistic with Dr Woolf; for I let her participate, and our camaraderie made me swell with pride and joy. When I confessed to her that I had sullied her scene, her face was impassive, but I think she was OK about it.

'Not telling you,' I said, 'but it is four down, hundreds to go, sis.'

The next one was 'risky but doable,' I said using the latest infuriating office speak.

'Do tell me' Sylvie pleaded. 'I know it is the one and only thing on your mind. Chop, chop, whose head is next on the block? Although you rather disturbingly hack at the limbs. Strange that you are into gore more than me, sis.'

'It doesn't appeal so much to vegan me, as you know, but I felt strangely compelled. I needed to obliterate all that gleam, glimmer and big lashes.'

Belatedly answering Sylvie's question, I told her that prey five was a young one – school bully Patrick Weber. He'd been in the papers the previous year for punching a boy and nearly killing him. His smirking 'it wasn't me' face was on the front pages, even on the broadsheets.

As you know, prey five was actually the judge, but he was hanging on for dear life and had wrecked my numbering system. When Dacres dies, I told myself, Patrick will be prey six, as originally planned. I could wait for the darn judge to expire.

Earlier that year, Patrick had assaulted a boy named Josh. His parents were taking civil action; but, in the meantime, the brute evaded retribution. His papa, Gary Weber, was known for hanging around with East London gangsters and minor celebs in his day and appearing in those mags as arm candy for a bunch of has-beens, soap actresses and Eurovision song contest singers.

SYLVIE

I look Patrick Weber up and try to dissuade Betty, it is one thing killing an adult, but killing a child is heinous.

'He maintains that Josh hit him first,' I tell her. 'Several others vouch for him too, though that poor boy is still in a coma.' For good measure, I add, 'Just like Tracy.'

I stifle my laugh, but I can see Betty's anger flare.

'Still, you need irrefutable proof,' I insist, 'before you go there.'

BETTY

'I am sure,' I replied, 'you can tell just by looking at him. This is serious Sylvie. Many children self-harm or worse after being bullied. I need to do something about it.'

'OK, but let's stop short of killing. We can teach him a lesson,' Sylvie proffered. 'He is a minor after all. We can take it to a certain limit – when we've finished with him, he won't be able to fight his way out of a paper bag.'

But I was reluctant and peeved. 'I have trouble with packaging that causes much swearing, as you know, but anyone can get out of a paper bag.'

She just stared at me, uncomprehending.

'What will happen,' I asked, 'if he doesn't change his spots, of which there are a smattering on his otherwise angelic face?'

'Happy to progress from paper to scissors, sis,' she replied. I left it at that.

*

It was a Monday again and regretfully I had to postpone my plans for Patrick. I was once again like a whirling dervish at work. All I did, I complained to Sylvie, was scatter the papers. The upshot: I was at melting point. Work was ruining my life!

'The French have this saying,' I said, 'that translates to something like I am so busy I can't even see my desk. Well, that is where I am. They say that when out sipping wine on the Rue Saint-Denis during their lunch breaks apparently. Why can't we be more like the French, Sylvie?'

'The French,' she cooed, 'have a lot of sayings, sissy dear. Some that I love, some that I hate but that's me through and through, in extremis. I love their shrugs and pouts and their passion for all things carnal. I hate their aloofness.'

She looked positively gleeful that I was floundering at work. Empathy was the one look Sylvie could never fake.

CHAPTER 36.

A Flock of Swooping Seagulls

BETTY

My next work day began with the high-pitched voice of my boss as she made a flailing attempt to keep her voice down. She was driving me back down the misery-and-failure path; too much interference and trying to 'hang on to my coat tails' derails.

'I have scheduled your appraisal,' she said.

B999 – Boss emergency! I thought as she turned on her sensible three-inch heels.

My results had been erratic: won one, lost one; drawn one. I was in danger of being sent off. She wanted to see if I was on top of things when we both knew I wasn't. I was particularly worried about the feedback forms some of those frightful colleagues would be completing. I was afraid I might have to make threats or tamper with the evidence.

Sadly, I couldn't afford to leave that vile, bile-inducing drudgery. Naturally, I didn't mean in a financial way; I meant I couldn't lose my cover for my extracurricular activities.

SYLVIE

I offer to help her. 'I'll save that bacon of yours,' I say, 'with a hack, hack here and a hack, hack there into your work systems. Don't worry about the feedback, sis. I will tweak a number here and a comment there.'

BETTY

Go for it I told her, thinking that (to compound it all) I had another mare to contend with: we had an office move. We were just going up a couple of floors, but there were crates everywhere. I stuck a few crates out at awkward angles; there had been the odd injury, but nothing too gory. Regretfully.

I needed something more gratifying to happen and turned my attentions to Patrick Weber again. Carlos was at the ready although he expressed concerns about the tender age, the wuss! Patrick was nearly fifteen (well, six months off). We all know what we were like at that age. Sylvie and I were adults by the time we were ten.

But I capitulated, trying to sound all sincere.

'Tomorrow, the tormenter will be tormented,' I said. 'But we will stop short of killing him. And I mean it this time.'

Sylvie did not seem convinced.

CHAPTER 37.

Dead Tired

DCI CALUM LYNCH

I had not slept for twenty-three hours.

It would have helped if I could at least be in the vicinity of my house or (even better) in my king-sized bed. I would have thrown myself on it and not gotten up again for a day.

I ordered a double mocha with three spoons of sugar stirred in. My brains felt like the watery scrambled eggs in front of me. Last time I was here, they served me an overcooked omelette that offended my palate and burnt my tongue. I didn't complain; it was my local, and the coffee was satisfactory.

Anyway, I was past caring about what I ate. My scrambled head wasn't working; my inferior colleagues talked behind my back, but it all got back to me. Even worse they were clearing up various misdemeanours.

I hadn't solved a single crime since I met Sylvia, that mystery woman who had got into my head and my bed. I believed I was onto something. I saw a connection but it had a loose wire.

I turned over another page of the case notes. That poor doctor; his murder was so macabre, redolent of poor butchered Baker. That's it! I jumped out of my chair and winced as its legs scraped the floor.

I needed to ask Sylvia where she was last night.

BETTY

I had taken on following Lynch on weekends in disguise (he was rather fascinating). He looked tired, like he hadn't slept for days. More than likely he was disturbed by Sylvie, she being sugar and spice and all things poisonous.

I watched him as he finished his coffee. He turned the page of the *Metro*, which was frayed around the edges, a bit like Lynch himself. I saw the other customers glare at him as he suddenly got up from his chair.

In a café opposite where he was, I was also reading a paper.

Let me share with you my latest gripe: The death of print media. We were going from dumber to dumber still; the 'digital goldfish' era had a lot to answer for. Apparently, most clicks were on 'showbiz' news. We wanted to see a famous David in his scanty, pricy panties and get a close up of the cellulite on the latest reality star, top model, forward slash (yes, I would have liked to forward slash them) talent show reject.

Who cares? Seriously; it was this banality that drove us to kill. If everyone kept their filthy shades of grey and their ripped or rippled flesh under the covers, behind closed doors, there would be no need to act in extremis. Well, at least, that was my excuse. Sylvie was another matter.

End of rant.

Lynch wasn't up to much so I went home and stayed in.

*

The next morning, I went to Euston train station. I was on the way to Leeds. Within minutes of sitting down on the train I had to move due to an offensive assault on the ears, another shrieking child. I was in the quiet coach, but phones rang, people yapped, and (the worst offence) furiously tapped keyboards. My gaskets blew past sky high, orbiting the earth and back. It felt like a spinning Jenny had been let lose in my hot little head.

I had laid a false trail relating to the murder of Dr Woolf and was peeking into Lynch's world for a day too. He had been on *Crimewatch* two nights before appealing for anyone on Harley Street on the night in question to blah do blah. They hadn't found the mysterious doctor that joined and left the practice before any appointments had been made with him. Luck was on our side again with that; Lynch had a big fat nada. To thwart Lynch further, Sylvie called the police hotline with an anonymous tip-off that wended its way to Lynch.

So there I was, following the DCI, tracing his lead to Leeds. In her call, sis named a couple of small fry from dark bygone days; said they were importing substandard Botox, mumbled about a botched jab job in London, and then hung up.

Good acting, sis; old school, scarf over the mouthpiece.

He must have realised he was in for a wasted day, but he was playing with the wrong ones and shouldn't have expected any less.

I watched him get off the train. He was met by a couple of local plods, one a fresh-faced petite thing. Sylvie was trailing me, also in disguise. I could almost feel her hackles rise and her teeth bare at the sight of the dainty cop.

I hadn't thought of that! *Avert your eyes now, now, NOW* she said in my earpiece.

I shuffled along the platform. I was dressed as a frump again; did the follow-that-car thing. (Try it one day; it either freaks or excites the driver.) I didn't need to 'follow' them; I knew where they were going, but it kept the cabbie's eyes off me. Even as a frumpy, dumpy old thing I still looked hot.

Just kidding.

Lynch and the petite plod went into a boarded-up old mill near Oakworth. I wouldn't have minded buying it and making it into luxury flats; it would be a good money-laundering opportunity. They battered their way in, as the criminals within did not let them enter. They spent twenty-seven minutes in there, came away Scooby Doo-less. Although I wasn't so confident when I saw the DCI's face. He looked pensive as if he was onto something. I hotfooted it back to London, first class this time, and tried not to think about all the noisy fucks in my carriage on the way up.

*

I began to have doubts about the bully Patrick and decided to park him (as they say at work). Geographically he was the wrong side of London, and that was too much of a faff. My thoughts, instead, were on my next kill (the new prey five) – Ricky Jennings, a TV presenter whom I despised. His sexist remarks, his infidelities, his faded, stonewashed jeans: they warranted his demise without the other gross offences.

I was overwhelmed with the many ideas swirling around my brain, I thought I'd head to Prada to distract myself.

Later that night I showed Sylvie my purchases. I don't know why, but I got the feeling she would steal them.

'Prada, not a brand that suits you,' she said. 'Meow, meow. Can you feel my tiger claws extending?'

'You do know we are identical? If it doesn't suit me, it won't suit you. Hands off!' I said.

I knew what that was all about; seeing the young female copper in proximity to Lynch had electrified a raw nerve.

'A nerve that runs to my eyes, heart and solar plexus. Boy, do I feel the urge in my bones, my pelvic bones to be precise. The bottle blonde police officer will soon be out of the equation,' she said.

I felt a chill in my bones.

SYLVIE

The first thing the petite blonde 'Lindy', for that is her name, does after the Leeds fiasco is check her emails whilst walking along – and she nearly walks into a lamppost. Two emails pique her interest: one marked 'personal' from DCI Lynch, the other also marked 'personal' from Human Resources. I know that because I hacked into her account.

LINDY

Two important emails in one day, how exciting. The burgeoning butterflies take the lead. I tap the email from the absolutely striking DCI.

Subject: Tonight
'Hey you, fancy meeting up, I could do with your help?'

Short, sweet and asking me to spend the night with him, in London, the city where the inhabitants don't sleep, too bloody polluted and noisy I reckon. Still, I am chuffed to bits – I caught his attention. The high-priced highlights and blow dry were worth every pound. I'll book an essential waxing appointment.

Now, what delights does the second email hold?

Subject: Transfer Request
We are pleased to inform you that your request to transfer to the Outer Hebrides crime team has been approved, effective week commencing 16th May.

What the fuck? That's in two weeks!

But the transfer I requested had been to Lynch's team. The Outer Hebrides! My application must have got muddled with someone else's. Talk about being inflated then deflated in a matter of seconds. Major balloon burst.

I'll fire off a quick reply to HR.

SYLVIE

Fortunately for me, in her haste to sort out the mix-up, Lindy forgot to reply to Lynch.

So I reply instead.

Subject: Tonight
10:53 @ the Soho Hotel bar.
Lindy

Why so precise with the time, you ask? I have a box at the opera where you can get up to all sorts and I nearly always do. All that goading, dick teasing, baiting and jealous rage; the cards don't lie.

My relationship with dear Calum, I decide, is turning out a bit like Betty's with Seb. It starts off all hearts and diamonds, but it will end with the spades the gravediggers will use to dig his final resting place.

Carmen. A night at the opera. What can I say?

I am always tempted to leap up on stage when watching Carmen to pry the knife away and kill Don Jose in real life. But that might get me a spell somewhere I do not want to be. As for the bubblehead in my line of sight that started bouncing during the overture: well, I look away, count to nine, but that does not help.

Second go at suspending my disbelief. OK I am there, I am not Carmen, I never will be; I am backstage Jenny, the understudy in the wings, a pesky presence. Jose, you know nothing about raging, possessive, insidious jealousy. I am the green-eyed honey monster.

Go on, I have to say it: no way, Don Jose!

Fast forward to 10.54, the hotel bar is buzzing. I feel a tap on my shoulder.

'Lindy, it's me.'

I turn, wide eyes. Calum's are even wider.

'What are *you* doing here, I was supposed to meet Lindy?' His words escape before he has a chance to think about them. Lindy-hopped off, I think, but keep that to myself. Wasn't even funny the first time.

'Same could be asked of you,' I retort.

DCI CALUM LYNCH

Once again, Sylvia caught me off guard. I knew it was her before one second was up. Her shape was inimitable. My forehead was dripping about two seconds later. I noted a change of appearance, different hair, and different barely discernible mask, softer. More natural-looking. Reminded me of Betty from court, but a lot prettier. But then Betty was staid; this one is unhinged and scary. I was drawn to the air of wild excitement that she exuded.

Feeling browbeaten, I managed a wry but distracted smile. Of course, I wanted to see Sylvia, she was fascinating, but I did not want a repeat encounter. I did not like being on the receiving end of pain, and the rest of it quite frankly wasn't worth it. She was just too weird and a bit creepy.

I was flustered and tongue-tied. My frown must have made her sense the confusion – the cogs of my brain were going around and round. Where was Lindy? What if she showed up? Had I somehow contacted the wrong girl?

Admittedly I had been feeling out of kilter. Oh Jesus, I needed to simplify my life: too many women after so few and too many stories. I had not planned on those stories interweaving; I wanted them compartmentalised. If I wanted them plaited together I would have set something up – a trap of sorts, maybe, with me and Lindy trying to psycho-analyse the strange woman in front of me.

I started to panic. How could I explain this one away? I composed myself and lied. It was easy to tell white lies; in fact, lying had become my modus operandi.

'It has been a long day and I fancy a drink,' I said, thinking at least I could ask her where she had been on the night of Dr Woolf's murder. That loose thread might be tightened.

SYLVIE

I tilt my head towards him.

'I just ordered two Gimlets so we can start with these.'

'Let me get the next round then,' the darling DCI interjects. 'I am expecting some colleagues to show up shortly. I would hate for them to be disappointed.' I sense that he is pleased that he has thought on his size 10s.

Lie number two of the evening: what 'colleagues'? He has no shame. I like that in a man. The lies are piling up, coming fast and freaking furious. I hope that will be what we will be doing in a few minutes' time – it has been a while and the usual deprivation desperation has kicked in, like a crack addict without a fix.

I know, I know, look who is talking: me desperate for Lynch; Betty, for the next kill.

There he is – so gently, so ineptly – preparing me for Lindy's entrance. He should not worry his pretty big head. Lindy would not enter the bar or any other bar that evening, for I texted her to cancel their rendezvous.

I, on the other hand, have booked a suite that certainly is not going to go to waste. I will drop the bombshell once he has consumed double figures in units. Then he will be ready for pain and pleasure in Soho.

Let me explain. Pain for me is not just about inflicting it on others; one also needs to experience a certain amount of pain to know how to cause it. I watch Lynch's eyes widening, for in each cocktail there is a quarter of something brain-addling, a precise amount guaranteed to both interfere with time and motion as well as many other things. Each time, he says he doesn't want any more, but that doesn't stop him gulping them down. He so reminds me of Betty.

I whisper that to her, for I know she is listening in. Like me, she plants devices everywhere.

BETTY

I was judge sober. I can play the newt sloshed drunk, I can be the disordered inebriate, I have it down to a fine Agnes B tee, but that night it was so not appropriate.

I admit I was listening; I had planted listening devices in ten of my handbags. This handbag was a vintage one that she pilfered from my cupboard before heading to the opera with a new latex face on, bah.

I was furious; Sylvie was really doing her worst. At least he wouldn't remember a thing; that was one consolation. I could tell. His words were so slurred they weren't even words, just primeval sounds; he was drugged up to his odd-looking eyeballs.

'Just wait till you get home, sis,' I muttered.

I was sure she heard me. She actually giggled.

'I can't wait,' she said. Was she talking to me or Lynch?

CHAPTER 38.

Atrophy

BETTY

The next day a toddler smiled at me, so I thought I would smile back. I knew for sure it did not suit my face; luckily, there was plenty to smirk about instead. The hot weather resulted in a veritable meat fest: an obnoxious display of flesh, lamb and mutton (applicable to all genders). Put it away, please. I did not like to see sausage legs or shoulders of pork.

There was a parade of fashion victims and perpetrators of fashion crimes. Of course, I was not immune to the occasional ill-conceived outfit myself. Tottering was not my ever best look. The stripper shoes I consigned to the charity shop were more suited to Sylvie, you're welcome.

'Do stop being the nastiest bitch in the UK, OK?' Sylvie screeched in my ear.

*

I turned my attentions back to Patrick Weber. To stir things up, I called Carlos and asked him if he could find out where Patrick went at night; bound to be outside an off-license, I thought. To my surprise, he muttered something about him being a child. What a wuss.

Later that morning I waited for Sylvie to stroll into my kitchen before I questioned her.

My ears had been blushing the previous night, redder than the delicious Epinard de something rosé that I was imbibing. The moans and the slurping sounds offended my ears. I gulped the rest of my rosé straight out of the bottle.

'I heard your disgusting hook up last night, vile twin. Do spill. Are you done with DCI Lynch now?' I began. 'It is time to focus on our next prey Patrick Weber.'

SYLVIE

'Vile sis, you need to stop it already with the Weber kid. As for Lynch, I will never finish or be finished with him – and stop eavesdropping,' I say as I rifle through *her* vintage bag and throw the device at her.

'I am cast under his spell, and he is tangled up in the web that I have intricately spun, you know. I am a scorpion with the tendencies of the black widow. The one fly in the unguent is Lindy, distant and soon to be dispatched up North, not far enough though.

Can we put her on the list?'

BETTY

Lindy would not be added to my list. Emotion and murder should always be long dead cousins and not close relatives. That's what I told Sylvie anyway.

Regarding Patrick, I reflected that maybe Carlos was right. But I still asked him to track him for a day though – intelligence gathering. I floundered as I thought it through. I should strike him off the list. But that would make me a wuss too. Still, I could delay until he was sixteen. He would simply need to be allocated a new prey number – prey nine perhaps. I would, of course, need to identify prey ten to even up the numbers. Feeling slightly uneasy, I made some amendments to the kill list and turned my thoughts to prey five – as freaking Dacres was still alive!

I decided that dreadful actor, Ricky Jennings, would be next.

*

Back in Marylebone I knocked on Sylvie's front door; she ushered me in and made me tea, but I didn't drink it. I glanced at her; she studiously ignored me, staring instead at a photograph of Lynch in a newspaper and cooing. Cue another nasty headache.

'Will you shut up about Lynch!' I shouted at her.

She assured me he still did not know who his Sylvie was, especially after all those substances she fed him.

Still, I reminded her, she was putting herself in his sights just by wheedling her way into his life. He was bound to have her DNA by now, stored at the ready.

She said that she had taken hardly anything with her, apart from my bag, and promised that she watched him like a hawk. Regrettably he was asleep for most of the night due to the quantity of alcohol and drugs he had taken; she shooed him out of her suite at dawn.

When I casually told her I had arranged to see him during recess the next day, she did not take it well.

I was tempted to flee, but I couldn't resist another little jab.

'Oh, did I tell you I laughed yesterday?' I whispered breathlessly. 'Weird feeling, it was. I saw a woman in the lift, one of those trophy wives. She had obviously tried to get her tattoos removed but chose an amateur removal clinic. I could still see a faded butterfly and a dolphin (of course, why people would want butterflies and dolphins all over them like some badly designed wallpaper for children was beyond me). Anyway, of course I slinked out all cheerful.'

SYLVIE

'Trophy wives,' I tell her. 'I never liked that label and like even less that many are wannabe trophies!'

I still do not understand what it is that these men get from these trophies. OK, they are nice to look at and cause envy with those that have last year's model (just like their flash cars), but that doesn't impress me, sis!

I don't tell Betty this, but I will tell you.

You may be wondering why I suddenly have a bone to pick with their bony asses. Well, a wannabe trophy wife, eyeing up Lynch at the hotel, hangout of models and minor celebrities. If only she knew what scalding water she would get herself into if she got those perfectly manicured claws on his back. I will remove them one by one, and that would only be the amuse bouche.

One bonus – for the trophies, the tragic and untimely death of the King of Botox has accelerated the ageing process for a lot of them. They will soon be collecting dust on the back shelf while a shinier model takes centre stage. No one could hold back the years as well as him. That should shake up their plastic snow globe worlds.

BETTY

One of my burner phones rang. It was Carlos; he called to say that Patrick was skulking outside an off-license in Essex. I told him that I no longer wanted to pursue the minor.

'Good decision ma'am, you cannot go after a child,' Carlos said.

Him calling me ma'am made me want to change my mind again. So I did.

I told him it wouldn't be long until Patrick was a full-fledged fucker. He was nearly an adult, and there was no time like the present. Carlos emitted an elongated sigh and hung up.

Much as it pained me, I needed Sylvie's help again. I told her that I was planning a rather sticky entrapment; for Ricky liked them young. 'He is a slippery eel. You cannot get near him unless you are a fifteen-year-old girl or in the media. Mask time, Sylvie. As young as you look, you need to look younger. I need you, Sylvie.'

'It will be wonderful, working together again,' I added. 'See how sweet I am, really.'

But then she crept up behind me and whispered in my ear. 'So sweet it is sickly. Turns my stomach: the candy floss saccharin sugar that you add to all your conversations. Why bother? Venom is just as effective, and it is calorie free. By the way, your entrapment plan is futile and stupid, what has got into you?'

'I am glad you have dropped your plans for Patrick,' Sylvie said, in a normal voice. 'You need to stop nitpicking. He is a teenager; you will be crucified, vilified, plus you might even catch nits.'

'No, I won't. I'll wear a wig, silly,' I said.

'Talking of sweets, Sylvie, you are a bag of marshmallows wrapped in candy floss.'

She did not reply.

'What is wrong with you now? I asked. 'Are you still sulking about me having lunch with wild-eyed Lynch?'

Her reply was yawn inducing.

SYLVIE

This is the speech that almost put Betty to sleep.

'I do not copy,' I declare. 'And I am no prissy pussy. Do not go badgering me into being your copycat murderous alter ego. You think you are the master puppeteer, pulling my strings – left, right, left leg pulled up, right leg pulled down, take that smack from the left hook "paw". I'm not your Punch and Judy show. You think you can lay the bait, and that I will scavenge rodent-like towards your little traps, laid out in sequence. Far too obvious for someone like me. Catch me you cannot.'

Then, to wake her up, I deliver the grand finale.

'I know you got boozy woozy with Lynch, and I'm going to give you your first formal warning. Keep your parasitic fingers off him, or I will maim and stuff you. That's a promise.'

BETTY

I, of course, was not impressed.

'Ooh, shoot that poison dart through my fluttering heart, bitch,' I said.

By the way, my Lynch lunch was fabulous; we sloped off to La Lanterna on an extended break of my making at court, threw a spanner and a monkey wrench into the works. The new judge looked thunderous when we walked in late for the afternoon. I was quite taken. He was much more pleasing on the eye than Dacres (RIP not, for he was still alive; the bad die old, sis).

CHAPTER 39

Crashed

BETTY

My download with Lynch over my penne all'arrabbiata with vegan cheese went like this.

I slipped a couple of droplets into his wine when he was in the toilet; he gulped it down and launched straight into his so-called progress. 'Five celebs have died in suspicious circumstances lately,' he began. 'None of them were in the same league as Christopher Lee.'

Then he literally sobbed into his minestrone soup. I'm not kidding.

'However, this latest spate of deaths,' he went on, after he composed himself, 'has thrown up some anomalies. It appears as if someone is targeting them. I am thinking serial killer.'

I laughed and met his fromage-faced grin, his fluorescent eyes giving me a bit of a start.

'I am deadly serious, Miss Ellard,' he said.

That was my cue to leave.

*

After I got back to the mews, I turned the radio on, listened to Luna 8 Radio and heard Leroy Menzies report on an accident in the Rotherhithe Tunnel, in South London. A man in his late 30s had died. Police had not yet confirmed his identity.

Then forty-three minutes later there was another announcement. Sylvie and I listened together.

LEROY MENZIES: LUNA 8 RADIO

Notorious former East End gang member Gary Weber has died in a crash in South East London. He made his fortune in the haulage truck business. He leaves behind his partner, Stella Wakefield, the ex-wife of Premiership footballer Darrell Hughes and a teenage son, who recently hit the headlines after an incident as his school.

BETTY

'Sylvie, what the fuck?' I sputtered. 'It could not possibly have been an accident.' I felt one of my migraines coming on. Lynch's stats were up the Suwannee again. 'I told you, sis, to keep your little pointy nose out of my business.'

'Nope, not my work. You know I hate cars,' she said.

CARLOS

As I listened to the news, I felt beatific. I would never let that weird woman, or two women even, harm a child.

But, when I stopped to think, killing the dad was not exactly doing said child any favours.

I wish I'd never had any dealings with her or them even, but I was handcuffed to them for life. Truth be told, they scared me. I wasn't sure which one was worse, the man-eating tiger in pussy cat clothing or the totally deranged one.

My thoughts began to run wild. It was a bit like *Jurassic Park*. I wondered whether it would be better to be killed by a whole load of Compsognathus; the little dinosaurs (ouch, painful, maybe a tad distressing) or just one big fuck-off Tyrannosaurus Rex. One bite and you'd be a goner. With the little ones there could be a chance to escape. The big ones were slow and stupid, maybe I'd run and hide…Argh, I thought, here I go again wasting time on something that isn't going to happen.

I had to put my wire cutters and garrotte away (always carry them for safety reasons).

It didn't take me long to get to Deptford and back; I'd been tailing Gary in his vintage Saab for a while. Never liked him. Our paths crossed once when he used to party like it was 1999

– back in 1999, in fact. That is when I blagged his way into every party I could – my size and looks helped lots.

'What did I get out of all that?' I asked myself and replied, 'At least my life has some direction with those two. Or is there only one?'

Ouch, that's when my head began to hurt.

BETTY

Three minutes after I heard the announcement about Patrick's gangster dad, Carlos called me.

'I have a confession to make,' he said.

Sylvie listened in on the whole sordid thing, of how Carlos got carried away.

With an erratically beating heart, I turned to my smug-looking sister and said with not much conviction, 'Oh, Sylvie, much as I do not like to apologise, I am slightly sorry for suspecting you.'

The question was, what to do with Carlos, going off-piste and ruining my plans. (I was not that fussed really, like father like son and all that).

Gary Weber was dead, and that evil son of his no longer had any parental control. But nothing had changed. I decided Patrick would stay on the list, and I immediately felt more upbeat.

It was a horrid rainy Sunday. I called Seb, but it went straight to voicemail. For once I didn't fancy shopping. I even thought of seeing the beastly mama. I missed France; mama could be entertaining. She always wanted to wipe someone off the face of the earth; she hated more types than I did.

I could hop in a cab to Heathrow; a short flight to Biarritz, I'd be back in time for work on Monday.

Bah, talking of work, I knew I would have to resign soon. My vile boss seemed to read me like a Biff and Chip book! Yes, taking a breather in France would give me time to work on my exit strategy. After that, a year abroad was due, or longer. Mexico appealed.

Once Ricky Jennings was no longer alive (I no longer cared if he was prey five or six), I was out, all aboard for a trip abroad, packing already.

'Are you game for it, sis?' I asked, but Sylvie was gone.

CHAPTER 40.

Crash Diet

SYLVIE

I am trying to pin Seb down, him and his freaking voicemail. I thought he would have learnt his lesson after dog-gate. I feel the need to retrain him, having enjoyed our time in the basement. Meanwhile I am a bit crazed. I am off sugar for the week, a bikini diet. Well bloated now; maybe it is the bread, but I cannot give up all my sins in one foul swoop. A girl needs some measures of sin, and a triple gin a day will not suffice. Does not have to be food-focused though, does it now?

There are other ways to sin, something close to our heart of hearts.

BETTY

It was Monday night and I was on my second double Plymouth gin and slim-line tonic (yuck to no sugar) with fresh lime. That was my new diet; sadly, no crisps allowed. Sylvie had swayed me. She was on a diet, so I had to be on one too. 'We need to remain identical,' she ordered. It was her way of taking control. Whatever. I was on a slosh fest.

The reason? First thing that Monday, I got it in my delicate unlined neck by that freak fuck that was my boss. And I wasn't over mama's clinging limpet thing over the weekend. Your fault, Sylvie. When was the last time you went there? Your turn will come. I was sick of acting the beloved.

I did a twelve-hour stint dealing with a French inquisition, including 'What have you done to your hair?' All asked with a snide disapproving look. 'You were our rising, bright, sparkling star whose lights have gone out. Pfffff, power cut,' mama said cruelly.

What's more, at work, I made some funny remarks about Martin and his painted eyebrows. What was he thinking? He was positively Spock-like – no one laughed. How was I meant to know his fiancé had (unsurprisingly) ditched him the other week? The fukunts never tell me anything.

In other news, I met Seb on Sunday night. He smiled his bared teeth smile. I swore I would have to bin him. We had a quick drink; I made an excuse and noted that he did not look at all disappointed.

When I got home I read more about the allegations against Ricky Jennings. I told Sylvie she could be the honey trap: twenty-eight going on sweet sixteen, she could do it. I told her I was ready with the long-distance lens, the hidden camera, the bug and the knife.

'Only pulling your pins about the last bit,' I said. 'I meant the scalpel.'

I felt drowsy. I lay down on my sofa, my train of thoughts went astray and askew as I heard Sylvie's voice resound.

SYLVIE

'Betty, let me bring Yuki in to join us, I love him, his yakuza roots give him street cred.'

Tailing Yuki is not easy; he is almost on to me. I have to jump lights. The man is a crouching tiger – rahhh! He is the dogs. I witness a broken back and a disarranged face thanks to two of his blackbelt chops. Bruce Lee, eat your heart out. Yuki probably would; we are twin flames.

Why am I trailing him? Let's call it intelligence gathering.

We are on a road to nowhere town with Carlos. I spot him standing out like a sore thumb outside Green Park tube station. Wearing a dark suit in thirty degrees with his pomade greasy shoulder length hair and shades. An oil slick is forming at his feet. He looks like a cross between Men in Black and a Mafia lackey. He stands out by not a mile but by 26.2 miles. What is he playing at?

'I have a plan,' I tell sleepy, drowsy Betty. 'It involves Yuki, an iron bar and an early start, only joking.'

What I do not tell her is that Yuki is tailing Ricky and I sporadically hack into his laptop. Between us we have gleaned that Ricky has an alter ego. His online shopping habits are brow raising, and I draw my own conclusion. Oh, and he is booked on a flight to Mykonos for the third time in a year.

That reminds me I must book a flight to Athens and a ferry from the Port of Piraeus. I will wear Betty's Prada sunglasses; I think as I pilfer them from her bag and bung them under my shirt with a couple of other items.

BETTY

I opened one eye to look at my annoying twin.

'Your stories are so tall,' I said. 'No one can see the top of them. You have gone so far off-piste you are on a different mountain altogether. I was here before you, so marshal the martial artist in.'

Inwardly, I liked that we could take more paths, two for the price of one; steal one, get one free. Sylvie's plan was tempting (what with me being a massive Jackie Chan fan), but it deviated so far from my LOUD and clear instructions that she gave me a big fat headache again.

'We will ruin his reputation first. You are going to lure Ricky to a hotel,' I explained one more time, 'with a hidden camera about your person. Take some shots. Then post the evidence online.'

I reclined again. Let's start, I told her, with exposing Ricky Jennings for the man he is. I want to raze his reputation and then I will kill him.

A few months ago, I told her, he was questioned by police and managed to weasel his way out of it. His excuses were pitiful: 'How was I supposed to know she was fourteen? She threw herself at me. I am a celebrity; you know; the wannabes want to make a name for themselves.'

There was no evidence; he had been careful; it went no further. He and Judge Dacres would get on like chalk and chalk.

'I can distract him, and then stick a scalpel in his gullet,' Sylvie said.

'Hold your fricking horses,' I replied.

I was outraged that she was trying to get ahead of me again but felt too drowsy to go into a characteristic tantrum. She stormed off. I tried to calm down. I thought of five animals beginning with A; aardvark, alligator, anteater, antelope and armadillo. I continued through the alphabet, I was asleep before I got could finish the letter F, ferret, fox, frog.

*

Tuesday was the usual drudge – I did not stop from the minute I slumped down at my desk at 7 am. I had a reputation to live up and down to.

After a long day of pretending to be normal, I decided to ditch the honey trap and exclude Sylvie altogether. I had the files and a hatpin; piercings were in order. I could film a confession and send it to a low brow newspaper. But not right then; I fancied a cold glass of champagne first. Easily diverted.

After finishing the bottle between us (so magnanimous, but it was a magnum), I told Sylvie that she was out of the picture – and relayed my new plan to her. I had blabbed again. Why could I not keep schtum? I bet she dropped some truth serum into my drink. I wrote 'buy a wine glass with a lid' on my chalk board as she lectured me.

'Using the hatpin will be a slow undertaking, but it might suffice for the hors d'oeuvre.'

I was suspicious that she yielded so easily to me going it alone.

SYLVIE

'Yuki could tattoo Ricky,' I tell her, 'with that special ink we bought from the back streets of Istanbul from that ramshackle place with the rickety door, two years back.'

I remember the shop filled with old musty smelling furniture. The front is a muddle of furniture that no one has been interested in for the six decades the shop has been open. Behind a desk at the far end, an old bearded man stands hunchbacked. He has piercing blue eyes and exquisite limbal rings.

BETTY

Sylvie was right, I had found him on the dark web, advertising 'deadly ink', I recalled. With her description a vivid image flooded into my head as she reminded me of that night. But I'll let her tell it.

SYLVIE

The old man ushers us through to the back room, which, in stark contrast to the chaos front of house, is Zen like and minimalistic. He gestures for us to remove our shoes and sit on tatami mats. We then engage in an elaborate tea ceremony. Over the course of the afternoon he talks to us in hushed words – to avoid any passers-by in the furniture shop. He divulges the secret ingredient of the ink and ways to deliver the poison, delivering his wisdom via his stories of success.

I remember Betty whispering, 'This man has likely penned many a death wish, unlikely written on paper.'

Having refreshed her memory, I tell her, 'I suspect you might not like this suggestion because you want everything to be your idea, but this is a clever one. You and I both know that our man in Istanbul is an enigma. We can be his ghost-writers.'

BETTY

'Loving your style, but it's back to me for a change!' I frowned as I watched her wipe my blackboard clean. My tram lines deepened as I realised I had forgotten what I'd written on it.

Back to Ricky Jennings, I had some thoughts – in fact, I had 23,000 thoughts or more piling up in my head. He was getting to me so much; he was everywhere, the self-aggrandising dick.

Jennings had recently appeared on a talk show. An overinflated ego dick was at the helm – the host, I mean. So many chat show hosts are: look at me, listen to my (rubbish) name dropping anecdotes; I'm so funny. I'm so much more talented than my guests and so quick witted. Ricky J, a lolling guest after a snifter and one for luck in the green room, was at his smarmy worst.

I had enough of Sylvie and booked a cab to Seb's. Fifteen minutes later, I was in his top-of-the-range kitchen making a gin cocktail. The sound of canned laughter traversed the airwaves. I hotfooted it up the stairs and asked him to turn it down.

From the TV screen, Jennings looked right at me, all sweetness and light, but his eyes told a different tale.

I had seen the allegations: a grope here, a few bruises and broken ribs there and a few accusations that surfaced only to be swept away. One day someone might come clean and confess.

I know, that was a bit rich coming from me.

I stopped to watch Jennings talking about his latest series and thought about his ex-trophy wife. Unhappily she must have felt like a runners-up medal after several years with him. He regaled, but it was a front. I had seen the back and the sides, and it was a true piece of abhorrent mess.

*

Although fired up, my plan had been a maze, with thorny bushes in the way, but that night it was straight and righteous. I put up with prickly behaviour from Sylvie, but I hated to admit a dependency. I could not go ahead with it without knowing if she would be about.

I needed an audience. I felt it was time to bring Carlos back into the fold too.

I had ditched the idea of traps, honeyed or otherwise, and started thinking about a freak accident. I mentioned lightning, but that was not freaky enough – and Sylvie would laugh at me again. Falling down a hole was good but sounded like a faff. Electrics, carbon monoxide, falling asleep in the bath – but not so easy to undertake; not high on the freaky scale either, but I could get away with it.

I could purchase deadly snakes, spiders or scorpions. Then there were faulty brakes, poisonous berries, a piano falling on his head (only joking; that was beyond a faff), alcohol poisoning or a caffeine overdose. Ooh, thinking up freak accidents was fun! Tampered parachute cords, a quick shove off the platform onto the tracks.

I could have gone on, but Sylvie rolled her eyes, not just up and down but from side-to-side too. It was distracting. I was drawn to caffeine; it would be easy to feed him the tablets! Drink a few espressos with the pills and some coffee cake with special icing to speed up the process.

'Let us book a morning coffee party, Sylvie dear.' I said.

Sylvie swore that she had the perfect ingredients to disguise the taste of the drugs. Hazelnut; almond and vanilla essence.

What we would do next was still under construction. I had such lofty expectations, sis. I would have tried the poisoned tattoo with some bacterium to create an infection that would cover up what lay beneath.

By then Sylvie started to entertain me with some even more fantastical scenarios.

SYLVIE

'I want to replicate a scene from one of the *Silence of the Lambs* sequels where someone's innards spill from a balcony. Allow me some artistic license, will you. They could be draped from the balcony above the café where Ricky Jennings will eat his last meal.

BETTY

Innards from a balcony had mess and chaos inked all over it.

'Remember candy necklaces, sis?' I said. 'Well, I have a candy watch, handed to me to promote a new website; I did not bother to see what exactly. I am thinking along the lines of homemade edible scanty pants. That would be a good way for our prey to ingest caffeine.

Such were the scenarios; the reality was different.

*

That Saturday, I took a train to Horsham in Surrey and met our Mr. Jennings at a café. I had donned a latex face and inflatable bottom. I resembled Jennifer Lopez I thought happily. Earlier in the week, I called Ricky's manager from my burner phone earlier and said I would like to discuss an idea for a new show to show case his talents. When Jennings arrived at the café, I quickly handed him an espresso. He made ugly with the face and said he did not drink coffee.

But I had a backup plan: I crushed several caffeine tablets and put them into a sugar packet. I stirred it into his tea when he was chatting to yet another fan of his. We had a brief one-to-one, I told him I would schedule an audition at the studios. He seemed happy, even though I was a bit vague about the show.

Within minutes, I was gratified to hear a panicky voice. 'Help, feel sick, heart racing'. There probably was not enough caffeine to kill him. Just a scaremonger's measure. I made my excuses and left, umbrella up and head down all the way to the station to avoid any cameras.

A short stint in the hospital gave him more of the fame he craved. Maybe his heart-quake would also shake him up enough to keep him out of the public eye whilst I worked out how to get him to eat the poisoned cake without me being nearby. I would work something out.

*

I planned to start baking that weekend. I had never tried it before, it couldn't be that hard, could it?

But when I got home, I inhaled aromas unknown to my delicate nostrils. I saw a sponge cake cooling. Before I knew it, I ate half of it. The next thing I knew I was reaching for my phone to call an ambulance. Back up, back up; yes, my heart was beating at nearly 200 beats per minute, one beat indistinguishable from another. How could I have been so stupid? Tiredness, no doubt. I collapsed on the kitchen floor.

My fukunt twin. Only after I had eaten it, did she bound in and say she had laced it already with speed. '¡Arriba, Arriba! ¡Ándale, Ándale! speedy Gonzales,' she said clapping, before booking a cab to A&E. My twin cheered as I lay dying.

*

Sixteen hours and twenty-two minutes later I was discharged.

Reeling, back at home and still groggy, I spotted an envelope and opened it gingerly. It was my sister's handwriting, unmistakable:

Dearest darling sissy,

There is no point begging for forgiveness. I know you will try to lock me up. I am in a lose–lose situation, but it was worth it.

Sylvie

Her grating voice slipped effortlessly into my head. *It must have done you some good to have a near-death experience. Maybe it will stop your obsession with killing. You might learn how to empathise.'*

I told the disembodied voice that she talked detritus. I was empathetic already. I even made the 'Aw, poor you' face with the tilted head. The one I made whenever anyone had a tale of woe (and that was often).

'Your abhorrent plan did not work,' I said aloud. 'You live in tra-la-la-la land, Sylvie.'

The voice also mentioned that, as I was thrashing about, I turned the needle on a doctor. The shame of it. I did wonder why that spotty, rather fetching, young doctor was asleep on the chair. I thought it was because he had been working for forty-eight million hours. I nicked his stethoscope. I know, what a bitch. I would send him a replacement in the post; might as well spend my large fortune, the best money can buy. I sent him two in case he lost another. You see, I couldn't stop going around doing good.

I did feel for the medical profession, so maybe I was not a lost cause. Saltiest of the salt of the earth, the lot of them. Well, maybe not the lot: Dr Woolf, for a start. But we did not need to worry about him anymore.

*

Anyway, I chalked that one up; I would not forgive or forget. When Sylvie finally got up the courage to come into my kitchen again, she did a little dance. I was baking a cake. I told her to watch her step for I totally, totally, really, really hated her, her guts and all the rest of her anatomy and physiology.

Having gotten that out of my poor ruined system, I asked her to pass the vanilla essence.

Amphetamines and ketamine were ground into the icing: Ricky's heart would go slow, slow, quick, quick, slow, dead. Yes, Lynch might well pitch up, but maybe he wouldn't. Ricky's death, like the judge's death (when he dies), would look like natural causes.

*

By the way, I forgot to tell you I was turning into one of those fukunts I hate! I suddenly found myself walking along looking at my mobile phone. I never even used the freaking thing much. I could not stop looking at my feed; it fed me until I wanted to throw it all back up. People were so rude, boring, funny and/or dumb.

Anyway, I needed to sleep. I had been awake for twenty-three hours and forty-three minutes. I heard Sylvie say, '*My intervention was for your own good. What doesn't kill you makes you stronger. Oh, and you are sending that doctor two stethoscopes, are you? I think you fancied him, though he is young, barely out of the medical school. Still, it makes a change from banal banker boy Seb.*'

I swore she was in the kitchen, but she wasn't.

'What did not kill ME made me weaker' was my screeched response. 'Your concoction made me parrot sick, but my stupidity for falling for it made me sicker. I exhibited more dicky judgement than Alice in blunder land. Eat this little girl, argh!'

Regrets are debilitating, and I was inert. I was pontificating, pensive, and plotting revenge, when she appeared by my side, making me jump.

'You will get your comeuppance, it will rain down on you, Sylvie, you will see.'

'Pah, I am so scared,' she said as I shooed her out.

*

Enough arguing and tail chasing I thought. I needed to move prey five, Ricky Jennings to the front burner. But alas and alack, I was easily diverted. I wasted away in my nasty phone habit; I could not stop checking those daily deals. 'Wait until you see what I bought!' I announced to no one.

Kitchen devils (for me the kitchen devil), a course of laser hair removal, a three-course meal at a top London restaurant, a 150-hour Teaching English as a Foreign Language course (it would take me a quarter of time to complete), tickets to see an 80s has been soloist who never was, yada, yada, yada. Bing!

I did not need any of this stuff, but I could not resist a bargain.

And sharp instruments were always useful. So, watch your back and front, Sylvie.

SYLVIE

I too have caught the shopping bug.

A poker, whether made from the toughest steel or iron clad, is the only instrument worthy of an afternoon spent scouring the local flea market. I am tempted by a cream paper label, tied around the handle of an 18th century handcrafted fire poker made from wrought iron. Holding it gets me whisked up into a frenzy. All I want is to take it into my hands and hold it close. I could use it to stoke the fire at night in the winter months, which would eliminate any suspicion or evidence of its usage by day.

Where others crave human touch and the feel of another's flesh against their skin for comfort, I yearn for dangerous weapons.

I recoil from the recoil, my delicate fingers a vibrato of movement that sets me a-thinking. Everyone must be petrified of pokers: the red, hot variety conjuring up images of inquisitions and medieval, evil torture, ouch, pain and slow (infectious) death (or fast from shock). For me, I am thinking that I can use it as a tuning fork and bash it against Professor

Grave's head. Nasty, but I am sure he would prefer it to a red, hot one up the derriere.

I remember a few similar up the derrière, and the Professor saying they were medical tests that I needed. The only upside: it's good to know what pain really is if you are going to inflict it on others.

When I am finished with it, I will use it again to stoke the fire that will destroy any and all of the professor's hairs or remaining brain matter.

CHAPTER 41.

This Big Piggy

BETTY

I found myself distracted by some very disturbing sights. Men (and some women) wearing flip-flops displaying toes that ought to be permanently covered. I am talking deformed, hirsute and/ or overlapping. Piggy phalanges that should be banned from the light of day or night for that matter. I felt so queasy, pig-sick of little piggies, I could not go on. REALLY, I could not.

One day, I swore to myself, I would manifest as a fashion avenger. I liked the sound of bye-bye passers-by.

Anyway, workload and managing the builders who kept giving me looks had kept me away from finishing Ricky off. Yes, I realised my home improvement plans were a bit bizarre, but I needed the work done for walling-in purposes.

Oh, I would let Professor Grave out – eventually. Just needed to give him a little kitty scare. I had plans for that professor who was so awful to Sylvie (and to pay him back for giving me unsettling looks), but I did not let her know that. Suffice to say, she could keep an eye on him by removing a purposefully loose brick or two.

I loved Sylvie, sometimes.

Although, it had crossed my mind to put her in there too.

CHAPTER 42.

Finding Her Religion

SYLVIE

Whilst Betty obsesses over phalanges (yes, of course I know about it; I know everything as she cannot keep her stupid opinions to herself), my new favourite people are those butter-would-not-melt lot who give up all worldly chattels, including lust and all mortal sins, to devote their lives to the cloth and all its simplicity. People gawp at them like goldfish. Devout, that is what they are: devout in their prayers, demeanour and behaviour. I see a group of them on the tube. They look like seraphs and remind me of myself.

I wonder why the fascination? Is it because I am eager to learn how to be virtuous?

No, I do not want a sensory bypass; I merely want to mirror them. It lulls people into a false sense of security. What good is goodness if you cannot learn from it?

'You could learn a thing or 200 from them,' I say to Betty. 'Have you noticed how they don't seem to want, they always smile, they have no anger. They are living, breathing examples of the Corinthians verses they chant in their sermons. They have a sense of calm, second to none, as if guided by a greater good.'

BETTY

Bah to her pseudo-religiosity. Sylvie had turned into a veritable ecclesiastical maniac. And pah to the eyes-to-the-skies lot. Only kidding, but I could do without any commandments, let alone ten! Let Sylvie be a copy kitty; I was on top form and ready to perform bad deeds. Ricky would soon be feeling so ill, I told myself, he would wish he was dead.

But not that day. Why? Because I saw a single magpie, no other in sight, so I had to turn back, cake tin and all. Eyeballing the one fukunt bird, forced me to delay dealing with my prey.

You know the Scottish myth that if a magpie (a defrocked priest incarnate) appeared outside your house with blood under its tongue, it was a sure sign of impending death within the dwelling. Well, it appeared outside MY window.

Sylvie sent that bad bird, I bet.

I was stuck in the house, a poker in one hand and her hammer in the other.

SYLVIE

I peek in through her window, she is enraged and tooled up. It is a sight that I never wished to behold. I escape whilst Betty is inert; I catch a morning flight to Athens and not long after I board the ferry to Mykonos.

In the blink of an eye I am on the sun-drenched Greek island. From a distance, the sun worshippers resemble lizards and dragon flies. I soak up the sun, feeling at one with the world, when Betty suddenly breaks the spell. I have a flash back to the sight of her clutching her weapons (my weapons) the night before. I wonder if she might use them on me.

A line from Father Dubois' service keeps echoing in my mind, '*Le bien triomphe du mal.*' GOOD triumphs over EVIL. He was the priest at the ancient chapel mama used to drag us to.

I could swear he looked her way when he said 'EVIL.'

I am like that too, but at the unit I learn how to hide it and how to blend in. Not many are willing and strong enough to alter their very beings, but I manage it. I usually do OK until Betty gets her claws into me.

Tomorrow, there will be blood and gore once more. Oh, how I have regressed, and it is all her doing.

BETTY

I didn't even get a blink of shut-eye until I'd reassured myself that no one was going to get me that night. The magpie incident was a momentary lapse; although there had been too many lapses and collapses of late. My mood did not lift when I received a call from Sylvie. She told me she felt the need for sunshine and was in Mykonos; I didn't bother asking for details. I was hopping mad.

'You best get home quickly or you will miss the frazzle-dazzle,' I told her.

What the freak? I had stopped making sense. It was all her fault for being so irksome.

I peeked out of my bedroom window. I was not going out in that downpour – especially with Sylvie far away glittering in the sun, and me shivering and a-glistening in the rain. It should have been bare-leg weather, and it wasn't. In an effort to manifest a rise in temperature, I went to work wearing a summer dress.

I froze for the whole day.

I decided to book a flight.

CHAPTER 43.

Love on the Rocks

BETTY

Another day passed, still no sign of Sylvie. I woke on Saturday, early, with a sense of unease. My flight was due to take off in three hours. I made myself an espresso, old school on the hob. Within minutes I was shaking again, not with the cold or fear that time, but with rage.

Ricky Jennings was dead – drowned. Leroy Menzies announced it on the breakfast show. What the fuck?

I avidly searched for more information, checking and rechecking Twitter. Freaking cattish hell. Turned out that the rumours I had heard about him and dismissed at the Black Bar turned out to be true, so the tabloids said.

But I knew that, once again, Sylvie got to my prey before I did. I called her. Predictably, she didn't answer.

I left a message on her voicemail, all the while knowing she was unlikely to come back any time soon: for she knew I would be mad. 'Do not think you have gotten away with it. I will hunt you down. In the meantime, I have money, both mews houses now and free reign on the next prey. Yay!' I told her voicemail.

My thoughts belied me. Silly, stupid me – I needed her. I wished I didn't. To be fair, she achieved the right result with the wrong execution.

Sylvie did not call me back. She left me alone with mixed emotions and vengeful thoughts. Eventually, she sent me an email recounting the whole sordid story. The subject line? The digit '3.' Intriguing. I grabbed my hand luggage and got in my cab. Stuff it, I needed to confront her.

This is a short re-creation of my email to Betty (more or less).

Ricky is in drag on the island of Mykonos, it began. I explain that he is at the Sunset Bar, but then to be totally exact, as she likes exactness, I add 'at the Elysium.'

No one knows Ricky's real identity apart from a couple of his close friends, I write, and now us and everyone else.

Details are such slippery things, and I have a slippery mind to begin with. Let me just say what happened and skip the email business.

To begin at the beginning: the day I arrive I spot a poster plastered on a wall by the beach.

'26 July – Elysium – After Dark Show
With Special Guest'

I am convinced I know who the special guest will be.

After a sleep filled night and morning, I sunbath. By the time I return to my room and shove a few items into my belt bag, it is show time. I tip the waiter 20 euros to get me a good seat, close to the exit but with an unimpeded view. I am in disguise. My hair is short and mousy and my attire not to my liking – men's cargo pants and a backless woman's Bretton T. It is not long before I see Ricky's alter ego take to the stage. I almost spit out my ouzo cocktail when I see the transformation.

He looks relaxed but dazed and confused. He has purple and blue hair. Nearly all five foot ten of him waxed, with a stage name to die for: Zaza Cartier. He sports what looks like a Lady Gaga tattoo across his hairless chest.

The macho, macho man is not quite who we thought he was.

Ricky (or should I say Zaza) does make a good first impression; I will give him that.

Fifteen minutes before curtains up I order a dirty martini and furtively spike it. I ask the waiter to take it to Zaza, saying it is from an admirer. By my reckoning he voraciously imbibes it within seconds of it being placed in his manicured hands. He is swaying up onstage. He mumbles that he needs some air and clumsily leaves through the emergency exit. I am several steps behind him and then three ahead. I catch his eye and ask him for makeup tips. His reply is incomprehensible as he staggers towards the rocks.

A quick shove in the dark is all it takes. There is a belly flop of a splash, but I am the only one to hear it. Seven hours later, I see his body in the distance. The sea has washed his 70s disco make up off and his false lashes and wig: detritus floating on that now sullied sea. Later, he is placed in a body bag, wearing a green Lurex thong. I hear that there were no signs of a struggle, according to the local police. They also say that he had imbibed a cocktail of, errrr, cocktails and drugs and that 'Zaza' had taken a lover on the island (an unwitting suspect, I suspect).

A bit of an aside here. Take a moment to learn something from all this, Betty. Take a cue from Ricky and mix up your disguises. A bit of drag never does anyone any harm, now does it. The queens at the Elysium look more alluring than many women I meet. Barbie dazzlers all round. I comment how talented at singing they are to the delicious man beside me. He is wearing a tight designer T-shirt and skimpy shorts, straight out of a Calvin Klein ad. He whispers that it is lip-synced. I feign that I was kidding, but my stupid remark means that he might remember me and report a 'newcomer' in the club with a Swedish accent.

To be on the safe side, I slip three droplets into his drink. He will not be up for at least a day – out of sight of anyone that might start digging around.

*

With a whiff of a crime (even though it looks like a tragic accident), I sense that Lynch is on his way. Ricky is a celebrity after all. I soon spot him in a café in the cobbled streets. That requires a second email. Do not worry, I write to Betty, I remain incognito and will tail him through the winding alleyways and throngs of gay bars. He is bound to linger. He is as straight as you are sane.

Ricky's demise is the talk of the island; his last movements are reported to have been by the protruding rocks on sunset beach. 'What was he doing there?' everyone asks. Use your vivid imagination, Lynch, and take a few wrong turns.

I always take care to leave no traces or trails. I have another false passport and a ferry booked to Athens, then a flight home. I just need a couple more days in the sun.

I conclude my snappy second email with these lines:

'It's three to me, two to you Betty. Note: I claim Dr Woolf; you merely turned up and ruined my aesthetic scene – and you mucked it up with the judge! See you, wouldn't want to be you. Ha, ta-ta for now.

'Unkind regards

'Sylvie'

BETTY

Even before I got the second email, I got my list of prey out and wrote her name in neat, tiny capital letters. Where is she on the list? I'm not one to kill and tell, not this minute anyway.

CHAPTER 44.

The Greek Goddess

DCI CALUM LYNCH

I flew to that small island in the Cyclades, having argued with my boss about it. As expected, I won.

Once I got there, I said to Dave Gorry, a sharp-eyed sergeant, 'I'm going to the Elysium tonight to check out the crowd. As for you, find the so-called Zaza Cartier's mystery girlfriend or boyfriend.'

I wasn't sure what word or words to use, maybe a 'dash' friend. That sounds about right, I decided, pleased with myself.

Unwilling and unable to step off the one track I'm on, I'm convinced Sylvia (if that is her real name) was involved; she had to be. She could be anyone that she wanted to be. What with all the distracting sights on the beach, I didn't put it past her. I could not shake the feeling she was there, watching me. I did a slow 360 turn, for it was hot, and I was tired. Short hauls were always more tiring somehow than long.

First things first: off to tan. I would stand out like a sore thumb otherwise. I booked myself a sun lounger at an extortionate rate.

Soon I found myself rubbing my lobster forehead. I had left my Panama at home, and my SPF 20 sunscreen was rendered inadequate minutes after being applied. After about eighteen minutes, I stood up, thinking I'd better do some work.

SKYLAR VERSAILLES

Let me introduce myself: I am Skylar Versailles, famous on the island. That is all you need to know.

I was the first to spot him: in the near-distance a statuesque figure looming and looking out to sea from the craggy rock face and perusing the basking sunbathers.

His bright eyes were visible from the rocks.

I clocked him in under a second and undressed him with my eyes in fewer than two.

Well, he was only wearing shorts and aviators on his head.

I did not move, his eyes rendered me inert. Out of the corner of my eye I saw him approach –albeit very slowly.

DCI CALUM LYNCH

I felt as though I could get used to beach life. I would have happily dropped out, like one of those hippies that arrived for a week and never returned home. Dereliction in the line of duty was where I was at.

But it was just a fleeting thought. Work cuffed me back in.

Before I left for Mykonos, I requested lists and pictures of all inbound and outbound passengers by air in the last seven days. I had not thought about anyone coming in by boat, and my heart sank.

There was no proof, only a hunch or two, even the circumstantial evidence lacked, errrrr, shall I say, 'evidence'. All I had were circumstances, lots of them, and the unyielding belief that Sylvia was behind this. I would have to keep it to myself until I had proof.

But I wasn't going to let anything go. The tracker I had placed in her bag was no longer functioning, so I only had a vague idea where Sylvia lived. Even before she discovered it, she may have laid false trails. She never stayed in the same place long enough and was always on the move. Nevertheless, I was still determined to comb London until I found her. Then I would ask her to account for her movements and check if she had a tan.

In the meantime, I would make the best of my time in Mykonos.

SKYLAR VERSAILLES

I sighed and turned my gaze to the glittering sea. Never again would I reach the lofty heights of the ecstasy I experienced many a time with Zaza. Since the initial shock at the death of my lover, sadness had encompassed me, mixed with bitter disappointment. The last few hours revealed secrets about Zaza Cartier beyond even my wildest suspicions. For a start, he was known to most other people as Ricky Jennings.

To me, Zaza was addictive, frightening and exciting in equal measure. I was both fuming and tearful after reading some of the stories online. I wondered why he never told me who he really was.

For Zaza (or so he told me) the sex was explosive, the best he had ever had. That alone perhaps kept him coming back for more. We swore to each other that Cartier-Versailles was a double-barrelled surname that only death would part; and now it had. I would have sobbed, but I was only then becoming fully abreast of the secrets that Zaza had kept so close to his smooth chest. They came in dribs and drabs. There were so many revelations about Ricky Jennings' life that I felt that I was on a roller coaster ride, one that I would never get off of.

The biggest one was that Zaza – or, as I mockingly and reluctantly think of him, 'Ricky' – was a philanderer who frequented the clubs of London to feed his voracious appetite for young girls. I wondered how many others there had been – and then realised that was why he was such an incredible lover. They must have been diversionary tactics, to lay a false trail.

DCI CALUM LYNCH

My heart leapt when I spied a beautiful woman near the scene of the crime. She was redolent of a blue morpho butterfly that is the dreadful woman Sylvia. It was immediately followed by crushing disenchantment, when I discovered the vision before me was not Sylvia, which was, in turn, offset in seconds. The mutual attraction was instant.

Her name was Skylar and I found out later she knew Ricky. How fortuitous.

SKYLAR VERSAILLES

My train of thought halted abruptly when the man I had seen from afar, in scanty shorts, reached his destination. Me.

I soon found out that he was a cop. Interesting, I thought as we walked to a bar. He was a rather fetching but blotchy looking male – heat rash, the poor dear. I was shocked that my thoughts turned to chamomile and rubbing it in gently, then more firmly. I was widowed, I was even wearing a black bra and still wearing the wedding ring Zaza had suggestively put on my ring finger earlier in the year.

The cop ordered us a drink at the bar. Simultaneously, my already fragile world was rocked by another story.

'Rocky Road for Ricky's Ex-spouse,' ran the headline on Sky News.

I listened intently. The next sentence chilled more than any drink: 'Ricky's eighteen-year-old love-child by soap star Amber Ventokele is contesting his estate.'

I felt paralysed. On top of an ex-wife, there was a love-child. I had visions of appearing in court and announcing that Ricky and I had secretly married at a Las Vegas chapel on a weekend in February when Mykonos was worth escaping. I would explain – gently, fiercely and compellingly that I wanted the share that had been promised me. There would be plenty for the ex-wife and the love-child by another lover.

I reminisced about the business-class flights, the Bellagio suite. I had never been treated that way. The rich trappings would come in useful. Rightfully mine.

I imagined departing for London, with Calum, for that was his name, in tow.

My only dilemma was the nagging question, 'What will I wear?'

CHAPTER 45.

Glitter in the Glittering Sea

BETTY

Another email from Sylvie. How skilfully she managed to send my system into fight and flight! I was alarmed, and my bloodstream felt like there was a high voltage electric current coursing through it. There wasn't any headline news in the email – just that she had watched Lynch from a recess in the rocks. She boasted that she could stay still for half a day and not get cramp. I did not need to read between the lines of her short email; she was a liability, always had been.

I booked the next flight out, having missed the one I'd booked because I cut it too fine.

SYLVIE

I am so incensed by the sight of Lynch's eyes meeting another across a crowded beach. I nearly sent her the way of Ricky: a surreptitious push and out to sea. With all that bling on she would sink before she could swim; the tide would do the rest. But heroic Lynch would dive in pronto to rescue the absolute stunner.

BETTY

I had no trouble finding Sylvie. She wore a floppy hat, atop a vile pink rinse wig, Prada shades (mine), covered by a rather cheap, drab sarong. My disguise was less flamboyant and more professional. Dressed in men's clothes, I brushed a few hairs above my lips with mascara. Wrap-round glasses, an XL T, Bermuda shorts and a Panama hat made me both unnoticeable and unrecognisable, even to my twin.

I was overheating for more than one reason and tried to work out what to do next. For once I had no plan. Sylvie should have returned to London, but she was playacting. I needed to get her back. Blood sisters stick together, and us two were like the platelets that rush and gush through our hearts.

I still wished that she was dead, mind.

I checked into the suite and topped up on my dwindling blood alcohol levels. I hadn't had a drink for at least three hours.

Oblivious to my presence, Sylvie texted to say that she was miffed about Lynch. His head was turned; not only by Skylar, but by a few of the top-heavy topless men and women too. A dog in heat in the heat had nothing on him; his predictability quickly disillusioned her. She was booked on a flight to Frankfurt that evening to evade Lynch's prying eyes and another from there.

*

One week after the Mykonos fiasco, Sylvie and I finally conversed. I had blocked her from my thoughts and from my house. I threw myself into my job and spent the rest of the time drinking myself into a stupor. Days passed fast and nights even faster. In spite of all that, the thought of killing again was never far from the forefront of my mind.

All was fine until the bombshell (aka, my twin) dropped not only a bombshell but a barrage of bombs in its wake.

SYLVIE

This is how I begin to explain things to her.

'Sis, you've seen the film *Girl, Interrupted*. Well, my interruption is a much, much bigger deal. Being in Mykonos spelt a rebirth, a new direction.'

Betty looks at me with her usual disbelief.

'OK, here goes,' I say. 'I am leaving you.'

No response. I keep talking.

'I know you want to kill me; I saw my name on your list. But I am going for good this time. I may come back to the recesses of your mind from time to time. I know you will hunt me down, so I concede that it may just be *au revoir*, but a loud bye-bye is longing to ring out on my perfectly plumped and sculpted lips.'

Betty positively squirms.

'What the fuck?' she screeches. 'We are in this together. There is no get-out clause, only a path forwards, towards the next kill. I am a compulsive finisher-completer and WE will not cease till I say so.'

I interrupt her interruption. I tell her that I want out; I insist on it.

'Because I got sick, very sick last week,' I tell her, almost pleading. I suspect she tried to poison me actually. 'For the first time in my life I tasted impending death. So, I took myself away to a forest, deep in the countryside, in the wilderness, to a festival where I had time to think and let myself go.'

Betty is a total blank. I'm not sure why I bother.

Put simply, the wilderness gives me time to think. The swallows, the creaky tree houses, the rainbow lights; and best of all, the warm, youthful naked bodies in the river swimming, writhing around in the mud, spray-painted with gold. I want to taste the life on their lips, feel the heat of their skin next to my cool, limp body. In short, I want to stop time and open myself up to the life elements in all their glory.

I make one last attempt. 'Don't you understand,' I tell her. 'Lynch has disappeared from my thoughts. I have broken the chains that bind me to our multidimensional world of breath and death.'

I finish by saying, 'I know you will not take my news well.'

BETTY

She was bloody right I didn't take it well.

'Cowardly custard,' I yelled at her, 'can't cut it! Ding, dong bell, you are a wussy pussy plummeting down the well.'

I was shaking so badly, I could barely point a finger, or stick for that matter, at my despicable twin.

So, I was reduced to croakily saying, 'Go fuck off!'

But there was a backup. All was not lost. I had Jodie, MY intern on a placement for a year. She just came to me. Everyone was beady eyeballing her, and she chose my perfect self to shadow. And, no, she was not an undercover cop.

When I revealed my little surprise, Sylvie was jealous; I could sense it.

'Do not come crawling back now because I have a new friend!' I told her. 'The day I met her was a collision of like-minded minds, and we had a double espresso addiction in common. Jodie and I were like twins!'

Sylvie stood in frozen shock.

'Anyway, sis, another thing,' I said. (Was I trying to win her back with one of my interesting but non sequitur facts?) 'In bonding with Jodie, I found out that the general public is more honest in daylight.'

Of course, I was not completely honest with her. For one thing, I was definitely not general or public, not if I could help it. The usual rules did not apply in my case simply because I did not accept the terms and conditions.

And now for a special confession.

Dear reader, wherever you are, here's me truth telling for once: I planned that moment all along. The split with Sylvie was from my side, not her side.

Forget conscious un-coupling; this was conscious un-twinning.

CHAPTER 46.

Seconds Out

BETTY

'Before you go,' I told Sylvie, 'be aware that prey six has 1440 minutes of inhalation and exhalation left, 1439, 1438.'

No, prey six was not Sylvie. She sheepishly entered my threshold. I did not let her stay for long; within minutes of her one woman show, I shooed her out.

Unfortunately, her voice still reverberated in my head. *'About this joker Jodie, your new soul mate, hah! Soul mates are so last season Betty. We still have the struggle, the endless fights, and the unfinished symphonies of each other's selfish, self-fulfilling destinies ahead of us. Twin flames burn the flame of the same fire till the last ember dies out. Doesn't take a rocket scientist to go figure that out, does it? We are two sides of one coin, we are one with two heads.*

Ingrate! I thought, 1436, 1435, 1434: the minutes were ticking away.

I wanted to be dark and mysterious, a fluttering femme fatale.

I reminded myself of the architect who designed that new long, narrow room in my basement. Possibly to put you in, dear sis, or that awful psychiatrist or prey six. Or maybe, it could be hidey hole for me, if things got too hot.

CHAPTER 47.

Sleep Deficit

DCI CALUM LYNCH

Back in my hotel room, I rubbed my peeling skin off with a flannel. I glanced back at the strange shape under my Ralph Lauren covered duvet: Skylar, what kind of name was that?

My head was crazy hazy again. I slapped some moisturiser for men on, getting some in my eyes.

SKYLAR

He was red, white and blue with two black micro-dot pupils, but still looked tasty.

'Honey, come back to bed for seconds,' I said.

DCI CALUM LYNCH

When she said that, of course, I had no idea if I had or had not. But the word going through my co-codamol smog-filled brain was grappling, grap perling, grap peeling, grappling. Followed by an uninvited image of Sylvia and a sharp oriental weapon.

I shivered.

I knew within hours of meeting Skylar that she was not involved in Ricky's death. She had a rock-solid alibi; she was getting her legs waxed, in readiness for her meeting with Ricky, aka Zaza. Still, I had no qualms about booking her on my flight back.

Dave Gorry looked bemused; so what, I was beyond caring. All I thought was that I couldn't wait to revisit her scrumptious exterior.

BETTY

You can imagine my joy when Sylvie came back!

She only left me for half a day. I knew she would never leave me, where would she go? Not back to the wet and windy wilderness. She needed me, she was but a shell without me. Anyway, she felt wretched that Lynch got together with Skylar – well, she put it more rudely than that. Then she added, 'We need to kill one of them or both, preferably.'

I was tempted: if I took Lynch out, we could rest easy. But it was a red line. Lynch wasn't up for grabs. I came to realise that it was the thrill of the chase that kept me feeling alive. If the chase ended, my blood would stop flowing, and I would be no more.

Yeah, right. Later that night, the count was finally over, two, one, zero. Another prey had bitten the dust. There was rather a lot of dust in his bedroom, I noted, how slovenly.

Over breakfast, my ears pricked in anticipation, I waited impatiently for the Luna 8 Radio news. I wondered if Lynch was listening.

LUNA I RADIO NEWS

A man has been found dead at his home in South East London following a break-in. He has been named as forty-seven-year-old Callum Lynch. The victim was found by his girlfriend who returned home in the early hours of this morning. Police have launched a murder investigation.

DCI CALUM LYNCH

I switched my phone on: thirty-nine missed calls, plus more texts than I could count. It did my head in.

No, I was not dead, and I'd never even been to Welling. Besides the spelling of the name was different, mine had one L. No, it wasn't me. Strewth, the cheek of it; I'm nowhere near forty-seven years old. Although my façade was a bit jaded, and I had spotted two furrows on my forehead yesterday, I didn't look much older than my actual age, thirty-three. The cheek, the cheek.

I could not shake the feeling the murder was a message to me.

Of course, I arrived on the scene late and dishevelled looking: Skylar's fault. I couldn't wait to rest my head in her lap again. I was feeling a wave of desire, such as I had never felt before.

BETTY

I felt that the killing of prey six forged a detachment that no other killing caused. There had been previous annoyances and suspicions with pushing of boundaries and the tug-of-war of our mutual power struggle, but this emotional hiatus was unprecedented. The thick red lines of do's and don'ts, the tacit agreement we may have once had, was substantively crossed.

The score was indisputably three all now. Sylvie could not argue with that. However, it was really four to me, two to her.

Why did I go off-track by killing a random man in Welling? What did he ever do? Never been on television, is not a wannabe anything.

I needed to shake things up. Six dead and counting.

DCI CALUM LYNCH

As soon as I stirred that morning and switched on my phone, I felt shaken. That feeling of invincibility evaporated, and my blood began to run cold with terror. My once warm hands shivered as I patted my gun, holstered and resting behind my right hip, for about the twentieth time in the last hour.

It was exhausting living like this, on tenterhooks.

As I stepped out of the car, detectives were milling around, huddled, droves of them. My armour of bravado was still on display, but it was only skin-deep.

'Chaps, live and let live. This cat's got nine lives; one down, eight left.'

Some of them laughed; others glared, jealousies piqued that I was the centre of attention again.

My thoughts were on Sylvia again; she must be obsessed with me. I was sure she was complicit and her death toll had gone up by one. My powerful hold over her could prevent any future killing. I wanted to burrow deep into her mind. And I wanted to see her face, the real one. To do that, I had to catch her and keep her – and I had to convince myself of the lawfulness of my intent.

It could not be perceived as a kidnapping. I would bring her in to help with investigations, at my place. Skylar may not be happy about it, but she would understand, or maybe not; perhaps she would kill Sylvia or vice-versa. I wouldn't put it past either of them. Of course, there was no proof that Ricky was murdered, the investigation had hit a dead-end. Although, someone mentioned a guy who spoke to a man in drag outside the club. He wasn't above 165 centimetres, short enough to be a woman, and there were no further sightings of either of them. Not much else had come to light. But I added it to my list of suspicious deaths – Ricky had a similar profile to the other murder victims.

It troubled me that I hadn't seen Sylvia for nearly two months, but I sensed that she was watching me. The last time I saw her, she appeared rather distant, like she was someone else altogether – like that Betty Ellard, come to think of it.

I had almost dismissed my belief that Sylvia and Betty were related; they were so unalike that I felt a modicum of shame about being mistaken. Betty would never wear a mask or a wig; and she would certainly not venture out in underwear and a cloak, like Sylvia did. She was too natural and normal; she was strait-laced; liked a drink, but that was about it. Still, I would if it was offered.

Groaning, I came back to the thought: I had Skylar now. She should be enough for me for forever. I wished I was back in bed with her, exploring.

But still, inexplicable and unwelcome lust tinged with fear came back at the thought of a sustained period in close contact with Sylvia, if I managed to catch her.

Now, where the devil was the she-devil?

CHAPTER 48.

Heads and Wagging Tails

BETTY

Like many people when they first heard the news of Callum Lynch's death – including, I suspect, DCI Lynch himself – Sylvie's first panicked thought was that her sporadic lover had been offed. Then came the confusion. I, of course, laughed at her.

'Hey, we could stuff Lynch,' I said when she walked into my kitchen wide-eyed and bewildered. 'There's a thought, sis. Ha-ha, taxidermy is in again – can't go anywhere without seeing a stuffed creature.'

I sat her down and said, "I want to tell you a delicious little story about last night, Sylvie. About prey six.'

First, I explained how I went undercover of rain, under a big, black umbrella at 10.36 pm. 'Lock picking is easy when you know how,' I said, feeling the thrill all over again. 'But it took a lot of practise mind and a few minor phalangeal injuries over the years. The killing itself was quick and nasty – my right shoulder hurt a bit afterwards. I had to ditch the hammer in the river. It's ok, don't you worry. I'll get a new one.'

Sylvie looked at me with total incomprehension.

'He didn't know what hit him,' I added. 'Blunt instruments are it!'

Then she started to have a go, said something about killing an innocent man, violating the principles of the very list I had created, etc. etc.

'Stop it,' I said firmly. (Hysteria does not sit well with me). 'No one is perfect. He'd been done for affray and assault in his teens. Once a yob, always a yob, I say.'

228

I hesitated to say much more in case she had a go again, but in the spirit of our reconciliation I did.

'I must admit, dear sis, it angered me tremendously that I couldn't find another suitable Calum spelt with one L, like the DCI. A flaw in an otherwise perfect crime. Still, the one I found was fit for the purpose. And what was my purpose, you ask?'

I paused for dramatic effect.

'Well, apart from scaring the bejeezus out of Lynch – or, at least, puzzling him – it was purely for entertainment. It was hilarious to think such a nothing, such a slob of a nonentity, shared the same name as your illustrious (at least in the shabbier media realms) and irrepressible detective Calum Lynch. (Plus, of course, an extra 'L,' the common spelling.) I was laughing so much I nearly woke the snoring, somnambulant, beer-bellied fuck up. A quick hammer blow was all it took before his hooded eyelids flickered for the last time.'

Sylvie was not paying attention. I felt as though she was planning something; she didn't like it when I got even. She wanted everything to be odd and skewed in her favour.

I continued relentlessly with my story.

'I was so freakishly clever, especially as I was in the office all night! There was security footage to prove it, if need be (I never swiped out of the building). That's the handy thing about fire exits and trade entrances and knowing what's what and what's where.'

Sylvie left without a word. She didn't even congratulate me.

*

After she left I felt exhausted.

I was tired from all that I had done the previous night. I had to sleep in one of the meeting rooms and only managed to get two hours of shut-eye before setting off for court errands in the morning.

'Look at me, I'm a bushy tailed squirrel this morning and bright eyed,' I said to Errol, the delish dish of a security guard. 'And look at you, poor darling Errol, you're soaked. Dreadful

weather. I've been working all night and am dry as bones, see.'
I did an uncharacteristic twirl. He rewarded me with one of his
smiles, my heart leapt.

I would have told Sylvie that part of the story, but she was gone.

Who needs Sylvie? I thought. My office could be my new
alibi, and it is not unusual for paralegals to pull an all-nighter.

DCI CALUM LYNCH

I was stuck in traffic for hours. By the time I got back to my
apartment I was surprised to find that Skylar was out. I was
disappointed; I imagined her leaping up to greet me in the
hallway with a long, lingering kiss that would lead to all sorts
of carnal bliss.

Instead, I called Dave Gorry. I had to discuss my latest
hunch with someone who wouldn't smirk and get all narky
with me.

'Maybe there are two murderers,' I told him. 'One with the
blunt instrument, one with the sharp. One Cruella, one callous.
I'm thinking a raging one and a patient, meticulous one.'

Truth was I didn't know what to think.

'Unfortunately, there's no evidence,' Dave said. 'Not yet
anyway. There was no sign of forced entry. Yet he or she got in
somehow.'

So much for sharing a confidence.

But I was convinced there was a connection with the other
deaths. It felt as though they were all linked, all done to thwart
me. I was a hooked worm. There was only one suspect, Sylvia.
She weaved her way onto the scene after Alby Fry's murder, a
sure sign of guilt. I'm convinced that she was there the night
he died. It had to be her that I glimpsed on the side-lines at the
XO Club; she was the sort that could take your breath away for
good. I could have wrapped it up there and then. If only.

I was reluctant to give voice to my thoughts at work; some
of my colleagues would laugh at me again. Losing it, or maybe
he has lost it already, they would say.

But I couldn't stop thinking about it.

Perhaps the raging beast of this meticulous killer was two sides of the same coin. A coin that spins round and round and sometimes lands on the raging head and other times the tolerant tail. It set the killer's modus operandi, which answered to the tune of patience or fury.

I was shaken and full of doubts. I tried to state my situation clearly. I was drawn to a woman, Sylvia with two sides, one side alluring and sexy and the other shady and highly dangerous. That clouded my usually impeccable judgement.

Yes: alluring and sexy but petrifying too. I had mainly witnessed the latter, there was a darkness to her soul. I saw it in the depths of her eyes; I sensed a danger that was both disturbing and becoming. She made love to me with careless abandon, scratching, biting, bruising, and violent. She even cut off my air supply for a few seconds. I still gasped at the memory. I had to grab her wrists and pry her hands apart. I fell asleep seconds after. I wonder now whether it wasn't so much sleep that welcomed me but unconsciousness after being starved of oxygen.

To complicate matters, Skylar appeared on the horizon. When she was near, my heartbeat broke all previous records – up to 200 beats per minute, according to my smartwatch. I hoped that didn't damage one of my five vital organs.

*

Although I was tired, dog-tired, and scared, I felt compelled to see Sylvia. I called, but there was no reply.

When I put my beanie hat and leather jacket on and left my flat, it was 1.26 in the morning. I walked and walked; I didn't know what to do. I felt bad thinking about Sylvia; it was as though I was being unfaithful to Skylar.

Where was Skylar anyway? I had not seen her since the previous morning. I headed home, in the hope that she would be waiting outside for me. My heartbeat surged. I wanted to do it right there on the path to my front door; I couldn't wait another second.

But even as my nerves tingled, I realised that what I thought would never happen, had: I was in love. Within seconds those same nerves jangled and my stomach lurched as I wondered where Sylvia was and whether she knew about Skylar. I tried to call one after the other, Sylvia, Skylar, Sylvia Skylar. All my attempts went straight to voicemail. I felt like weeping.

BETTY

The next time I heard from Sylvie, she called me in the middle of the night. She relayed that Lynch kept trying to call on one of her burner phones. She tried to put into words what she was feeling.

'Obsession with the flesh,' she half-whispered as if talking to herself instead of me, 'is entirely different from an obsession with me as a person. Calum has carnal desires towards me because he no longer has access. If I were on tap to do with as he wanted, he would long for another's flesh.'

Whoa, horsey what happened there? My twin sister had a rare moment of clarity.

'So funny and so true. Too much of a bad thing is a bad thing. And toxic relationships are, errrr, toxic,' I counselled, thinking it was odd that she hadn't mentioned Skylar. Was she erasing unpleasantness from her pretty little head again? Skylar was so striking, she was hotter than the sand on Mykonos; surely, Sylvie was seething with jealousy.

I didn't feel alarmed until she said, 'Bad news, by the way. I got caught in a torrential downpour earlier. The kind that no umbrella can withstand, no matter how premium. I just hope there are no cameras because my wig cannot endure this volume of precipitation, or my makeup.'

Where had she been I wondered. Had she done something to Skylar? Maybe she poisoned her too. I checked my newsfeed, there was no new news about Skylar Versailles, née Ciel Moreau. (I was totally jealous, by the way, that was a better name than mine.)

It was 2.32 am by then, I was not getting any more sleep. I got out of bed, annoyed. Another imperfect day had passed, and lack of sleep was impinging on the next that had yet to dawn.

CHAPTER 49.

It's Just a Delusion

DCI CALUM LYNCH

Nine days passed, and I had still not got over the shock of seeing a man who almost shared my name lying there with a crushed skull. It reinforced the need to catch the sick fuck. I was worried it could be my turn next, now that I had become a bit of a media celeb. I received several marriage proposals; so much so that Lindy, who I nearly had a fling with the last year, offered to be my bodyguard.

I spent the evening in watching my favourite flick *F/X – Murder by Illusion* thinking it might spark something. On my lap there were three tinfoil takeaway boxes on a lacquered tray. I had tasked my partner with trawling through the reams and reams of CCTV footage from several cameras, dashboard cams, doorbell cams, the lot, near the victim's home in Welling, South East London. I anxiously waited for a breakthrough.

There were eight suspicious deaths on my list. Most would say that I was on the wrong train, but I was convinced I was on the right train on the right track. There were patterns, two victims were hacked at: Terry Baker and Dr Hans Woolf. Two were poisoned: Alby Fry and Kevin Wilkins (but he was cremated so I could not prove it). Alby was problematic too. 'Bad trip from a bad batch,' the boss Superintendent Becker told me and said to let it lie. One, Gary Weber, had his car tampered with. Another came off his motorbike – Todd Dickson, talent show runner-up – although the crash investigation team drew a blank. And most recently a drug related drowning, Ricky Jennings.

Then there was my near namesake killed with a single fatal blow to the head, that had to be the marauding murderer sending a warning message to me, surely?

Tracy Wilkins was in a coma – should she be on the list? Although she is a woman and was still alive, the rest were men. Another link: they had all appeared on reality shows, apart from that poor chap, Callum Lynch, in Welling. I shuddered. I will tell my dismissive boss of my suspicion that a woman may be responsible, one adept at disguising herself. She wears latex masks that look as if they are made of real skin. A sure sign of criminal activity. I will leave out some salient details, including mentioning my two repugnant encounters with her.

The film ended and I flicked through mugshot after mugshot of some memorable and many unremarkable faces, all women that had done time. It was a waste of time and effort but at least I am doing something.

My hunger pains got the better of me, and my mouth was back to sucking in noodles. Without diverting my eyes from the pictures, I stabbed my chopsticks haphazardly into the cold noodles and gloopy sauce. More and more sauce droplets splattered the cellophane, as I took out my frustrations with the chopsticks. My mind diverted to memories of the hacked murder victims, and I spat out my food into the foil container and tossed it and the other leftovers into my wormery.

The sleepless nights since Callum Lynch was murdered took a toll. Luckily, Skylar turned up at my door. She stayed at mine one night (luckily, I had changed my sheets after all that peeling). Reminiscing about our reunion still had a physical impact on me as I remembered the sighs, the gasps and the soft moans. That morning she whispered that she was off to get what was rightfully hers and that she would be back in a few hours. She did not tell me where she was going, and I was afraid to ask.

Twelve hours later, I felt sick with anticipation; she still was not back. She was like the most striking magician's assistant ever; so far, she had appeared, disappeared, reappeared and disappeared again. I felt all morose.

I cast my mind back to 'the case'. In my mind's eye, the only real suspect was Sylvia. I imagined sharp but feline features underneath the masks. I recalled the gentle caress of my hands along the lines of her naked body, the lithe limbs and minimal body fat. Pinch an inch would have been an overestimate. There was no sign of anyone who resembled her on any footage or mugshots and no witnesses. Or maybe there was, all I needed to do was unmask her.

I reached for the rum and swigged it straight from the bottle; within seconds I felt woozy and fell asleep at my desk.

BETTY

We watched Lynch on a large screen in my basement. Paperwork strewn all over his living room, covering the table and some of it on the floor. He was so off-track. For a start, he was not on the lookout for a hunchbacked old woman in black with grey hair tied up in a loose bun. Even if usable images were found, state of the art technology could not expose me. In addition to a latex face, I had several helping hands – the dark, the rain, the massive umbrella and no sight of the moon to light the shadows. As well as throwing the hammer into the river, I had burnt the clothes I was wearing in my fireplace. I was also adept at changing my gait; that night I put a couple of small stones in both shoes and walked awkwardly (it was a little painful). That would fool DCI Lynch, if they ever found any useful footage.

I laughed at Lynch; old school won't cut it for too-cool-for-school me, fool! He was a mug looking at those mugshots!

*

Still, I wanted to see him in person, so I arranged to meet him at the Black Bar after a wearisome day at work. He let it slip over a glass of perfectly chilled Viognier that there was a woman of interest called Sylvia. I spluttered as I was gulping my drink down at the time. Not a good look.

I made my excuses after two drinks and headed straight to Sylvie's and barged in.

'He knows,' I told her. 'It is strange that he thinks you are called Sylvia.'

She was uncharacteristically silent, so I kept going and told her about my meeting with Lynch.

Here's the short version.

'What's your poison?' I asked after I dragged him to the Black Bar; he was not happy. Said he had been up all night, and his head was hurting. I handed him a pill.

'Have a painkiller' I said. Gullible or what?

I got all sorts of information from him: mainly that he knew nothing! He went on about a suspicious death in Penge that he was working on. I asked him about the death of the man in Welling.

'Wasn't it strange for someone to be murdered that has the same name as you?' I declared.

He was beyond talking by then. Nonetheless, I feared he was closing in and I would have to kill him.

Having laid it all out for her, I turned to my soundless twin and whispered, 'It was you he was after. You should move away. You said you were leaving, but you still haven't.'

She did not reply.

'Let me help, how would a place in the woods suit you? Oxleas Wood to be precise; I know exactly where.'

I knew I didn't need to worry. We had so many disguises that the DCI was no closer to finding any evidence. Anyway, he was permanently addled. When Carlos broke in, he spiked the rum and all the other spirits in his place. Skylar had imbibed some of the rum too but not neat like the DCI.

*

It helped us in our little escapades that we had so many wigs: one was syrup-coloured and there was a caramel, toffee and rose gold one. My current favourite was the cerise one. They were all untraceable. We even had one made of horse mane, not to mention grandmama's French belle bouffant wigs and several purloined from film studios and West End theatres.

We had thirty-four in total, all displayed on homemade papier-mâché heads, a bit grotesque some of them (I'm not good at the eye sockets). The wigs were lined up in shade order, starting with black and ending with the Marilyn Monroe platinum number. They were magnificent and were stored in Ms Godzikowska's attic next door. She was a tad deaf and there was a concealed door to her attic from my attic. My duckies were all in a row.

CHAPTER 50.

Hard Feelings

BETTY

For once, Sylvie was candid with me. But, no matter how candid, I was always and forever suspicious of her motives.

SYLVIE

If I were normal – in other words, were it not for the antisocial personality disorder and a few other syndromes I am purported to have – I would feel sympathy for Lynch and his inability to sleep, his obsessional nature, the lot.

At the same time, if I were normal, I wouldn't have charmed and beguiled my way into a relationship with the very man who seeks to curtail my days of freedom. Suffice to say, Betty, I do not feel the same way you do. I never have, although I occasionally try to convince myself otherwise.

I beguile, all the while wanting to do harm. I display most of the signs of 'psychopathic' behaviour. Lack of empathy the most prevalent. Mama tells me my detachment was evident from an early age. She cites the day I witnessed a classmate being run over by an out-of-control car outside our house in France. She says I seemed to find the scene to be of interest for a few seconds then carried on playing in my room.

BETTY

Once Sylvie finished going on and on about herself, I told her how empathetic I was.

'If someone welled up in tears, I welled up; they threw up, I threw up; if they were in pain, I felt their pain,' I said. 'But now, if someone fucks up, forget it; it is schadenfreude all the way. My face says, "Aw poor you" but inside I am a cat smirking. Naturally I don't feel empathy before a kill. That's when I feel like a balloon about to burst.'

There was a time and place for being empathic, that was the key, I told her. Anyway, just try it one day; you might become the person you've always wanted to be: me!'

*

That was enough depth for the day. I poured myself a pink gin.

In my head, Sylvie can't resist telling me off. *'Crying inside is for winners, you say, but your gin-soaked eyes tell a different story, a sob story, my dear Betty. I can't help but hear you; you try to keep it quiet, but it never works. You are weak. You blubber uncontrollably, it gets on my freaking nerves. What's more, keep away from Calum or I will scratch one of your eyes out or maybe two.'*

'Freak off, freak. Life itself and alcohol made me sob, but you wouldn't understand, vile Sylvie.'

Still, there was an upside: I was getting my five-a-day through my gin diet. Grapefruit with the first medicine of the day, cucumber mid morn, lime for lunch and kumquat as a digestive and straight up before bed! You must have heard that fruit in the morn is golden, silver in the afternoon and bronze in the eve.

Sylvie turned up not long after and had a go at me for thinking that gin was medication, that it cured all ills. Last night she told me that she has been out and about lots, she had even been hanging around at a stage door waiting for Rory Kinnear. 'What an actor. What a fine specimen with eyes like Calum.'

Yes, I know, sis.

'Now shut it, Sylvie, and go back to your hovel,' I said out loud.

She did not move. 'Delusional Betty,' she said, 'for you are inebriated. I am in charge now; you have gone soft. Alpha-me is at the helm. Anyway, finding prey is so easy, no skills are required. There are so many look-at-me, look-at-me-me's out there. I've found loads, some on my fake social media accounts for a start, seventy-nine notifications, twenty-seven friend requests. Who the freak are they, sis? Accepted them anyway. I even set up a brand-new account so I could track Skylar, for she is one to over share.'

'Sylvie,' I implored, 'get out, pronto.' Luckily she did.

Back to my prey. Prey seven. He should be prey eight, but everything has gone awry, sadly Dacres is still hanging on. Carlos killed Gary Weber, I can't chalk him up as one of mine. Prey seven has been on the list from the start. His name is Benjamin Briddell, known as Ben. Same first name as judge Dacres, a pleasing symmetry. Ben is a popular actor, a 'national treasure,' they say. Argh, I hate both of those words; let us bury those words forever.

Prey eight is that idiot that won that fukunt show even though he couldn't sing. It hurt my ears, sis. You know, the one on that dicky show, with the smug, snide judges, I wouldn't mind taking a few of them out too.'

Anyway, let us start with that actor.

There was a resounding silence, inner Sylvie was thankfully silent. I wondered what she was up to.

*

Briddell was filming on location not far from Brighton, in Peacehaven. I know it sounds a bit hippy, but, hey-ho, needs must.

Sylvie, the real one, surprised me by saying that she had to go to the theatre – to the Barbican in the City of London.

Late into the night she woke me up to tell me that she had walked past one of the dragons of London and read the motto beneath it *Domine dirige nos* – O Lord guide us. The winged, sharp-tongued monster made her think of me she said, 'Although you are more like a toxic toad,' how rude!

'Prolonged sitting is fattening and flattening,' I told her. 'You never catch me at rest at a play: no time to waste. I do not care for a hammy Hamlet or dicky Richard. Thane and Dane cause me pain.'

The next day Sylvie conveyed more unsolicited information – for over four hours, she had sat on her perfectly elongated, sought-after bones, inert.

'I was not at rest, I do not do "rest",' she added.

'You are so vain, Sylvie.' I reminded her.

I was worried that she would start posing online as the real her with her snakeskin cat suit on!

I told her I was going on a trip too, to the northern most tip of the country, but I was actually heading south.

CHAPTER 51.

The Wizard from Oz

BETTY

Carlos had returned from Australia, where he had suffered from sunstroke. In his incoherent calls there were mutterings of neck crushing from the land down under. He talked of gin monkeys and jockeys: a ghastly rum lot out there with their sneering, superior weather complex and hegemony.

Anyway, he was back in front of me on my mobile; larger than life and berry red of face.

'What is happening?' he asked.

'We are off to sea,' I said and switched my burner phone off.

When would Carlos learn? I wondered. A beast of a man like him getting sunstroke was pathetic.

*

Carlos, who was taller than most doors – and had the lumps and bumps to prove it – was the solitary advance party. He cased the film set and the crew. He took 'access all areas' literally and had already taken someone's outer and underwear off.

Anyway, I too had a pass thanks to his light-fingered work. On this production there was a stunt double; I sensed an opportunity.

I soon realised that posing as the man in question might be tricky. Dear Ben's stunt double looked out of bounds – a creepy, coffin-shaped fuck. I went back to the drawing board or rather the skirting board of the hotel floor where I crumbled to, thinking and drinking.

Hey, I was at the seaside after all.

*

Whilst on the floor, I thought of several ways to kill Ben. The first thought was to push him over into a large body of water; like Sylvie did to Ricky in Mykonos. That would result in a pleasing sense of equilibrium. However, Briddell deserved a Kafkaesque ending – a trial, mental torture and branding like you've never seen, and I knew how already!

Why? He had created a storm with his narrow-mindedness, homophobia and racist comments on unsocial media and he just announced he was thinking of going into politics! How did they keep getting away with it?

I was sick to my perfect white teeth of social media – the stalking, trolling, the following, the adoration, the envy, the self-congratulatory multibillion-dollar popularity of it. There was so much striving to ape the famous, to have what everyone else had; for everyone to be the same. We had one preferred look and we all latched on to it. That did not include me (not much, anyway). I was not a sucker for the overpriced sparkly eye shadow that one of the women that begins with K wore. It was all, 'I'll have what she has.' We winked the wink, talked the talk and, pffff, the hackers and the influencers won the human race.

Well, I'd had it with the show-offs who talked the fake talk and faked the walk just to get famous. Z List was better to them than no list, and there was always a buck or few in it too.

So, rather than displaying your air-brushed faces and bodies and your fun nights out or in and feeling proud that you had thousands of likes and hundreds of friends whom you'd never even met, what about an alter ego site? With the *real* you on it, not the glossy, filtered you. On second thoughts that was a rubbish idea.

I tried to calm down, for I had gone off on one again, no chance. Despite the fact that I had shaken Sylvie off, I heard her grating voice in my aching head as I relived the conversation I'd had with her the day before.

'*Enough about you. What about moi, mwah, mwah?*' she asked, then she had a go at me, saying I was out of control and talked rubbish. She stormed off, vaporised like a headache that finally goes away, and said she'd had enough. '*When will it end?*' she asked.

'WHEN I SAY IT ENDS!' I screamed.

*

Fast forward two days and I was nearing Brighton again.

Despite Sylvie's ranting, I was determined to continue on my killing spree.

Ben had been led to the slaughterhouse like a fox with thoughts of a chicken dinner in his cunning foxy mind. He was in the barn, rather confused no doubt, thinking there was a roll in the hay coming his way. He practically ran to his car after receiving a note from his 'most ardent fan' with detailed directions and the hint that it would be worth his while. Instead of a signature there were three red lipstick kisses.

Carlos was digging a human-shaped hole and looked like a toddler with a new digger toy, a delight to watch, not. The landscape was barren, and no one was about.

There I was, wearing a mask and horsehair wig, acting as a judge – a fit and proper judge mind, not like Dacres. Out of necessity I was the jury too. My latex face was that of a mature, solemn woman. I read out the charges one by one and read Ben's online posts to him in a sneering manner. The sly fox denied all charges, but I knew he was culpable. I left him there with Carlos threatening neck crushing if he moved and headed back to London.

*

The next morning at work I walked taller and attracted attention, a rare occurrence. Everyone looked at me. Getting away with murder made me turn more heads than usual in the office.

I was becoming like Sylvie.

I entered the meeting room with an arrogant swagger. Within minutes I was bored, my mind wandering. The next thing I knew I was clenching my fists and breathing rapidly.

'What's wrong, Betty?' they asked. I could not tell them; I'd be marched out of the building, suspended on full pay, then sacked with no pay. No biggie.

My breathing quickened; it was the thought of those fukunt fun runners I saw last week in the park that made me mad.

244

It was OK to go round and get some exercise and to run for charity. But all those freaks made me shake with anger.

In my mind I shouted at them. 'Yes, you! People dressed as all sorts. As for you over there wearing a bright pink tutu: how hysterical, never seen that before! I have a question for you all, have you been to visit your elderly neighbour, seen a long-forgotten and lonely relative or actually helped someone, anyone lately?'

Well, if I'd asked them that you wouldn't see them for dust; they'd be off doing their next marathon, faster than I could say 'run egotistical rabbit run.'

AND MY COLLEAGUES WONDERED WHY MY FISTS WERE CLENCHED – AND MY JAW!

'Oh Betty, they are not all like that and the money they raise all goes to charity,' Sylvie said. *'Charadee,'* she added to annoy me. She had a point, but still, my opinions were fixed.

*

I dashed out of the office to practise my new walk, crisscrossing at will – that way I could annoy as many mobile phone zombies as possible. They usually spotted you out of the corner of their eye just in time to avoid a collision. An unwelcome distraction undoubtedly from the so important it can't wait task at hand.

Try it, it is fun!

Anyway, I soon stopped smiling. I nearly collided with a man boy on a freaking scooter. Not far behind there was an obese person on a mobility scooter. Did you know they've got limo mobility scooters now? They were the size of those oversized prams.

Once more I went berserk. 'Oh gawd, here I go again! I don't need this pressure on – say no to freak-sized prams, scooters, cyclists and phone fucks. Hey, people, it is time to reclaim the pavements.

I felt relief and a modicum of excitement as I walked back into the office.

CHAPTER 52.

The Oversized Toddler

CARLOS

I was in a field near the disused barn when I spotted some ducks, got distracted, and became obsessed with their eggs. I told Ben I wanted to crack them and make scrambled eggs for him. He tried to explain, in his booming theatrical voice, that they would neither poach nor scramble well. He glared at me, I glared back, although he probably did not realise it as I had my shades on. Then I remembered that Sylvie called me a man-sized baby. I sat down on an old sack by the barn door and waited patiently. I wish that weirdo Sylvie could have witnessed how mature I was.

BETTY

I left work on time for once and caught the train to Brighton. I hailed a cab and asked to be dropped off a quarter of a mile from the barn. I nodded at Carlos who sat on the ground with his eyes trained on the captive. I guessed he might be hungry. I fed him one of Carlos' raw duck eggs. I noted that he was grinding his veneered teeth, probably from fear. That reminded me that it was time to administer a sedative. I heard a noise, something was scampering, and then I heard my twin. The real Sylvie gave me quite a start. She must have followed me, that was very careless of me to slip up like that.

'I'm taking over here,' she said.

'So how come you pitched up? I thought you were founding a new cult or taking over the world,' I said, blatantly displaying my anger that she was not.

I turned back to Ben who was retching from the raw egg. The closing arguments in my makeshift court were over. There was no stenographer of course, but you couldn't have everything. What with me arguing for Ben and against him – it was quite confusing. In the end I let him represent himself. He said his accounts had been hacked into; he didn't believe any of those things that were posted online. He was not like that, he cried, like a baby.

He said that someone had a vendetta – he yowled something about an incident at school and a bully wanting vengeance. Haters got him into this fix, he said. They all wanted their moment in the sun, bringing down a star was their goal in life.

I was hit with the fact that there could be some veracity in what he said. People's accounts were hacked into all the time.

In short, I let him go.

But before doing so, I fed him more mind-altering, memory-blocking substances. Sylvie gave me an odd look. I headed for home, knowing there was no point trying to shake her off.

*

On the train back to London, I reflected that I had learned a lesson, that just a few words in someone's ears can set off a viral avalanche. One false fingernail or two pointing his way may have led to lurid headlines, poor Ben.

He was so right about people wanting fame. Boys wanted to be premiership footballers, even if they were fat or lazy fucks who couldn't kick a ball without getting a stitch or experiencing some sort of spasm. Too many of the girls wanted to marry them. Forget reality TV; reality check modules should be on the curriculum. For every footballer's wife, there were hundreds lining up – the nannies, the hairdressers, the TV reporters, even the spouses of other footballers – to take their place.

Ben had been let out in the open. He saw Carlos; the silly sod hadn't kept his wig and mask on! So, Carlos was lying low. The story I whispered in Ben's ear was that it was a fresher's week prank.

Ben looked happy when he left and so he should. I fed him happy pills, sedatives, a bit of speed and a few other addling tabs. I didn't keep track as such, but I handed him a large glass of Muscat. He gulped them down with the pills. I left.

*

Later that day, Sylvie called me to ask if I was sure Ben was still alive; she told me that after the Muscat and the pills, she dropped some drops in his mouth.

'I can just see your screwed-up scowling face with the fury seeping in and your pupils dilating to the "Don't mess with me bitch" look. I knew you wouldn't react well to that little change of plan,' she said laughing. 'You know I never stick to a plan. Pity he didn't die, for I have been trailing him, but he will another day. For it turns out he duped you, fished in.'

Oh frick it! Turned out I had been fooled by fake news about fake news. Oh, the mendacity! I cannot even describe how angry I was, so the lucky escapee was back on the list. I fell for the sob story; what a sucker, but he would not see the light of many days.

So 3,928 minutes and counting, prey seven.

CHAPTER 53.

It's Almost Where We Finish

BETTY

I spent three days thinking about what happened. I experienced despair, unhappiness and debilitating ruefulness simultaneously. It didn't get me anywhere, just left me inert. I just broke one rule and misinterpreted an email, two thoughtless actions at work. Got it in my swan-like neck and a kick up the ass too, a painful awkward position to be in. Next time I wouldn't click send.

*

Nearly two days after letting Ben 'escape', I was looking through my binoculars, right through the window of Briddell's trailer. It wasn't Hollywood flash, more trailer park trash. He was pawing and gnawing at Miranda Mills as she glanced at the clock. I heard her say 'shit' as she wiggled out, grabbed a plain grey T, and then ran to wardrobe in a similar trailer only shabbier where she got her makeup done. Not that she needed any in real life, but the makeup artist thought she looked so much younger than her onscreen age. Maybe a tattoo would give her some edge. Miranda rooted around in a large silver box pulling out a sheet after sheet of temporary tattoos.

Carlos, who happened to by hanging around in the trailer, fumbled in the pockets of his too-tight drainpipe jeans, and offered Miranda a sheet of paper, 'You want one of these?' he asked.

Cut! That was the clumsiest un-rehearsed act ever. Carlos had handed Miranda the poisoned tattoos that I had saved in case my other plans for Ben failed.

I wondered how the hell he got hold of them. My next thought was that Sylvie must have given them to him. Maybe she was showing off, how immature. What a dire dysfunctional infantile duo.

'Sylvie,' I said, because I knew she could hear me. 'I can't believe you gave them to the man-sized infant, for freaks sake?'

She crept up behind me.

'Oh, yikes about Miranda. I'm sure it will come out in the wash,' she said.

'Yeah? Well, let's see.'

*

Miranda, with pie wide eyes, looked at one of the tattoos Carlos was offering. It was a glittering star with a python's head and partial body flung out on a trajectory from the centre of the celestial beauty.

'Awesome,' she said.

Sally, the makeup artist, agreed. 'True artistry,' she said as she pressed the tattoo on Miranda's youthful skin. Carlos, a bit slow through lack of sleep, was a sleepy giant – until he leapt up as if stung by a bee, or bitten by an actual snake. He grabbed a baby wipe and smudged the tattoo, making the snake look grotesque, writhing almost alive, and slanting the star.

'Wow, gothic chic,' he exclaimed.

What the freak? This is a freaking catastrophe, I thought.

By then Sylvie had strolled unobtrusively near the wardrobe trailer.

'You, out!' she exclaimed pointing at Carlos. What a fuck up. He sidled off.

Sylvie grabbed a gown and escorted Miss Mills to her trailer where she locked the door and removed the poisonous tattoo. I watched from afar, binoculars in hand.

I thought it might be too late. Miranda looked like she was wheezing. Not surprised, Sylvie had a 3D face on, was dressed in her pushy mama's clothes, and Miranda's mama's visage was her visage. In her new latex face, she could walk around the set, unnoticed. Miranda's clingy, fame-hungry mama was tied up and gagged in the toilets.

Sylvie has obviously been doing her research, she will not kill Ben, if she does, I will kill her. I mean it this time.

Ten minutes later, Miranda emerged from her trailer. I watched the scene; she was a true star.

Inexplicably, I felt maternal pride, I really did. Odd. What with me having no plans to reproduce. Two versions of me were more than enough, let alone three. Although if I killed Sylvie, I might change my mind.

*

It took ages, the filming. Sylvie had skulked off, but I stuck around and did the phone twitch fuckery thing – hand curled, head bowed, eyes down. No texts from that fukunt Seb. He said he was in New York on business again. There had never been such a misused, overused excuse. I forgot how many times I'd heard it. Sometimes he was there, sometimes he wasn't. Truth and lies; once the latter had been embraced, it was difficult to tell one from the other, for him and me.

It didn't really matter what he said because the tracking device gave his actual location. I decided to cut my losses – I turned it on, tuned it in, and burned up time. Stalking Seb was taking up so much of every day that I considered dumping him just so I could stop this idiotic phone twitch thing.

I knew Sylvie would be up for an end to that distraction; she never liked him.

Lights flashed, and it showed him off the East Coast. The device hadn't failed me; it honed in on his exact location, a strip bar. Close enough, but not in New York. Really! Seb. Somehow, it reassured me to know where he was – even it confirmed what a lying, cheating viper he was.

They say knowledge is power, and that's sometimes true. I liked nothing better than dropping his real location into conversation just to hear his nervous laugh and see the look of terror in his eyes, which at other times reflected pure and filthy guilt. Guilt was a lonely look.

Of course, when I confronted him, he said it was a work do. He took to saying he had not only peer pressure but beer pressure; they made him go to these places and drink vast quantities. Yeah, right.

He would suffer; soon, I would name the day.

*

As for my plans, they changed again. Carlos was out of the equation after the poisoned tattoo fiasco; I could not afford any more slip-ups. It was lucky that I had a Plan B and a Plan C, plans that excluded him. It was always sensible to have a back-up for your backup plan, especially when working with clowns.

My head pounded as I focused on Ben again. I was still outraged that Briddell had committed perjury in my makeshift court.

Let's play merry.

'Marry, shag or over a cliff?' I asked Sylvie. Sadly, she was shadowing me again. I could not shake her.

'Over a cliff,' she said not surprisingly.

Right answer, my twin. Time to get the motorbike out and head for the seaside again.

'How does a poke in the back with the blunt end of my new hammer sound?' I added. 'Let's go for a short walk on a cliff. Get your fetching Hunters on, country dweller garb, oversized Barbour, wigs and grab a terrier!'

Terror instilled in terriers, across the country!

Later that day, Sylvie emailed me. She seemed to be playing nicely, making me wary. I guessed that she was after my prey, now that I was in the lead…

SYLVIE

Full disclosure: here's my email to Betty.

Subject: Dirty Ben and the far reaches of his dark soul:

Your 'over a cliff' plan will never work sis. How, then, will you capture him? Have you etched out a plan?

I can just picture you holding that notorious instrument of terror (that hatpin of yours), chalk attached to the sharp end, large, shaky hand-drawn letters etched sporadically, non-uniform on the wall sized blackboard across the exposed brickwork of the mews house:

YOU CAN RUN, YOU CAN HIDE,
WE WILL FIND YOU
BEN, THE FISHES, THE FISHES;
YOU'LL BE SEEING THEM SOON!

BETTY

More irritation from my pessimistic, doubting sister. Yes, I wanted Ben out of the picture, out of the miniseries, out of the undeserving best actor in a drama nomination, again! He would still be around when he's dead though, on all those repeats on those less watched channels. 'Unfortunately, after those acting and reality star fukunts die, they don't disappear from our screens.'

Sylvie blinked looking at me in my new rather costly new walk-in wardrobe mirror with Bluetooth speakers and lights built in.

'The freak fucks, sis,' I snarled. 'They come back and they keep on coming. It is a veritable parade of unstoppable freakishness. I can only take out five or six a year; there are not enough of us to get rid of them all. The snake-headed freakshow goes on.'

'Oh, Betty, we can keep going or we can go on holiday,' Sylvie suggested. 'Let's go on a trip to Angmering-On-Sea. Let's go play, or bite the bullet between your poker-straight, whiter-than-white teeth and we can bucket-and-spade it to Broadstairs instead.'

She was almost impossible to resist when she got that imploring look.

'If we are lucky,' she said, 'the rain will set in to wash away the bodies of lies of the sugar-coated demons.'

What the Dickens? I thought as I readied and steadied myself. It was time to execute my backup plan. Plan C.

*

That evening – dressed like an old dear, face lined, with a sprightly of paw Chanel collared pooch in tow (borrowed from outside a shop) – I walked the cliff path at Peacehaven. There was no sign of Ben at first. Then I spotted him approaching about nine km per hour, headphones on, never getting too close to the edge, but near enough.

'Fetch doggy!' I whispered as I expertly threw a sizeable branch at Ben's legs. He stumbled. Regrettably, there was no over the cliff wailing. That so did not go down well when he saw the rather elderly, frail owner. I walked over to him. The borrowed pooch sniffed at the branch that was way too big for him.

'Please, can I have your autograph for my mama? She's your number one fan.'

He squinted, I pointed up at the sky. 'What's that?' I asked.

That really was the oldest trick. I was going to shove him under cover of darkness as he looked up, but I thought better of it – he was too far from the edge so I skedaddled into the shadows as he rubbed his shin.

Ben's house was bleak alright, that night, after his brush with death so soon after his kidnapping. I could imagine the cogs of that mud-murky mind of his working, round and round like crop circles.

Exasperatingly, my failed attempt to kill him made the news. The upshot was that the police were looking for a woman in her late sixties who was walking her dog late that night, blah, blah, wah, wah. Briddell reported that a woman targeted him deliberately. He kept quiet about the fresher's week prank though. As his recollection was too hazy, all he remembered was a gigantic man and ingesting a raw egg.

Sylvie called me and said, 'Told you so, you faff around and show off too much.' And then she cackled.

*

I wasn't worried; it would be third time lucky for me. I took stock. Six were dead. Thankfully, Tracy was still alive, still in a coma (sob, I so missed her). That left two Bens, Ben Briddell and Benjamin Dacres, the judge (it was gutting that he was made of such stern stuff). A trip to the hospital was pencilled in to dispatch of Dacres. I would hold a pillow over his hideous head until he could breathe no more. I perked up at the thought.

I had a new plan, Plan C. I bided my time and seated myself in a chain Italian restaurant in Brighton. It was difficult to concentrate because there was a freakish gaggle of screaming, unruly *enfants terribles* at a table near me. Like an immovable beast, my anger would not subside. Several local parents could end up on the kill list before long! When all that was left of Ben was a smoking pile of ashes, I might pay them a visit. I knew where they lived after all. (Do you fancy a risotto al funghi? Chop, chop!)

Upwards and onward to Plan C. Mushrooms: deadly ones. All chopped up erratically, piled up on toast, sautéed in herbs and butter, smelling delicious, whetting the buds. I heard Ben liked nothing better for the first meal of the day, so his demise could come about before he could make any more incendiary comments.

Since the dog and stick trick did not work, I went after him the old-fashioned way. Bacon and mushrooms on sourdough coming up. The catering van was no barrier to the well-thought-out deviation of the plan. I sneaked in and out again in seconds. I hoped no one else would order the mushrooms. How thoughtful of me to think of others, I felt warm inside.

I almost pitied the chef too. Never trusted a thin one, but a fat one was bound to eat into the profits. Recklessness, carelessness and many other charges would come his way for killing the national treasure. He would be a lean cut of a prime suspect.

I longed to go home and rest. I had some Nordic noir to watch; but, before then, my entertainment was in the restaurant. By the looks of it, there would be drama aplenty. I pressed the fire alarm button on my way out of the toilets.

*

I was focused on executing my plans, when a preachy voice invaded, the voice of my terrible twin. *Does breakfast service go like this: nine mushrooms and three rashers, all grilled to the same shade of brown?*

'That is for me to know and for you not to find out,' I whispered.

'Oh sulking, skulking sister, with your headaches that are all in your thought-crammed head. If you must know, it is simple. No one has eye-to-eye contact any more. Eye to iPhone eye to iPad even at breakfast. No one saw you sprinkle a unique blend of spices. Bit boring of you to kill him the same way as you killed that lovely man, Kevin. Still well done, we are even.'

I screeched inwardly as I left the scene, no we are not, I killed Woolf not her, she weakened him only. It is four to me and soon to be five and two to her, Alby and Ricky. So there!

I was unnerved though – if she thinks we are even, then she must be up to something to get ahead. Not knowing what it was made my head swim.

*

Don't you hate it when a critical voice in your head gives you uncalled for opinions and advice? Her voice wouldn't stop, it berated me again:

'As for phones: please, everyone, desist. Put down your pesky walking, talking, life support device you THINK you can't live without and smell the skinny, flat white that's right under your blooming nose! Yes, I am talking to you. If you need a translation, I'm saying wake up and look up; you might see something interesting.

'As for you Betty, I am ignoring your cranky crammed thoughts and will treat you with the contempt you rightly deserve. You are a mind-bleeding, hatpin-carrying, fancy-dressed freakunt.'

Sylvie's opinions did my head in (even though some of them were similar to mine).

I ignored her.

*

Moments later, I wished I had ignored her advice too. As I walked down the road, looking up, I saw a mischief of magpies flying to the new build today from all directions. Also collectively known as a gulp, I gulped. Going off for a rooftop party and pairing off they were! Get them! My least favourite bird swarming around me – like a scene from *The Birds*, help! Is it an omen?

'*Bound to be*,' said the voice in my head, gleefully.

'*Voodoo is for amateurs. Sticking pins in for real is much more satisfying. I do not need a real pin; I can just push and push and push and push. See, your head is splitting, is it not? Have you thought that it could be me getting you back for being obsessed with Calum and for all your other ills against me? I am coming for you with a crown of magpies, like a medusa screaming and replicating!*'

*

Instead of obsessing about magpies, I took on one of their traits. I was into bright, shiny new desirous objects. I needed some new adornments, so I headed to Bond Street.

When I got home, I took stock, for that is good practice. Prey seven, Ben Briddell was dead – more of that later. I felt the need to celebrate; I tried on my new Chanel dress, nodded at myself in the mirror and called a cab. On the way to the Black Bar, I contemplated that Seb might be prey eight before Dacres (another deviation, but he had pushed me to my limit). If Dacres didn't die first, I'd turn my sights to him, in time for Christmas methinks, which had started already. There were baubles and trees everywhere, and it was only September! The freakunts!

As I returned home from the bar, I conceded that everything had to go on hold. My headache was debilitating and my thoughts had no semblance of order. The only thing I could hear in my fried head was Sylvie telling me that she was going to win. '*I am second to none, you have always known that*,' she said in my ear-muffed head.

I called her a liar. She was second to *one*; she was second to me!

CHAPTER 54.

Banged Up

BETTY

Stop the presses: I was making my third coffee of the day when I heard a news alert and joined the dots. They had arrested sullen Carlos.

NICKY ROWLAND, LUNA 8 RADIO

'A man in his 30s was arrested in Central London this morning on suspicion of the murder of Ben Briddell. New evidence has come to light placing the suspect on the set several times during the filming of A War in Peacehaven *even though he was not part of the production team.*

I was alarmed to find out minutes later from Sylvie that a load of cops had turned up at Carlos's porch.

CARLOS

I was going about my usual Saturday morning routine: huge yawn, quick hose around the toilet bowl with the trouser snake, revelling after a night out with the boys. The temporary absence of a woman to berate my childish ways felt like a dream come true. I ruffled my lustrous gelled hair and shuffled across to the kitchen wistfully thinking 'bacon and beans on toast for breakfast'. I was full of joy at the thought until the doorbell rang.

Who the Jesus is this at this time of the morning? Don't they know I've got a hangover from hell?

I made the mistake of opening the door, without looking outside first.

BETTY

I went into panic mode as I scrolled through snippets related to his arrest on my newsfeed, heart racing. The end might be nigh, a tabloid journalist recognised Carlos and wrote about it at some length, this is a short extract:

'Carlos Smith made headlines in February last year after he heroically tried to resuscitate Terry Baker the former 80s popstar and father of thirteen, the newest arrival Charli Page Turner born six months after his demise.

'Little is known about the six-foot-six bachelor.'

There was little of note after that.

Beneath the incriminating words was an unflattering image of Carlos being arrested.

Oh, Carlos, did we not teach you anything, son? He greeted the police and paparazzi wearing pyjama bottoms and a beer-stained T-shirt.

Bloodhound Lynch would be straining at the leash to question him.

CARLOS

A mean-looking cop tried unsuccessfully to stare me down, but my height gave me a distinct advantage.

'Carlos Smith we are arresting you under the (blah Act) for the murder of (blah). Anything you do or say will be taken down in evidence.'

I zoned out after I heard 'You have a right to,' bowed my head and complied. Waving at the photographers as I put my sunglasses on and feeling confident because they had nothing on me.

BETTY

Carlos let the side down. What was the point of us in our designer get up when he couldn't even wash his clothes? I thought as I looked at the article online.

But they would never ever join the dots to us.

I only met Carlos three times, once in Wales where I was covered from head to toe in surgeons' garb, face obscured too.

Once with Judge Dacres when he dumped him in the shower and took him back out again, and finally at Ben's fake trial. Each time I was disguised so well that I did not even recognise myself when walking past shop windows. There was a paparazzi feeding frenzy. What a scrumptious scrum, not. They scrambled to speak to the spotty lithe chef from the film set too – he had been freed.

I had to get busy and sort the Carlos mess out ASAP. Naturally I thought that Sylvie had squealed. She probably called *Crime Stoppers*, rat-on-a-rat they say. She denied being a snitch. She had no idea why they were there either. Not sure if I believed her; all I knew was that we needed to hatch an escape plan for Carlos. He was far too dangerous on the inside.

I made a call to the police station and told them that Martin Briars-Hedley would represent the suspect. With it being a high-profile case, he jumped at the chance. We shared a cab to the police station. I waited patiently outside, tapping my foot.

DCI CALUM LYNCH

I stared at my prime-sized suspect; he had a strange expression on his attractive face. He looked as if the situation he found himself in was surreal. Martin Briars-Hedley, Carlos legal representative looked familiar. I knew him from somewhere. Oh yes, court and he was at Betty's birthday party.

'It wasn't me,' he whined. 'It was Sylvie. She is a real looker. We had sex, she paid me.'

I stifled a laugh. Carlos stopped mid-sentence and blushed as I looked down at my notes.

'She paid me to follow you. Or they did, her and the other woman, if there is another one, that is. I don't know her name, but I work for them, or her,' he said. He looked addled and he had run out of breath.

Practically every hair on my body pricked upwards. It was too much of a coincidence, Sylvia had to be Sylvie; and, as I suspected, she has an accomplice. One was a poisoner and the other a violent hacker who bludgeoned my namesake to death. My heart was a-stirring, beating faster than an out-of-control semi-automatic rifle. My brain was whirring too. I was right all along. I wanted to shout it out loud in the interrogation room, in reception, and then from the police station rooftop. 'Suck it up dudes, I'm right again!' I imagined myself shrieking to everyone I knew. Immature but gratifying methinks.

His next panted words bought me back to ground level and shook me to my core, 'There are cameras in your flat.'

I suspended the interview to call an old university acquaintance, who worked for MI5.

'Can you sweep my flat please? I owe you.'

She would do anything for another romp with me, I sensed from the way she purred, 'Hello, sexy.' I was a-stirred again but for a different reason. I was agitated, like cat on a hot plate. I didn't want my Skylar antics out there. My sex life flashed before me.

I re-entered interview room six. I wondered if he noticed a glaze of sweat on my face.

'What is this looker's address?' I asked frowning.

'Easy,' said Carlos. '17 Devil Gate Drive.'

He supplied the postcode too: OX8 D1K. I tried not to laugh as I read it back. I could hold it in no longer.

I made an odd noise. He must have decided he had said something funny and beamed at me.

Totally ignoring the young constable sat beside me, who looked puzzled, I let out a guffaw. I thought I had forgotten how to laugh it had been so long. Once I started I couldn't stop.

'What's so funny?' Carlos finally asked.

'I think you are making it up.'

I got my phone out and searched. That address was in one of the fragrant Suzi Quatro's songs. Nevertheless, I made a note to check out the address.

He stared at me, and blinked a couple of times as I told him that he'd been hoodwinked. His eyelashes were so alluring, fluttering at great speed.

An hour later, the call came in from my MI5 contact. No cameras, no listening devices, my place was clean. Another nail in liar Carlos' casket: bang, bang, bang.

Minutes after, Carlos real name was uncovered, George Littlewood. More guffaws, he should be George Bigwood; I cried with laughter. Although it was a deadly serious business. The officer, the solicitor and I tried to keep straight faces. I had enough to charge him with murder, but I was waiting for DNA evidence from the scene of the crime.

Although George Littlewood and his alias Carlos Smith had a clean record, I was sure his DNA would be found in the kitchen of that filmset – or match DNA found at other crime scenes (excluding the obscene Terry Baker scene that he clomped all over). It had to, I'm never wrong. My conviction record speaks for itself. (We don't talk about the few where a verdict was not reached, they are still a bugbear.) Anyway, his hearing was scheduled on Monday.

I would question Mr. Littlewood again the following day about Sylvie and her accomplice, once I had searched his property myself (not much of interest was found that morning, he must have a hidey-hole somewhere). I would surely find evidence that linked him to those despicable women.

I left the station, after he was transported out of there, and headed for home. Doubts were burrowing their way into my brain. Maybe I should have let him go, then I could have tailed and nailed him – and caught scary Sylvia – or should I say Sylvie and her accomplice too.

Later, I heard that Carlos was struggling – no, understatement – Carlos was TERRIFIED. Not only was he in a grubby cell, it was also an old Victorian building – and we all know what that means. Squeak, squeak: MICE infested. In the toilets, behind the walls, under his feet. Maybe he will squeal.

CARLOS

Within minutes of arriving, I heard a scurry going on by my bunk. I opened my eyes and was shocked to see a hulk casting a shadow above me. I shrieked. Poor me, the robes of my Don Juan Carlos disguise had been yanked away, what was there to live for?

I shared a cell with Big Dave (all six foot seven of him). He had lived a colourful two decades. Not a moment lost on the good side. Dave had two loves, his mum and himself. He was sacked from the only job he had ever had as an apprentice butcher. He was good at the job, but unreliable, he informed me. He has an inflated sense of self-worth too, I thought, when he conceitedly announced that almost every part of his body had been tattooed. I tried to look impressed. He said he had been inside a few times for several crimes and misdemeanours, usually drug or alcohol fuelled.

Most recently Big Dave had once again been charged with grievous bodily harm, this time against yet another man who got on the wrong side of him, he said. 'Never killed anyone, like,' he confessed to me as he rudely invaded my personal space. I managed to stop myself from squirming. The guards knew he had the potential to cause chaos and liked to put the newbies in with him to see how far they could push him. He terrified me to the point that I lay on the way-too-narrow bed and pulled the scratchy blanket up to my chest, my feet sticking out the other end. I dared not close my eyes whilst reflecting on what I heard on the way to my cell – Big Dave liked the showers. I faked food poisoning to avoid an inevitable horror show.

I was proud of my adaptability and ability to plan. I would reinvent myself as Big Dave's right-hand man or I could take charge. I would have to see who would win in the battle of David versus Goliath, but with both of us playing the part of the giant. I decided things had to come to a head, after a short nap. I lay my heavy head on the lumpy, malodourous hard pillow and fell asleep in seconds.

*

What seemed like minutes later, I woke with a start and whispered, 'What the fuck's that noise?'

'How the fuck do I know?' Dave snarled. 'My balls might be big, but they aren't made of crystal.'

'Please don't tell me it's a mouse. I have a phobia and I'm allergic to them too.'

DAVE

My new cellmate did not make a good impression.

'Dear Carlos has a phobia,' I said. 'What to do about that? Don't worry mate, I'll take care of you.'

I am one of those people who never lets the other man know he has pissed me off. I like to keep the element of surprise to daily life. After all, if they knew what was coming, they would get out of harm's way. Anyway, what was the point of being inside if you didn't have all of those unsuspecting fools to play tricks on?

I soon had the perfect idea to get rid of Carlos' phobia and hopefully get the moaning pussy moved to some other cell.

CARLOS

When Big Dave returned from breakfast, he informed me that he had taken his A-level law exam and was eager to learn more. Maybe I could persuade him that we should join forces. I could drum up some business for him. He seemed friendly enough. As I was not sure who would win in hand-to-hand combat, I hoped that Big Dave didn't want to find out either.

Before that, a tale of mouse tail terror, just the tail. Big Dave collected them he announced without further explanation. I wondered if he killed the mice or let them go about tailless.

He gently caressed my pallid face with what felt like skin. Squeal, squeal – I made, a short of mewling sound, how embarrassing.

'Shut it, bitch. Yes, you, wuss. Big Dave will help you get over your fear.'

I felt the blood drain from my itchy face and had that sick feeling in my stomach. I felt as though I was going to faint. I heard the disembodied voices of the woman or women who got me into this mess. There was too much going on in my tired head.

'I feel like a stitched-up kipper. What a sucker, I thought, as I howled before I blacked out.

My dreams were lucid. They terrified me, and when I woke the terror had turned into panic. My breathing was laboured, and I started to wheeze. Through the darkness, I saw Big Dave looming over me, larger than he was in real life (and that was large). He laughed to himself, the orange tip of his illicit cigarette menacing. It wasn't even lunch time.

*

One hour later, I had a visitor, a lawyer, I think: Betty something or other, some French name. A pale, fey looking dude was at her side, that Martin something-something that visited me at the station; inept and pecked were the words that sprang to my mind. I dripped with perspiration.

The woman said that if I didn't accept her help that I would go to jail. 'You won't pass go, won't pass anywhere, apart from the showers and the canteen,' she said. (Silent shriek on my part.) 'You are stuck here forever or until death dost part you.' That was a bit much I thought, I was already in a bad place, physically and mentally.

She grimaced, although it could have been a smile as she told me not to worry, she would get me out. The Martin bloke looked puzzled, as did I.

Later in my cell, I reflected that she sounded like the woman who spoke to me on the phone and who I'd met in Wales and at the barn. But she was in scrubs and then dressed as a judge and in both cases she had a fake face on and it was difficult to discern a shape.

'What are those marks on your face?' she asked me.

'Allergy, alcohol withdrawal, stress, separation anxiety. You name it, I have it.'

I started to blub again, wistfully thinking of sneaking up and using my garrotte on Big Dave. I had a few new other names for that cruel freak! Not nice names or particularly imaginative because my sinuses were blocked and my head and my face ached. 'Dead Dave', or 'Dodo Dave'. I digress, it didn't matter, my freedom did.

I dreamed of having that cell to myself. Not long now, I told myself. But there was a good chance that Big Dave could be the one going it alone if my plan went awry and I ended up dead instead.

'I have always depended on the kindness of strangers. You should too,' the haughty one said to me at one point. She winked at me, it might have been a twitch though.

I knew that line from somewhere. It was from *A Streetcar Named Desire*. I remembered reading it at school. Blanche somebody said it. I wasn't convinced; I would probably spend the rest of my life in Dave's small sphere of influence. I retained the lawyer's words of hope in my mind to help me through this awful ordeal.

'Mr. Littlewood, try not to worry, they only have a set of circumstances and no evidence,' she assured me. 'A few coincidences albeit, but nothing that will stand up in court. DCI Lynch will not be able to make the charges stick. There is nothing to indicate culpability.'

Was it too late for me? Did the law have its squeezing, sweaty hands round my oversized neck? Having gotten over my fear of mice, it wasn't so bad, apart from the facial abomination. But sharing a cell with them and their biggest fan was not ideal. Although my face was rather red, 'Ah, it's just tail-rash,' Big Dave declared gleefully. He said he was trying to condition me. He said that he had 'helpfully' left some more tails about.

Before lights out I looked at the plastic mirror in my cell, a mirror almost the size of my head. I felt alarmed as I became rather breathless – a tad wheezy. I gasped for stale air.

Oh whatever. I might be a boy in man's clothing, but the antics that got me banged up had been a blast.

BETTY

Martin and I left the prison in silence. He drove his expensive-looking white car, too slowly for my liking. I had not even glanced at it that morning; he probably wanted me to say something about it, but that's why I did not. As expected, he lived down to my expectations and drove like the timid creature he was. A point in his favour – he did not attempt to make small talk. It gave me time to think about Carlos (I will never call him George). He really was a man of extraordinary beauty in his prison gear, even with a blotchy face.

What a shame about his predicament. Admittedly he needed development, as they said in my circus of an office.

But let's back up a bit.

As you might know, I am a criminal and I'm a lawyer (qualifications pending), but I was not a criminal lawyer, ha-ha. OK, maybe I am not that funny.

It would be convenient to let him take the fall, but that could bring us crashing down too. It was time to act, I pulled a lot of strings to wheedle my way in.

For the visit with Carlos, Martin fukunt thought he would be in charge. I cajoled and then blackmailed my odious manager to work on the case. It was an interesting case that could form part of my career and personal development programme, I told that freak bossy boss, whilst she cried at the unfairness. It was not my fault she was partial to the white stuff.

So now you know: I had a hold over her. A little white speck in the nose hairs was so easy to spot, what carelessness on her part. Weakness is pitiful, what did she expect?

She denied it, said she had some fluff up her nose and that she had never taken drugs. I scoffed and exited her office as she protested her innocence. Maybe she is, doesn't matter, I'll be leaving soon.

*

We would get Carlos off. The so-called evidence would yield little. Lynch knew it and I knew it.

Sylvie had a go when I got home. 'You are too eager to get him out,' she said. 'Bad idea. We need an escape goat, and he is a liability.'

I didn't bother correcting her.

I wanted to get Carlos out as soon as I could – he knew too much and was dangerous. I had also grown fond of him, but I was a professional and would keep it strictly so.

That night, I inexplicably became reflective.

There was a whole world out there for us to explore; the world was but our mirror. Temptation, opportunity and motive were all necessary for an offence to take place. Like oxidation, a spark and fuel were enough to start a fire. Those three things were my life's blood. Like popping bubble wrap; once you started, you could not stop.

Seeing Carlos incarcerated had shaken me; I had to spring him and then kill him or send him to a far-flung land with a new identity and a pile of cash. After that, I would have to learn to contain and restrain myself.

It was time to go straight.

Or so I kept telling myself.

Oh, and it was also time to throw Sylvie under the bus (a real one). It was her own stupid fault for telling Carlos her real first name and sending Lynch into a tailspin. She had already shoved me unceremoniously under one, a double decker or one of those monstrous bendy ones. My hair follicles felt as though they each had a tiny fire burning in them as I read Carlos's statement. Lynch extracted way too much information, particularly about Sylvie. Pffff, it was but an unset trifle. Ingenious me would sort that dreadful mess out.

CHAPTER 55.

That's the Wonder of Me

BETTY

Carlos the jackass would be out before long; the case against him was collapsing.

(Aside from that, I found out that you – yes, you, phone twitch over there – you have exceeded yourself, snubbing your life for your phone. Ninety-eight times a day! It was the new nicotine.)

The same day I visited Carlos last week, a new colleague was dumped by text by a man she had never even met! I had to spend two minutes doing the tilted head 'Aw, poor you' thing act. I was in tears by the end of it. I needed to destroy a few phone masts!

Fast forward to that evening. A woman – thin, steely, toweringly tall and just a little bit scary; almost machine-like in her brilliance and her machine gun fire delivery – made an appearance at her local bistro. Not many had been cunning enough to compete with Madeleine Byers (except once when she had an off day). As the devil was in the detail, she found the devil every time – and no, she doesn't wear Prada. She was tireless in her pursuit of justice and her latest case, the Crown versus George Littlewood, formerly known as Carlos Smith. If it gets that far.

I took a deep breath. 'I have got this,' I said to myself.

CHAPTER 56.

Going Straight on a Winding Path

BETTY

Not so long ago I was a coiled spring. Now the spring had sprung and the sharp pointy end of it was twirling about dangerously. The odds were stacked against me – what with blubbing Carlos blabbing about Sylvie. My previously suppressed pessimism that stemmed from mama was back. She set me up to fail with her constant undermining. Having to put up with a rotten twin did not help either. But I moved out and put it all behind me; I embarked on a new path. I even started to treat every day as if it were my first and last. Yes, that is rather clichéd and contradictory, but what people mean when they bandy that phrase about is to approach life with wonder as if it were the first day and enjoy it as if it were your last.

Regardless, I hadn't counted on Byers pitching up for the CPS in the case against Carlos. The hope was that Carlos would be freed before it got that far. Contingency planning was now vital. We needed to take him out of the equation, fast, and her out of the picture, in case we couldn't free him before the hearing. Unfortunately, due to time constraints that meant collaborating with my dreadful twin. She was tasked with the task. That evening she watched the impeccable lawyer.

'Will the proof be in the pudding?' I asked Sylvie, from the comfort of my sofa. 'Speaking of which, which course is she on, main course?'

'No, she hasn't even ordered the starters yet. She has spent too much time preening in the toilets. She's another one that doesn't wash her hands properly,' was Sylvie's reply straight into my ear piece.

I thought about work as I waited patiently. Gushing (on my part) had been going on that day: tears, not a Hollywood production but nearly. Work and my colleagues got to me. Vengeful thoughts were making their way in, in droves. Sylvie told me to stop, but I couldn't. I never would. Cross me, cross yourself, for I will come after you.

'Not washing your hands could lead to all sort of germs, sis. You know I am a clean freak,' I said. 'Maybe she would learn a lesson.'

Naturally, Sylvie had enough poison left over from the rancid basement.

And it was already on the brilliant lawyer's plate. Job done.

*

'Oh dear, she looks awful; went from dove grey to pea green in seconds.' Sylvie said as I continued to listen in on the events unfolding in the bistro from the comfort of my own home.

'Is there something wrong with your eyes?' I heard the waitress ask. 'Flu perhaps?'

'I feel like I'm going to be sick,' Madeleine Byers said weakly.

'You can't leave me hanging like that!' I told Sylvie. 'What happened next? '

SYLVIE

'Let's just say, that along with her phone twitch she has developed a hand sniffing tic. She will feel like she has the worst hangover ever, a bit like one of yours, and then some. Of course, there is not enough of those spiky bacteria to cause death.'

BETTY

Madeleine Byers had no choice but to call in sick. That was confirmed the next day.

If it came to a hearing, we would have a weaker opponent in play, although the hearing would never be seen or heard. It was time to intervene. Lynch had gone too far with his flimsy case.

The contents of a special delivery brown envelope provided Carlos with an airtight alibi. The file handed swiftly to Lynch's flinty boss set in motion a request for the blotchy man's immediate release. The envelope contained time-stamped images from within his abode, proving that he was nowhere near the film set at the time of the murder. Coupled with the fact that there were no traces of his presence in the catering van. The allegations against him would have to be dropped. Oh dear, DCI Lynch made several false moves. All those drugs he had been unwittingly taking must have addled him. Meeting Skylar cannot have helped either.

Yet Carlos wasn't even aware of it. For he was being transported straight to the Emergency Department at the local hospital.

A short time later, Carlos was in the High Dependency Unit, a drip dripping clear liquid into his left arm and one of those horrid bisected plastic tube thingies up his hairless nostrils.

*

I arrived at the hospital and asked where he was. 'Are you the next of kin?' the nurse asked.

'Yes,' I said, 'I am his sister.'

I noted there was no guard at the door, a good sign. I entered the ward with an orange scarf over my mouth. (I didn't want to catch anything.) I was also sporting a pink wig, green contact lenses, oversized pink-tinted glasses, a 1970s floaty dress that made me look like I was expecting triplets and one of Sylvie's floppy hats. It was not a good look. I soon found out that Carlos had a severe allergy to mouse hair.

The mouse tail had caused a rash; and the saliva-coated hairs that Big Dave repeatedly dropped onto this face like the first dustings of dandruff exacerbated his rash and caused severe respiratory distress.

Turned out, Carlos would need to carry an adrenaline shot with him at all times. He would like that I suspected. He squinted at me a couple of times but did not ask any questions. I told him through my covered mouth that he needed to keep it shut or I would shut him up for good.

'You wouldn't want to wind up in jail for killing Gary Weber or meet the same end as Terry Baker, for that matter,' I said.

He yelped in reply.

It was time for Carlos to go to ground, somewhere Lynch would never find him. I handed him the keys to a studio flat in New Cross. I told him to stay in for at least a week. I reminded him of what would happen, if he did not comply. After that he was only to go out at night, avoid CCTV, and only use cash – tricky these days, but he would have to manage. I handed him two bags of groceries and fine wine from Fortnum's, no less.

As I left, a call from the office informed me that Lynch's superior told him to let the case against George Littlewood go – he had practically nothing to go on apparently.

Through the bug planted in the inner pocket of Lynch's leather jacket, I heard one of his colleagues say that he was looking rather peaky and recommended that he took another holiday. He yelled that Mykonos had not been a holiday and told him that he refused to let the case lie. Then I heard a door slam. Temper, temper, Lynch.

SYLVIE

Given my strict instructions to look but not touch I reinstall a couple of spy cams at my dear Calum's place whilst he and his new girlfriend (I growl and howl at the thought) were out. I simply put them back where there were before. I did not like what I saw.

DCI LYNCH

I headed for home, where as luck would have it, Skylar was waiting. I swear I could feel the flow of my aorta and ventricles slow down to a safe rate. She was extraordinary, I thought as she kissed me softly and handed me a scrumptious rum punch. Within minutes I felt drained and staggered to bed where I slept for eighteen hours. When I woke up, she had gone. I felt so rough, I made myself cheese on toast and went back to bed. Some holiday that was!

SYLVIE

After Lynch takes an unsteady path to his bedroom, I watch Skylar on my tablet. She obviously feels miffed about the potency of her cocktail; she pours the remainder of the bottle down the sink. What a waste.

We are going to have to addle him another way, I tell Betty. I am tracking Carlos too at her behest. I hate my twin, she is a bossy mare, but I love simultaneous spying.

Whilst Lynch is sleeping, Carlos steps out of the hospital, standing tall and looking rather rugged. Within an hour, he goes all out for his twenty seconds of fame, it looks like. He turns up at a salubrious looking establishment to get his modelling portfolio done! Really! Betty's threats have gone in one big ear and out the other, I see. I follow him in and ask for a brochure.

'We just upped our fee,' I hear Anne, the photographer, say, gazing up at him through her bifocals and giving him a withering stare.

Not long after, from behind an old filing cabinet, I witness Anne succumbing to Carlos wily ways straight after the photo-shoot. His beau-in-tow cleans him at a makeshift Turkish bath in the basement where there is a grubby looking shower; she uses what looks like wire wool instead of a flannel. I feel a pang. I do not know what that signifies, I scuttle out, meeting a few stares along the way. When Carlos emerges, I follow him to his New Cross safe house. I had already put a note through his door.

STAY IN AND STAY INCOMMUNICADO
UNTIL YOU HEAR OTHERWISE –
OR YOU WILL MEET A STICKY, PAINFUL END!

I also drew a picture of a man with blood spurting from his neck and from each limb. I used real blood from a pig's heart in my fridge.

BETTY

The next day in the office, I had an unsavoury interaction with the boss.

Our standpoints were something like this:

Boss: 'I am not here to make friends.'

Me: 'Well, me neither. There is no way forward, and I am not going back to the under-the-stiletto days. Remember, I can squeal about your drug snorting habit.'

Boss: 'I am clean, and you know it. You have a choice, resign or get an epic fail on your records for incompetency.'

However, I am going nowhere, yet. It would be an admission of defeat.

Although, my odious boss will feel relief soon as I will leave her in the lurch, that will teach her. Not long now. In the meantime, I kept my glossy head down.

A few minutes later I was back to my best, juggling and not struggling, but who gives a howler monkey when you are swinging from the top of the tree? It was when you blundered that they pounced. That miserable load of misfits would not be braying any time soon, there would be no more slip-ups, ever. I was hyper-focused. The upshot was that not long after my boss let me be, apart from throwing sporadic dagger looks my way. I was sorely tempted to add her to my list of prey but I may have to settle for a take down.

CHAPTER 57.

It Doesn't All Come Out in the Wash

BETTY

Second things first, work again. My case load engulfed me, my boss piled the files up on my desk – punishment for catching her out taking class A drugs. The white powder on her nostril hairs (I preferred to call them vibrissae as that made me less queasy) betrayed her. She swore she was clean and as I have no evidence, I did not protest, even though she was trying to take me down. The extra work was opportune. The longer I rested between murders the colder the trail.

I only had time to take three short breaks a day to quaff expressos. Exhaustion compelled me to go straight to bed when I got home. The upside was that I rarely saw Sylvie. All I knew was that she made a big fat mess in her basement (not a great place for a studio). She took to painting monstrosities on slashed canvasses. Achromatic black and red oils were the only colours on her palette. She sold several online for a small fortune.

Carlos hardly ever left his safe house flat, he usually sat watching boxsets and lifting weights simultaneously as he did not want to appear slovenly.

DCI Lynch appeared to have dropped his search for Sylvie and Carlos. Busy investigating several murders, he worked seven days a week and slept an hour or two at a time. He was not at the top of his game, he had been listless since Skylar went back to Mykonos. After being informed that making a claim on Ricky's estate would be futile, she focused on raising her profile.

She did several 'exclusive' interviews to various magazines and newspapers. She particularly enjoyed the photoshoots and planned to go into fashion as many celebs do. She also made a sizeable sum from various brands due to her now two million plus followers. Before she left, Skylar pleaded with Lynch to pack it all in. With tears in his eyes; he told her he could not leave the force, 'Not until I solve this case.' She hugged him forcefully and left without turning to look back at the one, one last time.

I too was too busy to think about him or anyone else for that matter. That was how it remained. All was uneventful and ticking along until the first Tuesday of November, a wet day. My hair looked dreadful. I stopped in my tracks, literally. I could barely splutter.

The fateful event that caused my short stupor happened in court after Seb dropped by to tell me we were over, again.

'It will be over when I say it is over,' I told him in no uncertain terms. I must say I did not see that coming – the last time he called he told me to stop harassing him, but he always said things like that.

After storming off after our impolite conversation, he walked right into Lynch and nearly fell over, an inconvenient reunion after their odd dog-related encounter outside the Black Bar last year.

It was a worrying moment. Never the twain shall meet again, except that they had.

It felt like I had been electrified with a cattle prod, as I heard them arrange a night out.

These two little birdies had landed in the wrong cage. I held their fate in my hands. I could set them free or poison them.

That evening, I sat on the floor and wrote Seb, Lynch, Carlos and Sylvie in block capitals on a new page in my note book. They were all obvious threats to my occasionally pleasing existence.

I debated: I might kill two and spare two. I was taken with Carlos, despite his immaturity and lack of foresight. Perhaps we could go on a date. There was definitely a spark; when I visited him on remand, he gazed at me intensely, I must say. That meant that Carlos had a stay of execution. Sylvie would be dealt with another day – or in the dead of night (for that matter).

That left my unreliable boyfriend Seb (sob) and Lynch. They would have to die on the same day or thereabouts so that Lynch did not start to investigate and make even more connections. As always, there was an alternative path – I could leave the country, forever. I felt mildly excited about taking on a new identity and eluding my infuriating twin again. I liked the name Betsy Boucher. I made some calls and started packing, in case I decided to make a run for it.

I hated sitting on the fence, not knowing which side I would land. Being indecisive equates to being a wuss. I needed to make my mind up and act fast.

'I ought to kill Seb for two reasons. For a start he befriended Lynch or vice-versa. He knew way too much. Worse still, since that woeful day in court he hadn't contacted me for five hours and seventeen minutes.' The two odd numbers in close succession made me shudder.

Oh good,' Sylvie said, giving me a shock. *Sacré bleu*, she had crept into my kitchen while I voiced my plan out loud. I did not even hear her come in.

'I thought you had disappeared again,' I said, wishing she had gone for good. I felt relieved that I had not blabbed about Lynch, at least.

SYLVIE

So I explain to Betty, 'I have not done a disappearing act. I have been busy. Now see me as your conscious-clearer and risk assessor; your very own mind-sweeper.'

Betty asks me what the devil has gotten into me? She has no idea what I'm on about.

I do not bother elaborating, instead I say, 'Are you sure you want to kill Seb; he is unlikely to spill, trust me. Imagine this.' As I say it I re-enact the scene, 'First pretend you are Seb.'

Betty reluctantly stands up, staring daggers sharper than the one I am holding. 'I threaten him, at hunting knife point,' I whisper, 'the tip barely touches his Adam's apple. He trembles as I tell him that I will use the knife on him and everyone that he knows if he ever breathes a word of my existence.'

I do not mention to Betty my plans for Carlos. He promised much and delivered a freakshow. He killed Gary Weber. Not that I am bothered about that, but the fiasco with the poisoned tattoo and catching Lynch's arresting eyes, prove he is nothing but a liability. After him I will kill Betty and live her life, as I planned all along. I will do a far better job of it than her. I won't wear prim clothes though (although sometimes she gets it right). She really is a miserable specimen. Then I will enrapture Calum Lynch, playing the part of the respectable paralegal, wearing a pearl necklace over my buttoned up to the top transparent blouse. This time Calum and I can have a proper relationship, out in the open. I am ecstatic that Skylar is gone, I celebrate it in style by drinking a whole bottle of Betty's favourite champagne, Pol Roger. I steal it from her well-stocked wine fridge. That will be mine too.

Unfortunately, I feel a magnetic pull towards her and her bizarre ideas. I also worry that I will not have it in me to commit twin-icide – no such word, looked it up, sororicide then, there you go.

BETTY

Sylvie's voice was unpleasant music to my ears. I was livid, no wonder Seb wanted to leave me, after she threatened him at knifepoint, poor darling Seb. I was no longer on the fence – I would have one last killing spree after I ensnared the luscious Carlos. He would be delighted to accompany me to Mexico; I am certain of it. I decided not to waste any more of my precious thoughts on Sylvie.

What was her game anyway? She couldn't stand Seb, now she wanted me to spare him?

I wanted happy-ever-after for Seb and I, not happy ever aftershocks. I knew from the start the fairy tale would have a sting or two in its tail.

I heard her say, *'Can't we keep Seb as a pet? Please, pretty please? I will take care of him.'*

Sylvie was once again nestled comfortably in my head. I desperately tried to remove her malevolent presence from my whirling brain.

That minute, I felt like taking no further action, ever. I had a terrifying sense of foreboding.

I changed the subject in my head to some very important research I had been doing. Outside of work, I avidly studied addiction; you could say I'd become addicted! One theory was that there was no such thing as addiction; instead, life was a series of choices based on wants, not needs. Not sure about it myself, but admittedly in my case, enough wasn't enough. All my choices were want-based too, and the hate part of the love-hate continuum reared its ugly head.

Now my choices are needs based. Evading detection by the dogged detective propels me. Lynch, you are next and Seb, it will be painless, I promise. It was bosh that my list of prey had grown to ten. I was driven to distraction as I tried not to think of the mishaps along the way. Eight was my chosen number of dead. Carlos had ruined it by killing Gary Weber and Dacres is hanging on, I must pay him a visit soon. That's not even factoring in Sylvie's meddling.

Soon I would sort it all out but at that moment it was all getting on top of me. So much so, I looked haggard. I will stop after that for the sake of my visage if nothing else.

I promise on my twin's life.

CHAPTER 58

Match Point

BETTY

The next evening, I was with Lynch at the Black Bar. I wanted to question him and find out where his head was at, as they say nowadays. As was my new customary practice, I spiked his drink. He was working on a new case and barely had a second to think; he mentioned frequent headaches too. He added that Carlos was still a person of interest but he had gone to ground. As I rose to leave, he noticed my beauty spots. They looked totally real, and he swore blind they were not there the last time he saw me. Hypervigilance; he didn't miss a single trick or error, even when he had unknowingly imbibed unwelcome psychoactive substances.

I had been in such a rush I forgot to remove the fabulous beauty spots. I had been experimenting with some new looks. 'Do you like changing your appearance?' he asked, alarming me. 'The many faces of Betty' was my latest compulsion. Time to go. I wasn't going to get anything more out of him anyway. His head slumped onto a bowl of roasted almonds; luckily, I had eaten most of them. I poured some ice-cold water over his fetching looking neck to rouse him, and he was upright in seconds. I grabbed my coat and bag and waved goodbye. I would be turning up at his flat later.

As I exited the bar, I saw Seb get out of a cab. He kept his distance as he said that he was meeting Lynch. *Mon dieu*! I walked back into the bar and slipped something into his drink as I reached for more almonds, had to. Seb looked up out of his beer glass, but the goggles had long since clouded his judgement. Easily distracted, he focused on the music, making moves like Tom Cruise in Cocktail. Lynch had stirred and looked bemused, but perhaps their nascent relationship would be over shortly.

There was no time to brainstorm, sis; the synchronicity was perfect. I went with my gut on this one.

'It is getting late, either of you fancy a digestif?' I offered.

Game, set and match. There were addling drugs in play and no hidden cameras, not at the Black Bar. Neither dose was fatal. I was just having some fun, for now. Seb, having downed two shots and still a jittery wreck, was to my left and a less drowsy Lynch was to my right.

We were ensconced on a carmine-coloured velvet banquette. Seb stirred and called the delicious gay waiter over. Pity for me. For I was deluded, as always, thinking I could turn everyone's head. I did not wait for a reply. I ought to ask Sylvie for help, although as sisters we were not doing it for each other right then. She had gone one way, me the other; both of us hidden from the other's view. That was the trouble.

After one more drink each I walked out with the inebriated pair, one on each arm. Seb got into a cab mumbling. Lynch loitered outside. 'Coooooweeee DCI Lynch, this way,' I said.

I bundled him into a cab; drinks, drugs and lack of food were not a good mix. He would be out of action for at least a day. Maybe he would be sacked. Whatever happened, I would have to spend more time working out my next steps.

I was unable to dispatch the pair of them that night – too many witnesses at the bar, where I was a regular. The caged birds can flap about for another day.

*

That night as I lay in bed, I thought about Seb. He reminded me of a child who made you laugh until tears streamed down your face after saying something sweet and silly, out-of-the-mouths-of-babes funny. Their laughter and their beauty make you howl with joy. The second time they tell it – and it will be repeated more than once, it still warms you. Then it starts to wear thin and grates. That was how I felt about Seb, yet I had clung on to him for dear life.

Sylvie always said that I needed to ditch him. Well, I guess he was what I wanted before I embarked on a much more exciting murderous path. But when you're stuck with Peter Pan man and you are nearly thirty... well, what to do?

Do without or get a new model, methinks.

The morning after that night, my phone rang. It was Seb! He apologised for his behaviour and asked to meet up. Maybe he wanted us to get back together; I felt a surge within me, Oh, Seb, I knew you would come running back, who could resist?

But within seconds I felt suspicious of his motives – was he so scared of Sylvie that he was trying to get on the right side of me or had Lynch put him up to it? Maybe Seb told Lynch everything that he knows about me. I felt nauseated. What freakish hell.

*

As I walked to the bus stop the next day, after about an hour's sleep, I glared angrily at the perpetrators of the dick-phone-twitch-thing: eyes down when walking, commuting, in lifts, queuing for coffee, waiting for lifts and missing what was really going on. No one glowered back, they didn't even see me. They must be doing really urgent stuff. Distracted drivers and distracted pedestrians, I noted as I waited to cross the road – a double whammy!

Ok, maybe I got a bit carried away; I had also been known to be glued to the device.

After a double-shot espresso and a veggie sausage sandwich, I got on the first bus that came along. I spent an hour phone snooping. Shoulder surfing. What a fey day! I'd feasted on bitching, cheating, ditching and lying and felt gleeful. Enough skulduggery to see me through another day.

Then I heard Sylvie's voice, moaning, *'Phone snooping and shoulder surfing is no different from twitchy-curtain voyeur.'* She was spot-on. The Nosy Parker had been around forever. They had only left the comfort of their own homes and taken curtain twitching global – on tubes, trains, and in cafés.

There was a veritable epidemic of twitchers. They were here to stay – unless privacy laws get up close and personal with injunctions for snooping.

'Oh, what fun, a goldmine for the legal profession, Betty!'

That took me back to the start of our escapades and our frustrations with the frantic fame game. The need for attention from everyone, the pathetic excuses for constant updates, followers, 'likes', and the 'I have to use social media, I've got friends and relatives all over the world.'

Really, fancy that? When did you last see them? Do you know what is simmering under their glossy exteriors? And when did they last see you?

Anyway, enough of the seething and sweeping generalisations. Shamefully I had to admit that there was a distinct possibility that I protested too much.

*

Two weeks later I decided that Seb would be crossed off my kill list. We were back together. I had changed — it was an act, and he liked it. I played the sweet, smiling other half. I even met some of his overbearing oafish colleagues. I became proficient at smiling, although my face ached a lot afterwards. I even laughed, although I did not get any of their so-called jokes and 'funny' stories.

Seb had stopped all lines of communication with Lynch. It must have been after that night at the Black Bar, my boyfriend was so embarrassing. No wonder Lynch didn't want to be seen with him again.

Yet I remained on high alert – in case Lynch and Seb were in cahoots. Seb could be watching my every move – but neither would get the better of me. Sylvie would not be traced. She had disappeared again – surfacing rarely and when she did it was in my head and not in person.

I thought about Carlos occasionally, could not help it. I swore there was some chemistry there. If Seb was flaky again or betrayed me, Carlos was my back up. And if Seb did betray me, I would teach him a big, fat lesson after putting him back on the kill list.

Two more weeks passed, Christmas was over again – you could say I lived a normal life – not much of interest happened for what felt like years. Lynch was busier than ever. Tragically, the murder rates were higher than ever with all the gang violence, drug-related killings, domestic violence and random homicides. He did not have a minute to himself, but I continued to monitor him. I often worried that he had something up his sleeve, like the time he surprised me by arresting Carlos. I felt safer in the knowledge that he was still on the kill list. Mess with me and you mess it up for yourself, same applies to Sylvie.

CHAPTER 59.

The Whirling Waltzer

CARLOS

For months after I was in that awful cell, some said I had well and truly gone downhill. I played the little-boy-lost, hard-done-by gig and was spotted in the less appealing haunts, on jaunts to find love – or something like that. I had a new identity, bleached long hair and a beard too. Not exactly matchy-matchy with my tresses, but I bear less resemblance to my mugshot. I was informed it was safe to go out by that psycho freak woman. She slid a piece of paper under my door. The writing was scary in itself and the shouty caps!

'IT IS SAFE FOR YOU TO GO OUT. USE CASH, ONLY GO OUT AT NIGHT. AVOID CAMERAS AND NO SOCIAL MEDIA. YOU DO NOT WANT TO FIND OUT WHAT WILL HAPPEN IF YOU FAIL TO COMPLY.'

There was a remarkable drawing beneath the block capital words. I recognised myself smiling and ambling into a bar. But as I squinted at the picture, there was also a stick man in the room upstairs having a group selfie taken. Seeing red paint dripping from his blond hair and down his face, I gulped.

Unfortunately, when I finally left home, I discovered that the wiry hair I sprouted on my scarred face and the peroxide hair did not do the trick. My notoriety was no barrier, rather the opposite; a selfie queue forms wherever I parked my frame. I felt itchy and fidgety as I imagined being watched from above, behind and front like a hawk stalking a sparrow. I made a mental note not to go back to that bar or go out again, too risky. Still, I told myself, now that I'm out I might as well make a night of it.

'I'm in a good place,' I said to the 34 double G's that I was ogling; lovely tree trunk legs too, strapping lass. Well, this is fun, I thought, much better than being stuck in that poky flat or being banged up. Stuff Big Dave and eat him for tea. Mice and men (apart from DCI Lynch) did nothing for me!

SYLVIE

I watch Carlos from the crowded bar. He is a liability, and I am going to kill him. Afterwards, I will tell Betty that I did it for her. She wants to eradicate everyone who desires fame and he is going down that route again. OK, infamy was thrust upon him but still. Also, it will up my tally.

Worryingly, Betty appears to be oblivious to his new-found renown – she is too distracted by work and pallid Seb. Apparently, they've kissed and made up. Yawn!

Time passes. A week later, Carlos leaves his flat. I follow him (you can spot him a mile off with his swagger and mirrored sunglasses in the grey mid-winter) to a dodgy ambulance-chaser law firm in East London. Afterwards, I overhear him boasting about big bucks in a nearby bar. He is going to sue the Met Police for the stress and ailments he sustained whilst banged up. You can imagine how many extra selfie-requests and declarations of love that little 'poor me' routine will boost. That is a pitiful party I really do not want to watch.

This boy has had his chance and his five minutes of fame. Regretfully, his time is up.

CARLOS

My life felt like a Waltzer that had spun off its axis. I could not bear staying in any longer; I wanted my old life back.

OK, let's get serious. The unfair funfair that I foisted upon myself had to stop. I needed some excitement to take my mind of everything. I needed a sizeable sum of money too. I fancied a long, beach holiday and a stay in a five-star hotel to help me get over my ordeal in prison. Maybe I would rob that Sebastian Spiers guy. Sylvie told me all about him the night we met. She sounded as if she was obsessed by him, even though she hardly had a nice word to say about him. I needed to find out more, get his address too. She told me that he was an odd man and showed me a picture – lovely head of hair, cute nose. Oh, and filthy rich too.

I saw myself rifling through drawers full of cash in all denominations, him coming in and disturbing me: it would look like a burglary gone wrong. I would take my garrotte with me, just in case.

I made mental notes then typed them up, imagining myself as the leading man in a Hollywood movie.

SYLVIE

As Betty has gone all soft with her nauseating romance with Seb, I continue to keep her safe, for now. I do not know why – I hate her guts. Maybe because her days are numbered. I watch Carlos about ten hours a day. Keystroke monitoring reveals his innermost thoughts, what an amateur. He is going off-piste again.

No, it is way more serious than that. It is a fatal system error. So, I need to get Carlos and get him fast – and fairgrounds have always held an attraction for me.

His latest fantasy is Crystal, a lithe, but curvaceous bubbly girl with flowing curls.

CARLOS

I couldn't believe my luck when I met Crystal.

She appeared one night as I was downing my seventh pint, holding court, telling everyone about my time inside. She seemed rapt. As I was leaving, she asked me if I would like to go to the funfair with her. I readily acceded. Odd that, as I had been thinking about all the fun of the fair lately.

No one had ever paid that much attention to me – not since the night I met Sylvie. I was hooked. As I left the bar, I swore I saw that cop that arrested me in the distance. He must be tailing me, I thought. My face reddened as I hailed a passing cab, I got out at Oxford Street and ran into the throng of people listlessly walking past shops, then I got back into another cab relieved I had shaken the DCI. What a relief.

SYLVIE

It isn't difficult to persuade Crystal to lure Carlos to the fairground. A wad of twenties is all it takes; she is saving up for a deposit on a flat. She fancies him too, who doesn't? So that helps.

It is officially bye-bye Carlos time. His demise will take an epithelial route, through skin, muscles, vessels and through other portals to the maw of the matter.

Don't worry; it will be quick. I think about using Betty's hatpin on him, to aggravate her. It has been glowing, and I swear it is drawing me in. Like hypnotic Kaa – trust in me, my pretty. I trust you Kaa, more than I trust the other snakes, slithering, low bellied reptiles that stare blankly.

OK, maybe that will be too much of a hat full and head full of horror show. I should play nicely. Carlos will be Gulliver-downed first – with a pill, disguised as a mint, nestling in my faux pony skinned purse. I will hand it to Crystal and she pops it in his mouth after he downs his second beer, so far, so swell.

CARLOS

When I stepped onto the Waltzer, I was still in a Crystal whirl. My imagination was running wild. My mind fast forwarded to afterwards – we would head back to Carlos Towers (I planned to move back to my place) for a night to remember. Before the ride started, I whispered, 'Come back to my place after this ride.' She nodded; although inexplicably she looked a little sad.

Crystal grabbed my hand, and held it tightly. It was the first physical contact we had, and I didn't want it to end. I never felt so happy to be alive.

SYLVIE

The ride starts to move, slowly. I am a latex-masked hooded figure outside Carlos's field of vision as I perch myself in the car next to the pair.

Crystal knows that she has to distract him to avoid him spotting me. She disarms me by shaking her head, barely perceptible. Jeez, she has fallen for him. Time for a spin, then I will go in for the kill at the end of the ride.

CARLOS

'Woooooo,' I shouted at the top of my lungs as we spun faster and faster.

Woozy, whoosh. Thankfully the ride had stopped. I tried to get off the whirly thing, but my legs did not obey.

With a craft beer hangover looming after the chips and dips and with my jelly legs, maybe it was not a good time to stand up anyway. Out of the corner of one of my twitching eyes, I saw a figure with the same shape as Sylvie. At least I thought it was her. Clocked her – there she was, something glinting in her hand. I noted an arm swinging movement. A child wailed loudly in post-parental admonishment. A fat fuck just missed the bus. It started to rain, torrential rain, not that annoying drizzle.

My wooziness made my thoughts turn to the cross-looking bus driver that just departed at speed. I imagined that he wasn't in the mood for anything and that included stopping, opening the door, closing the door ad infinitum until death parts him from it. I told myself that if he ever heard that the freaking wheels go round and round again, he was going to puncture them and just walk off and leave the passengers fuming. I laughed at the thought and stopped abruptly as I thought – maybe that piffle would be my last thought, ever.

SYLVIE

The sharpened umbrella tip, dear sis, does the trick: straight through Carlos' belly, almost leaves him pinned to the ride. Not original, but in the driving rain, in a latex mask, you can get away with anything.

DCI CALUM LYNCH

I was last on the scene. Surprisingly Carlos was in the ambulance inert, swift, efficient paramedics either side of him. Strange that, I was expecting a tent and Forensics, there was one police car and an ambulance and the gawping small crowd, of course. I remembered the stirring I felt for him in Wales and in the interrogation room. 'Lovely lashes' was the unbidden thought that flashed in my mind. My face clouded over; I rarely forgave anyone (victim or not) for a seventy-mile drive to a fair.

There had been numerous online threats on Carlos's life since he was accused of killing the national treasure Ben Briddell, notwithstanding that he had been released. This was not a huge surprise; it was only a matter of time.

I walked around the Waltzer and spotted a pair of black shades lying abandoned within the cordon. I trouser-pocketed a souvenir of a man I'd become rather fond of. When I sat down I wasn't feeling crushed, but muffled. My head still wasn't quite right. I needed forensic evidence and phone images; but with the torrential rain, there wouldn't be much. Strange, going to a fair on a day when the weather was so atrocious. I felt deflated. I shook my head and identified myself to the one of the paramedics. I glanced at Carlos and was shocked to see a flicker and the white of one of his eyes. Two hours ago I was informed he was dead. I felt ecstatic.

I was going to follow the ambulance but stopped for a hotdog first. As I was eating it the local constable read witness statements from his notebook. A person was seen walking fast from the scene carrying an umbrella, but not one of the witnesses bought anything else to the table. Not one distinguishing feature. He said Carlos, I mean George, was with a woman as yet identified and she too was at the hospital, my heart beat so fast. I ran to my car making it beat even faster, not a good thing to do after scoffing fast food.

CHAPTER 60.

This is Where We Finish, for Now

BETTY

Dear sis, as you know, I booked us both on the late flight to Cancun. I felt the need to escape. Even though no one was closing in and it had been months since Briddell died. I would plan our next steps from the beach. My boss blinked furiously when I said I was going on immediate leave for two weeks. I did not mention that I would never see her again, tempting as it was.

Certain that you still wanted me out of the picture, so that you could cuckoo your way in, I sent you an e-ticket; first class it was, pricy but I felt that would tempt you. I told you that I would be on the same flight (I swore on Seb's life). You scoffed. 'I plan to go away for some time, it is up to you if you want to join me, I don't give a fuck.'

You said you would see me there. I felt a wave of relief. I had grown accustomed to having you around. Plus, I admit, you would be less likely to creep up on me in the middle of the night and murder me if we were to call a truce. I was sure that once you became party to my new plans – you would willingly join me. I will tell you about my new kill list. There are ten names in it. Each one a narcissistic, talentless loser. I cannot wait to tell you about the next chapter in our lives

*

Before executing my exit strategy, I visited Tracy, my one friend. She had been in a coma for months, and then one day, she blinked. Astonishingly, within hours of waking, she had made a full recovery. I read in the tabloids that when she woke, she noted with satisfaction that although her body was lacking in tone, it was a few kilos lighter. She was so hungry that she felt like shovelling the unpalatable hospital food down, yet she refrained.

She told the reporters waiting outside that she could not remember ordering any pills or ingesting them. She became famous all over again and was commissioned to write an autobiography, even though she had not actually done much of note – other than to appear on that *Great Fat Britain* show, lose her husband and then nearly die. She readily agreed, she had two mouths to feed, her own and her daughter's. Both now ate 'mindfully,' as they now call it, and that incurred massive costs. A book deal and tabloid features would fund that and more.

Pity they had not eaten well before, I thought, or Kevin would still be here. My eyes welled with tears that soon dried up.

Tracy had no shortage of admirers, her feed was full of heart emoji's, proposals, and requests for her to do photoshoots and interviews.

I felt happy for her, or at least my mind told me that I did.

See Sylvie, you went on about the consequences, but you never foresaw that some good would come of it, did you?

SYLVIE

Whatever! Game, set and match It is four to me: Alby, Dr Woolf (even though Betty is claiming him as her kill), Ricky and Carlos versus four to her: Kevin, Terry, Ben and Lynch's namesake. I will tell her about my trip to the fair later and shake on it. It is a draw, we are sisters-in-arms and equals.

On the way to the airport, I feel disconcerted, I cannot get an image out of my head. At the fair I walk past a man with a heart-shaped face, and I mean an anatomical heart. He is a creepy fuck, not to mention the leaning and watching, sly-eyed sideways glances aplenty. I am sure others noticed him. There were a few prime beef suspects about that day, hanging around the fair. As for evidence, forget it, neither hide nor hair was lost. No slip-ups, just a result!

What a scene it is! I think it is the best one yet. It will make front page news. The scream queens will be out in force. Sales of Aviators will no doubt be sky high; the hipsters and the squares all have a pair, even though the weather was grey and all a drizzle. I cannot wait to tell you about it, I feel the need to crow. I text, four all, with our facilitator down.

BETTY

Anyway, the question was, what to do now in my last few hours in London? Then I remembered, vintage champagne! Two hundred quid a pop at the Black Bar. Seb was buying. Yes, he did turn up to wish me well.

I was going to miss him, flaky as he was. I thought about our destination, Mexico. It was more me right then. The Day of the Dead celebrations are seasons away but I had my own version of it a few times here. I was after some piquant achiote and mescal.

*

I read the puzzling, nonsensical text from you before boarding the plane. I was on a flip-up seat disguised as crew. I know it sounds far-fetched for most people but not for me, I have always had the ways and means. My heart raced as I clocked the latest breaking news:

'Two Seriously Injured at the Fair'

I felt my blood pressure soar as I read about Carlos, what the freak. I had plans for Carlos. You had screwed up again. That mean, it was four – three to me, yippee or five – two more like. Although I felt nauseated – yet again Sylvie had put me in jeopardy.

I scrolled through the article. George Littlewood also known as Carlos Smith was in Intensive Care for the second time in four months, his condition critical. He was recovering from a seven-hour operation following an abdominal injury.

His partner Crystal Waters (really) had tripped; she felt dizzy as she descended the steps of the Waltzer and hit her head. She was in hospital too. There was the usual appeal for witnesses to a crime.

I was livid. But it would be ten hours thirty minutes before I could speak to Sylvie out of earshot.

I clocked her quickly enough; my dear Sylvie was dressed like our mama, face to match.

'Champagne please,' she demanded. 'Two bottles, saves you coming back.' I pulled a face, as well as I could with the amount of makeup I had on, wearing a wig and a face covering helped disguise me further. In reply, you said, 'why the look? They are only those little bottles.'

It was gratifying to know that she clearly hadn't recognised me.

I sat down again, thinking my dear, treacherous sister, I will deal with you shortly.

SYLVIE

I fondly look back on my last few hours in London. An Irish, down-but-not-yet-out man stares at me in a friendly way; surprising, as hardly anyone in this beast of a city looks anyone in the eye. 'I like your top, lady.' Oh, the joy of being a London girl and a head-turning one at that.

OK, maybe my head, like Betty's, has swelled too much, and the cranium just about contains it.

Anyways, this is before I lay down beside an A-lister self-inflated reality star fukunt on the plane on his way to try and make it big in America, probably. My fingers twitch as I try to sleep. One eye open, eyeing him. Betty's toxic influence has made me loathe him and his ilk. He is easy prey, but not a good idea. I imagine Betty having the same thought, if she is on this flight. I've not spotted her yet. Although one of the hostesses has the same slim ankles and hands, the rest of her is different.

Hours later my lips are pursed: too many deaths or not enough. Something is not quite right.

I am horrified to discover, when I switch my phone on after a smooth landing, that Carlos is still alive and that Crystal is injured. I like her, she is a good laugh. Yes, having a laugh is where it is at. I lay my plan to kill Betty to one side until we are even. She is not so bad, sometimes anyway. It has been a ball, a masked one at that.

One day I will go back for Lynch. In the meantime, I feel a buzz. I do love Mexico. One annoyance – my sis; where is she? Is that you in seat 2A or are you the scowling hostess? Or not on this flight at all?

BETTY

You thought I would be that obvious; you don't know me, that was not my game. Remember the film Lynch was watching, *F/X – Murder by Illusion*, the masks and the costumes? Not to mention that hypnotically memorable theme tune. Whatever you saw was 'Just an Illusion'.

Think my dearest, think. Who on the plane had my build, my height? I watched you as you settled in with your eye mask, mouth guard and ear plugs. I had been on my feet for minutes already and hours later I was sick to the back teeth of waiting on people.

Enough was enough; only another hour left. It was not all bad though; I had had two business cards slipped my way. Some interesting characters; wealthy ones at that.

*

A mere twenty-eight hours after leaving London I felt well and swell. Breakfast was delicious, especially the coffee. I was looking gorgeous in my Prada bikini, naturally. I headed for the beach, my eyes peeled behind my Burberry shades on the lookout for Sylvie.

'I spotted a few likely prey on the plane yesterday sis,' I said, as I tiptoed towards her on the scorching sand.

'Oh, so did I,' said Sylvie, irritatingly clapping her hands and not staring daggers for a change.

Maybe I was right all along – she won't kill me, after all; maybe she was addicted to the thought of it as I was. We had a fabulous time last night in the hotel bar. I gloated for hours last night about her ineptitude at the fair. She took being put in her place well, I thought. My superiority shone through yet again.

*

I thought of all the paths we had taken, together and separately. Where to now? Another spree, ten were in my sights, who knows when it would end. I knew when it would start, soon. I had withdrawal symptoms already, and nothing had changed. I didn't know why I thought it would. There were louts everywhere. I reflected on Robert Frost's poem, 'The Road Not Taken'. Sylvie and I had gone down a path that was seldom taken, to the point that I felt we *were* one traveller, or so it seemed. Between us we had taken some ridiculous paths, some that had made me laugh, some that made me cry.

I looked at my twin, and she looked back. She had thawed I could tell. She knew that I had won again.

'How many more names are in your new book?' she whispered as I threw my towel down on the lounger beside her. 'Would you like to see my list too? How about a kill collaboration, crime noir style? We both love the glamour of the 1940s,' she added.

I so do not! She knows I can't stand historic stuff.

I seethed at my irritating, competitive, copycat sister. I attempted a smile as I said, 'Yes please.'

Milton Keynes UK
Ingram Content Group UK Ltd.
UKHW040905171123
432750UK00004B/286